MASQUERADE

MASQUERADE

© Diane McNeele

2018

Once upon a time, there was a girl who dreamt of being a writer but was working as a sale employee. She created stories in her mind, and one day, in the tramway, she thought about the most famous actor in the world. What it would be like if he would meet a shy librarian ? 1 year later, she posts her novel online and discovers the reviews and comments about Masquerade.

Now, your turn to write a few words. Please, if you enjoyed the story of Olen and Candice, spread the words and let me know it on Amazon and anywhere else ☺

If you want to read more about me, join my clan on www.dianemcneele.com

Thank you dear reader,

Lots of love

Diane

Dedication

To Sylvie, Charlotte, Danielle, Tiphaine, Mylène, Juliette, Stéphanie, Leila, Wendy, Angella, Archcena, Isy, and many others: all these wonderful women who inspire me. Here's hoping this story surpasses your wildest dreams, adventurers of love!

Chapter 1

Anna Wintour would crucify me for only daring to look at them. But I'm wearing grandmother's old rubber boots ... in the mud. A shapeless dress with small flowers that I wore every summer since the age of fifteen ... It fit without any unwanted surprises, because I hadn't eaten for three days. Grandma almost had to threaten me to make me eat her carrot stew.

Candice Evans is back in town. The town where it all began for my mother and father. I can hear my grandmother talking to the donkey and talking about men. I'll spare you the insults and other colorful expressions that I wouldn't be able to translate into English. Yes, because I'm in France, where my mother grew up. The village where I spent almost all my summer holidays, wonderful memories between the chickens, the rabbits, the tamed doves. Dad created amusement parks and came to scout the area, his eyes fell upon the most beautiful sight he'd ever seen: my mother, a piquant brunette with shaped eyebrows. Apparently, I look a lot like her. Mom fell in love with this handsome, slightly eccentric American who was crazy about her, and flew with him to the New World. For now though, I'm trying not to think about my love life. About that lousy adventure. To try and forget it all. Forgetting even his name by feeding the hens. Just as I did when I was little. I actually named them all. If only they could eat his eyes and face.

Olen Van Cliff ... I'd managed to pull myself together, I vowed not to make the same mistakes. Life didn't smile back. As simple as that. And I loved you. And you knocked me down. Winner by Knockout. But the pain is still there, and resurfaces, nagging. Sign that I'm still alive.

"Olen, I'm afraid.

- Afraid of what ?

- Can't you see: I don't want to get hurt.

- Candice I swear, I'd never hurt you."

How could I have been so blind ? Actor, liar. Wondering how it came to this, huh?

When you lose everything, when you think you've hit rock bottom. Well nope. You know what, there was a hidden crevice!

I'm a survivor. I bend but never break. So that's why I came back here. Far from the States. To stop seeing him at every turn, to not be haunted by the memories. Because obviously I couldn't fall in love with the average guy. No. I had to fall in love with the most inaccessible type, the craziest, the most revered around the world ... and the most loved of women. And he's probably the one that loves them the most. All of them. Olen Van Cliff, the greatest of this generation of Hollywood actors and the biggest playboy. I thought he hung the moon only to realize I had stars in my eyes.

Blondes, brunettes, redheads ... a different woman every night and with witnesses: all the paparazzi in New York ! He moved on quickly, the bastard. Whenever I see his handsome face before my eyes, everytime I feel his hands cupping my face, everytime I feel like I smell his cologne ... I see the memories flash before my eyes. And each time, it's like a knife cut through our bond. Well, the bond I thought we had. Olen, did you ever truly love me ? Every time I ask myself that, it's like a knife to the heart. No, he enjoyed the distraction that I procured. I made a nice change from his day to day life. But he's a junkie, addicted to women, to parties, to the nightlife, one of those fallen angels that haunt the nights of Los Angeles or New York ...

My life was perfect before I met him, just perfect. Meaning? Well, an extroverted roommate, party girl, financially stable, in short my complete opposite. An easy job in a rather stylish bookstore where I simply had to open boxes, press three buttons and stack books. Occasionally, forced to be nice to Archibald, an old pain in the ass and to smooth out the edges with Niels, my petty colleague. I occasionally accompanied Liza during seminars abroad, so a dream vacation, for free. To make a long story short.

Perfect. Maybe it seems boring to you. Might be a little to me too. But perfect, you know?

When I think about it, it's in Indonesia that it all blew up in my face. Why did I agree to go to the beach with him?

Because you wanted to. You wanted to feel that again. And, deep down, you believed that you could change him.

There you go. Bottom line? Complete and utter social suicide. Career on the rocks. Love life obliterated forever. Heart? Nonexistent. As if a black hole had swallowed all that I was and my whole life.

But damn, what am I going to do with my life now that Olen Van Cliff screwed it all up? He got under my skin, and it's as if I can constantly smell his cologne. But let me tell you how it all began. How a poor insignificant girl was able to meet and fall in love with the biggest star of American cinema.

***

When I see Liza Cole, man-eater, my roommate, and best friend, enter the library where I work in New York like a hysterical puppy, I know that she's either got the scoop of the century, or that she's won the jackpot. She leans over the counter, and looks at me, raising a perfectly shaped eyebrow. She shakes her white pearl earrings which beautifully contrast with her dark complexion, and bring out the sparkle in her eyes. Tall, muscular, always wearing a dress, Liza doesn't talk, she sings, she clamours, she gives orders, but never falters. Never, in my life, have I seen Liza whisper. And when she turns on the charm, she tilts her head and gives her voice a whole set of soft inflections that give it a playful quality, never tame.

"Tonight, 7 pm at the apartment! Don't be late !

- What?" I said with a deliberately nonchalant look to annoy her.

"Masquerade, the annual event. The one percent will be there.

- I don't have a mask Liza...

- I'll take care of everything. We'll be hot, don't you worry!

- I always worry when you say "don't you worry".

- It'll be fun, sexy, glamorous. It'll make a change from nightclubs.

- But it's on invitation only."

Liza looks conspiratorially around.

"I got this at work."

And she waved a black card in front of me. I grabbed it : just by the custom print on this sort of glossy paper I could tell it had to have cost a small fortune. A few words written in white font. A mask with arabesques. Quite mysterious, I had to admit.

"Plus, it's a personal invitation. But I can bring a plus one, it says so here.

- Alright then.

- I didn't ask your opinion. It was obvious you were coming with me."

Liza takes the invite with a small disdainful pout, which made me laugh, and she storms towards the exit. When Liza has an idea, nothing gets in her way. I'm surprised that she hasn't already given her boss the boot to take his place.

Niels slams his hand down on the counter startling me:

"Come on, Evans! There's still two boxes that need to be opened and stacked."

He's not a bad person but ever since I made it clear that I wouldn't go out with him, Niels tends to act like a little general.

I'm tempted to grab the scissors and stab the palm of his hand with them. Hmm. What would Doctor Tran have to say about all this? When I become too aggressive, it doesn't take me long to give into old habits.

I leave the shop. Niels can kiss my ass. I don't smoke, I'm entitled to some fresh air.

"Hi Grandma ! How's it going ? Oh, are you off to the market ? Did the chickens lay some eggs? Yes, I'll try to pop over in December. You know that in business the end of year is hard... Yes,

I'm... I'm fine. Love you." What a great woman, my gran! Manning her small farm on her own... A French woman who didn't have it easy growing up during the war, I hope I got some of her genes. And what if that wasn't the case ? What if I was just a run of the mill woman, who's actually feeble and who'll never fit in? I close my eyes, and try to forget the noise of traffic.

"Hello, I would like to make an appointment with Dr. Tran. Candice Evans. Tomorrow morning sounds perfect. Just tell him "hard version". Thank you."

I hang up, letting out a deep sigh. Better safe than sorry. Niels looks at me speechless while holding the door. He's obviously trying to think of something to say, but changes his mind, looking pale, he goes back in. I didn't see him again for the rest of the day. While emptying the boxes of newly delivered mugs, I giggle, thinking back to his confused face. If he knew what hard version meant he never would have asked me out for a drink. And then looking at my wrist, I sneer feeling a pang. No, no one would ask me out for a drink if they knew.

"Candice? Wow! I didn't recognize you there."

I look up and stop short in scanning the books.

"I don't think I've changed that much.

- I don't know, I think I've never seen you in jeans and sneakers! "

Loretta Blossom. High school. She wasn't in my group of friends, but I recognised her. The invisible girl who sat in the back and who was forever looking out the window, daydreaming.

"Hey Loretta! How are you?

- You remember me?

- Yes. I remember you. What are you up to these days?

- I did an MBA in international relations and I just spent six months in London, and now I'm off to Canada for six months, I'm leaving in a few days.

- Congratulations, sounds exciting.

- What about you ? Are... are you okay? I'm sorry about your parents... and your boyfriend.

- Thanks, Loretta.

- We should... well, we could go for lunch and do some shopping one of these days, if you'd like?"

I pause for a second, searching for the right words, and go back to scanning books before taking it all in.

"That Candice she ... doesn't really exist anymore Loretta. I ... And sneakers are really comfortable.

- Oh. Okay.

-We can do something else if you want, how about..."

No matter how much I think about it, anything I say is going to sound incredibly condescending or boring, and that no matter what

I end up saying. Like an exhibit, feeding the ducks in Central Park. Because truth is, I wouldn't be able to stand doing the things I used to do. Loretta watched me for a moment and had the mind to put an end to the conversation which was becoming uncomfortable for the both of us. She must think that I'm too broke to go shopping because she smiles at me sympathetically and tilts her head to the side.

"I understand. I hope everything will turn out alright for you, Candice.

- Yeah. Me too."

She smiles at me kindly, and picking up the bag containing her books, she leaves. Some people are like that. They're like ghosts: you can't pay too much attention to them, they might lead you to believe that it's possible to get your old life back.

***

Forty minutes. I have forty minutes to write in this damned journal. I haven't written in it for years. It's more than just writer's block; no, it's just that nothing's coming to me. I could pick up any excerpt of story I started in my teens, but it's not coming to me. Dr. Tran advised me to write ten pages a day to let off steam. The session I had with him did me good. Where to start ? I close my eyes and the first thing that comes to mind is his silhouette in the doorway. He runs a hand through his brown disheveled hair and casually leans against the door.

"Hi, I'm Danny."

I look up from my computer, and lean back in my chair. I've been so bored since this morning, with this second rate thriller, I need to find something to do to keep myself entertained.

"You're the intern, right?

- Uh yes.

- Alright, I'm Candice, bring me some tea, and make a copy of this please.

- Um ok.

- Why are you still here?"

I laugh internally hearing his hurried footsteps in the hallway. I love to scare the shit out of newcomers. And seeing as I just signed a contract, I can afford it. But Danny drops off the pile of papers barely five minutes later. I pretend not to notice him, keeping my eyes fixed on the book report that I've just finished.

"And what about my tea, trainee?

- Is her Majesty going to keep giving me a hard time?

- Yes.

- And if I fight back?

- Why would you do that?

- Because you're a junior and just three or six months ago you were in my shoes.

- And how can you be so sure?

- If you were a confirmed editor you'd be at the meeting I heard upstairs."

I looked up and watched him. He's cute, and smart too.

"Well, come on tigress, come get your tea."

He leaves without further comment. I finally figure out what it is about his gait that I like. Danny doesn't walk, he drags his feet slightly. From the coffee machine, he looks me in the eye, despite the relatively tight blouse that I put on this morning:

"Alright... a part from being bossy at work, what do you like doing?

- Writing.

- Yeah? Me too. But I prefer writing songs.

- Really? What kind?

- Jazz.

- But there aren't any lyrics in Jazz.

- Oh really? So what did Cole Tran and Nina Simone do then?

- Well sure but ... I was talking about modern jazz.

- Stop playing around princess, admit it, you know nothing about jazz.

- No. I have to admit I didn't really care ... until now."

Now that I have a handsome nonchalant brunet watching me intently with his unblinking eyes hidden behind his glasses. I walk towards him and remove them so that I can look into his eyes. He shudders. Could he be different from the rest?

"Are you a good guy, Danny?

- I think so.

- And gentle?

- That too."

I smile at him, and he smiles back. And that's how Danny tamed the tigress within me. We were a cute couple. He brought me the bohemia I needed, and soon I was introducing him to all of my friends. I let myself be swept away by our love, and I encouraged him in his passion for jazz. I put aside writing to club-crawl with him, support him, introduce him to everyone who could help him in his passion.

Thirty minutes. Right. Liza will be here soon. Who else can I write about? The other man in my life comes to mind. Dad kisses the top of my head while I finish getting ready for my birthday party. I was jumping up and down from excitement.

"Did you see out the window?

- Has Danny arrived?

- Not yet.

- Oh my God Dad !! You had a huge slide delivered?"

Dad went to sit on my bed, and I could feel his gaze on my back. I don't like it when he's lost in thought. It's not like him.

"About Danny ... I don't think he's very attentive."

I don't answer. I persevere in my battle of put my earring in. But I feel irritation bubbling under the surface. He then pushes on:

"Will my daughter stoop so low as to stay with a man who doesn't love her? You can have anyone you want, you can get anything you want and do what you want. So don't waste your time with timid boys. Find a man who's worthy of you, you're passionate, vivacious: you need someone who can keep up with you. Is Danny up to the job?

- Dad !! If you say one more word... I won't go down!

- Don't get on your high horse, I know you well, Candice, darling. I just want you to be happy.

- I know Dad. Please, please be nice to Danny. He means a lot to me.

- I am nice. I only want what's best for the second love of my life."

Good. He'll be nice. I have a small victorious smile, something I notice in the mirror, while adjusting my hair. Yes, I have everything, and I want even more. I want Danny on my arm walking down the aisle, and I want to have a kid with him. He's the only one I've been myself with. Not Candice the champ. But the Candice who just wants to be loved for who she is.

"My question is simple: does he love you as much as you love him ... with as much passion?"

My smile falters. If I had listened to Dad that day, maybe it wouldn't have happened. Not our argument, nor Christmas.

Liza shouts almost breaking down the door to the apartment,

"I have the masks! I have our dresses! Quiiiiick!"

Exactly an hour and a half later, I'm sitting next to my talkative roommate, in the back seat of a taxi. Today it's Liza who insists on doing my makeup. I must admit, I've become lazy.

"Stop moving.

- God, you're impossible, stop it, it feels like a Madame preparing her new charge. It isn't the oscars for God's sake!"

Liza readjusts my mask after having put lipstick on me.

"You better believe it!

- What's that supposed to mean?

- Each year the event is organized by a different person, remember?"

Liza's busying herself in her lamé dress that contrasts beautifully with her dark ebony skin and her golden earrings worthy of a Bollywood film. I relax into the taxi's seat, sighing, reciting off by heart, eyes looking to the sky:

"Yes, each year the Masquerade ball must be increasingly depraved, lust, alcohol, an amazing show... it's what the rich do. The competition that will provide the most pleasure.

- Speaking of pleasure..."

Liza runs her tongue across the right corner of her lips seeing a devilishly well put together man adjusting his suit while getting out of the black limousine in front of us. I know all to well about Liza's huntress' instincts,

"Hey! You're not going to abandon me after only five minutes, right? I won't know anyone else here.

- But you'll be wearing a mask, Candice! You can say anything you want, your most secret fantasies, at the bar or at the buffet, tonight everything goes. You don't even have to talk if that's what you want. It's a secret party after all, held by a mysterious host, the location kept a secret until the last minute... You can be a mysterious woman tonight if that's really what you want.

- Ok."

The mysterious woman, that suits me fine. I grab the handle to open the car door when Liza holds me back.

"I was going to say, speaking of the Oscars: it seems that this year there'll be a lot of Hollywood names.

- What?

- Yessss!

- And apparently the host is a very famous actor.

- Who told you that?

- The person who gave me the address over the phone, just now. I asked if there was a theme this year ... well I prodded him a bit.

- I have no doubt that you can get all sorts of information when you're this excited."

She pushed me out of the taxi, wearing a tight dress of the mermaid by Kenzo type. She had picked out a shimmering black 50's style dress for me to wear, it was fitted at the waist, slightly covering my shoulders, which went well with my brown hair, pulled back in a high bun. Liza can't help it, she loves everything that's shiny.

I let her go in front, and give the invitation to the muscle guarding the entrance and screening. People stop at the street corner to watch us, intrigued.

The two dark doors open ... and I discover a hallway.

"Is this ... it's a hotel.

- Yes. A former hotel converted into a private residence. I wonder who normally lives here..."

The walls are black, and the only thing on them are protruding arms as white as marble, holding candles.

A butler with immaculate gloves calls the lift for us. I give Liza a nudge. I don't want to be noticed giggling like a schoolgirl! This design... I've got a strange feeling getting into the elevator.

The wrought iron gates are closing when it hits me. It's the setting from Beauty and the Beast by Jean Cocteau.

Wow... this is going to be interesting.

When the elevator doors open, music fills the air. High marble columns stand tall on a white floor... there are long red curtains and at the far end, a stage. We're obviously some of the last people here. A waiter comes straight away and a few minutes after enjoying a glass of champagne with delicious rose and lychee ice, the music stops. Three gongs ring out, and the crowd rushes to the foot of the stage, whispering excitedly. Silence settles in, and a blond man, with broad shoulders under an impeccable black shirt emerges in front of the curtain.

"Ladies and gentlemen. Thank you for your punctuality. I've planned an evening full of surprises. Let's go crazy, let's be depraved, let's be above the law and above everything else tonight! What do you say?"

Cheers resound. We're about three hundred. Liza whispers suddenly very serious,

"That voice... it sounds familiar..."

Suddenly, guitar chords sound and John Travolta and Uma Thurman look-alikes tear up the dancefloor. Safe behind my mask, eyes closed, I sway to the rhythm of the music. I see Liza tighten a tie in her fist and reel in her first victim of the evening to kiss him. I laugh foolishly to myself and stop at the buffet that is, of course, delicious: it was time, I think I'm on my fifth glass of champagne. I opt for a glass of white wine to drink while I explore the place. A cover of "Toxic" by Nael Yaim resonates in the air when I enter a hallway. I finish my glass of Colombelle, and place it on the first surface I find. Through my mask, and in the semi-darkness, I can barely make out the floor, so I have to feel my way along the walls to keep myself from falling. I hear chuckling to my right. No doors or curtains, just an archway that beckons you to go in: I see a beautiful redhead lying on a sofa and four men drawing her. She isn't wearing a mask. In fact, she isn't wearing anything at all... except a necklace with a huge blue diamond.

"Come on, gentlemen, the one that draws the most resembling portrait will get a surprise."

I don't recognize my own voice it's that bold:

"And what would that be?

- A champagne bath with me." And she stretches out like a cat.

"Oh no! You broke the pose!

- Don't worry, we have all night." she chuckles, winking at me.

I smile behind my mask. Is she really here for the fun or just because she's being paid? Maybe both... Kate Winslet had more curves, but this Rose has a mischievous insolence that would see a monk break his vows.

The music is louder in the next room. I left the redhead and the men trying to draw her, and trying to focus, their tongues poking out. By now, I'm very intrigued, but I stop in my tracks at the doorway to the next room. It really feels like I'm in a jungle with fake plants and vines tumbling from the ceiling forming a thick wall in front of me. I enter the jungle in which there's no particular animation, that is, except for the sounds of machine guns and screams that make me jump more than once. The rooms go on forever, couples emerge from corners giggling between two sighs. I have to admit... our mystery guest has made a big deal. How much did it cost?

"A kiss to build a dream on" by Louis Armstrong sounds. Syrupy saxophone notes seep into the hallway.

The warm and reassuring voice of Louis continues "Give your lips just for a moment... and". A hairy creature, machine gun in hand, suddenly jumps out at me screaming.

Chapter 2

I immediately crouch down and elbow him in the crotch.

When I stand up, heart racing, a huge chewbacca is squirming on the ground moaning. I start screaming,

"Are you insane?!

- Crazy bitch!"

The host knew his cinematic history, I had to admit, but he was obsessed and an immature kid.

"Sorry. Come on, get up.

- I'll have bruised balls tomorrow.

- You were lucky I didn't have anything to chop them off with. Really, I'm sorry."

I stupidly pat his shoulder. He stands up, hands on his knees, and exhales loudly.

"Damn, where did you learn that?

- I watched Buffy the vampire slayer a lot when I was a teenager.

- What's your name?

- Candice." He picks up his fake gun.

"Okay. I'll avoid any Candice that crosses my path from now on.

- I'm really sorry.

- I'm William. William West." He holds out a hairy hand to shake mine.

"Candice who?

- Candice Evans."

I turn to leave but he holds onto my hand, and gives it a theatrical kiss all his hair tickling me, before skulking back between the dark curtains in silence.

I turn on my heel and after a few feet, I open the last door of the hall and I remain speechless. It's completely black except a giant green curtain descending from the ceiling, cleverly lit by spotlights. Green smoke spreads in wisps on the ground, giving me the impression that I'm floating. I let the door close behind me. I've already guessed the name of the movie which is reenacted here. I jump a little when a deep voice resounds.

"I am the Wizard of Oz. Great and Almighty. Who might you be?

- Don't you feel a bit lonely waiting for people to end up in this room?

- The great and powerful Oz knows why you came here."

Let's see in the Wizard of Oz, Dorothy enters the lair of the wizard, accompanied by a cowardly lion, a scarecrow without a brain, and a tin man without a heart.

"Well I already have a brain: I wondered why I agreed to come to this party, but the fact that I recognized all the movies depicted comforts me in my mental capacities, at least about some things. I have a heart ... and as for courage ... well, yes, I'd like a bit more of that.

- State all the movies you recognized tonight!

- Beauty and the Beast in the entrance. That was well done... Pulp Fiction to start with, not bad either. Titanic was the easiest. A car with fogged up windows would have been funnier, I think. Apocalypse Now was the least obvious, but the coolest one of them all. And finally Star Wars in the hallway.

- Good. You can access the Holy of Holies.

- The Holy of Holies? Because you still have something staged behind your curtain? What's behind there? The Eyes Wide Shut of the evening?"

An awkward silence fell. I obviously guessed right.

"I'm not interested in naked women.

- You prefer men? That's good to know..."

A man came out from behind the curtain. Tall, with perfectly styled strawberry blond hair, bright eyes behind a black mask. A simple wolf, without any frills. A suit tailored to perfection. Muscles evidently present under it. The man who launched the festivities earlier on stage.

I instinctively take a few steps back. He smiles. And God... what a smile. One of those lopsided smirks, and it brings out an adorable dimple. As someone was drumming on a closed door, something told me that I knew that voice. I'd heard it somewhere before.

"Seriously, what's this all about?

- All this what?

- This set up that costs at least as much as the GDP of an African country.

- For fun, the pleasure of entering an unknown world that seems so familiar." He closes the distance, close enough to touch me.

"The beauty of living in the present,"

He touched his index finger to my cheek and traced it along my jaw. Heat pools in my stomach.

"If you don't want to go any further ... is there anything else I can do?"

I answer boldly:

"Not really. Since you've failed in all your duties as host, I'll take care of myself.

- What do you mean ?

- I was bored. I had to deck Chewbacca.

- My friends bore you?

- Those who pretend they are, yes. I've got to say, I didn't look into it."

I compose myself, despite my mask. He remains silent, observing me. I smile and go on insolently:

"You're not going to ask me who I am?

- If you're here, there's a reason.

- You personally take care of security here?

- You got past my security guards right outside the house, so it's supposed to be enough.

- Supposed to?

- Well you didn't go through a body search... yet."

I'm suddenly very hot. He burst out laughing. I recognize that smile, that laugh. Glimpsed on television and on the red carpet. Olen Van Cliff. The most pursued bachelor in Hollywood, by women and by producers. My God. Now, I understand why women swoon before him. He's insolent, refreshing, a laugh that warms you and a smile to die for, with perfect white teeth. His laughter puts you at ease in a matter of seconds. A smile that makes you feel like you're a part of his inner circle. But his sparkling eyes and penetrating gaze make it seem like he sees deep into your soul, taking a hold, never to let go. I could see why all the directors fought over him: he looked like an adorable wild animal that no screen could tame. Keep it together,, Candice. Breathe. I change the subject.

"Do you have a library?

- A library?

- Yes.

- It's a party, you're not supposed to read at a party.

- I'm curious to see what books you have.

- What makes you think I have any?

- A huge house like this? It takes all kinds to impress women.

- I don't think I impress you.

- You're right.

- And that's what it would take?

- At the very least," I muttered.

"Philosophy Books?

- You like philosophy?

- I have a very simple one.

- Really? I thought philosophy was old speeches made by decrepit old men.

- Old people can teach us a lot.

- That's true. Teach me.

- Ouch. That hurts."

I burst out laughing.

"It was just too tempting...

- You want to know my life philosophy?

- Go for it. Surprise me.

- Carpe Diem.

- Well I'm definitely not surprised.

- Seize the day, what's better than that?

- Come on, are there really people who believe this?

- Most do.

- I think you've become lazy, Mr. Van Cliff."

He recovers from the accusation. I reach out to pull his mask off, but he grabs both my wrists and I remain at his mercy. Body tense and burning up, I wait.

"Lazy?

- Lazy! You'll have to start practicing the art of seduction again.

- It's just... I have a very old wound that prevents me from any form of overly exerting practice," he said pulling me gently against him.

"I'll be careful not to tire you out."

I sigh softly, letting myself relax into him. What's the matter with you, Candice? I feebly try to free myself and he felt it. He takes a step closer, tilting his head and now staring at my lips:

"Why not give yourself over to the beauty of the present?

- I don't need to give myself over to the present to prove that I'm cool or a real woman. I leave that to your female entourage laying in wait behind the door.

- You don't like men, do you?

- And you, you've known so many foolish girls you don't even know what a woman is anymore... Why don't you go and see how many flowers you can get your hands on in that jungle out there.

- And what plant are you?

- A cactus."

When I smell his cologne mixed with the fragrance of his skin, it drives me crazy. He holds my arm behind my back, and grabs my neck, then my hair. He leans down and is about to kiss me, his lips parting, when I feel his fingers undoing the ribbon holding my mask in place. Not so fast. I throw my head back shooting him a defying look.

"Why?

- Why what?

- Why me? You could have any girl here. So why me?

- You're different.

- You don't know me.

- Can't you feel it... this thing between us?

- Hormonal compatibility.

- You talk funny.

- It's not my fault if you don't take the time to talk to women.

- Are you resisting me?

- Does it seem like I've resigned myself?

- I wouldn't want a resigned woman in my arms..."

Every inch holding my mask in place that he undoes chips away at my resolve a bit more.

"I think you'd have any woman in your arms...

- You really have such a low opinion of me?

- I'd have an opinion if I were interested in you. Which isn't the case.

- You would have made a pitiful actress, you're a bad liar... Your body tells a different story. I can read it like an open book.

- You've got a lot of years of experience on women's bodies, I suppose.

- I'll have to go back to the basics with you, I reckon."

Just for a moment, I'm under the impression he isn't only talking about seduction. He wants to break me, bring me to heel like all his little bimbos. I feel my mask slip on my nose, while his smile widens.

The door opens with a bang, and surprised, Olen relaxes his hold on me. A group of giggling girls scream when they discover Olen, in a tone that reminds me of group of geese. But I don't give myself time to think, and I rush to the open door, trying to readjust my mask.

I pass through the jungle, and casting a glance behind me, I catch a glimpse of a blond head of shiny hair from in between two vines. I quicken my pace, driven by adrenaline that I didn't know I had. I grab Liza as I rush passed the buffet. She has time to shove an appetizer in her mouth but has to run with her glass of champagne and high heels.

"What's going on?

- I did something stupid!"

Liza grabs me by the arm at the entrance and stops in front of a security guard listening to something in his earpiece.

"Hey ! Can I have your invitation please ? As a souvenir ?

- No.

- Come on ! Liza Cole. It only takes a second..."

I drag Liza hailing a taxi and shove her inside so she can give the driver the address.

"Go on then... what did you do? Did you wreck a Ming vase dancing or something?

- The host was... Olen Van Cliff."

Liza looks at me bewildered. She looks like a crumpled rag doll in the back seat, while the lights of New York fly past the window.

"Really? Did you talk to him?

- We almost kissed..."

Liza straightens up, the effects of alcohol dissipating in a nanosecond.

"Hun! Something stupid? This is the best thing that's happened to you since you got that crappy job at the bookstore!

- Pffff, yeah right. There's nothing to be proud of.

- What are you talking about?

- There's no reason to be proud in being kissed by the man who makes out with all the bimbos, models and actresses of the country.

- He kissed you?

- Yes.

- Every woman wants to kiss Olen Van Cliff.

- Even you?

- No. I'd suck him off though."

The taxi driver turns around I shove some money into his hand blushing at Liza's vulgarity and get out.

"All the women in the world throw themselves at Olen Van Cliff. But I bet there aren't many he actually tries to kiss."

I undo my dress, and the let it pool at my feet like a veil of broken illusions. Forget about it Candice. No one has ever resisted him. And it's that very resistance that intrigued him about you. I want him, but if I let myself give in, I'll just be another name added to his list of conquests. Such is the ruthless rules of this business.

Sitting on my bed, I gently stroke the satin mask. And I vow to myself that tomorrow morning this evening will be just a dream. The kind of dream that escapes in wisps of smoke when you awake.

Chapter 3

Focus Candice. Focus. How I would have liked to pull off that mask and see his face. God gave him his half smile, but he had the beauty of the devil. That perfect smile stinks of sulfur and it haunts me. I still have his scent on my skin... I would have eaten him up! At noon, I'm in such a state of nervousness that I make an appointment with Dr Tran.

Pull yourself together. How can a guy like that have such an effect on me? Because the dream hasn't dissolved. Just as I try to think of something else: suddenly, I see his eyes again, his forefinger stroking my cheek. He probably ended his glamourous evening with at least three girls. I take a deep breath and unlock my phone, standing on the street corner, drinking my coffee. That's it : fight evil with evil. I open the news page and tap in his name. An onslaught of photos appear: all beautiful, obviously. Or rather he's what makes them beautiful. Perfect white teeth, his irresistible smile, photographs of his first job, Hawaiian shirt open all the way down to his belly button. An article says: "Olen Van Cliff's crazy New York parties, the King of debauchery?"

I hesitate. Is trying to find out more about him really a good idea? When I know most of it's just bullshit? The devil on my shoulder clicked the link for me seeing as a large picture appeared: five men, masks half ripped off in most cases, their white shirts bearing alcohol stains, beaming at the camera, Olen occupying the place of honor in the center, his mask worn as sunglasses with his hair tousled and pushed back. I can't help my contemptuous grimace. A brunette in the middle, laughing riotously, showing all her teeth. At least he contented himself of just one woman... Maybe he prefers brunettes?

My colleague Niels gives me a sinister look as I walk by.

"So, did you have fun last night?"

What's his problem? I answer with a yawn:

"Oh yes, I'm exhausted.

-Yeah, well as long as it doesn't interfere with your work."

Jerk.

"Sorry, since when are you the boss, I must of missed the memo."

He gives me a dirty look as I do the same. He returns to the storage room and hits me with a,

"Go to the front desk for packaging."

I put my phone between two book-piles, and wait patiently for the customer who would come back here. That's to say no one. This is the most depressing station of the entire floor, but who cares? I click the link to Olen's Wikipedia biography : strange. For an international star who was almost nominated for a golden globe, there's barely anything on him. Maybe he has a lawyer who keeps close watch on these things? He has an impressive filmography for his age: I took him for a pretty boy who wouldn't last long despite his undeniable talent: I was mind-blown by his artistic choices navigating between independent films by directors who had already been noticed, and major super production adventure films. I go back to the previous page and a video appears a little way down. I cast a quick glance around: I'm alone. Well, might as well go for it! I click on it: it's one of the small special features you find on DVD's. It shows Olen, as a young lad, barely twenty.

"Ambition? I don't think it's a bad thing. After all, that's all my character, John, has in life. You have to understand that. He's just a kid trying to find his place in the world, a merciless world. That's a universal concept. And I mean, ambition is in our DNA, as Americans. And I hope this storyline will make it into American cinematic history.

Love? ha ha ha ... I don't know. I'm not sure this a romance movie. Sure Silvia loves him, Amanda does too, and he loves her. But he sacrifices it all to gain power. The love of power."

The video ends with an excerpt of the film. Shouting on a sailboat, pouting, wisps of hair in his eyes, a Hawaiian shirt opened to reveal a perfect and toned body, eyes as blue and as mischievous as the Mediterranean. The mix had the desired effect. I vaguely remember the pitch of the film that launched his career roughly ten years ago: a young man seduced the wife of a wealthy shipowner.

He managed through a play of manipulation to be entrusted with certain duties and then kills the person who saw him as a son. And subjugating the widow completely under his youthful charm, he gave up his highschool sweetheart to stay in power. It was unclear whether the widow committed suicide or if Olen's character helped her along. The glistening skin under the Italian sun was preparing him to be the star that would hit Hollywood like a freight train and who would make teenage girls quiver. A few sassy interviews, the beauty of an angel and his irresistible smile, did the rest: a star was born. Another video, slightly below the first caught my attention. You could see Olen walking down the street in a video filmed on the go by a paparazzi.

"So Olen? On the prowl tonight?"

Olen laughs.

"Go on then, Olen! Give us a tip to get girls! How do you do it ?

- Well you either need to have some dough or... you mistreat them a bit.

- And they like it?

- Yep, they all do!"

He leaves with a roar of laughter dodging the paparazzi to get into the club.

I'm mortified. Disgusted. But it's like a drug, either that or a part of me just doesn't want to believe it. I couldn't have fallen for a jerk like that! I click furiously on a link to another video, an interview dating from around the same time apparently. The background is different, it seems like a more intimate interview:

"The first time I stepped out onto the red carpet... it was crazy. The girls... Well people in general were pressed up against the barriers. Some of them actually fainted. When I got closer to them for autographs or whatnot... They literally wanted to tear my clothes off. It was so intense... It was like making love...

- So it's the power of seduction that appeals to you in acting?

- No... it's... You don't understand... It's a job that demands you give it your all, and I'm willing to do that to make it work.

- And what about starting a family? Do you ever think about that?

- I'll think about it when the time comes. I have all the time in the world for that!" Another video caught my eye: Olen is sprawled out on a sofa, it looks like a video taken unwittingly during a party. He has a cigarette in his hand, his rebellious lock of hair falling in his eyes, and an inebriated look :

"Why is it that the admiration of the hairdresser and the concierge aren't enough?

- Because the feeling I get on set, what I see in the eyes of passersby, being on the cover of a magazine, all that... it makes me feel as if I hold the world in the palm of my hand. And that's something nothing and nobody can replace. People say fame's useless. Bullshit! It's recognition. It's power. It's the antidote to the fucking shitty life I used to have. And nothing and no one will make me go back to that.

- Even if it can destroy you?

- Nothing can destroy me, man. I'm immortal now! This is the antidote I've been waiting for. I'm going to inject it to myself in small doses every day, and I'm willing to pay the price.

- At what cost?

- I have sure-fire survival instincts."

The video stops and freezes on Olen's proud face. What an arrogant jerk. He was young then Candice, relax. And anyway why do you care? It's not like you're going to see him again. I let out a shout of frustration, throwing my phone in my purse,

"Nope, I'm definitely not going to see him again!"

Niels poked his head out from behind a shelf.

"What?

- Nothing!!"

I furiously punch a book that had nothing to do with it all. I need to do something. Keep myself busy. I come out from behind the counter, and route through the shelves. That's what I need. To be methodical. I need concentration. I check that each author is in his rightful place and it keeps me busy for much of the afternoon ... when I hear my phone vibrate.

"Hello beautiful.

- Who's this?"

My heart's pounding in my chest. How did he get my number?

"William."

Well I wasn't expecting that. I bite my lip when I realize that I'm disappointed.

"Oh, hi!

- Do you want to grab a drink tonight?

- Why not..."

Don't look at me like that. You'd do the same. I need to clear my head after the night I had yesterday. Olen only took me by the waist, and he's got my mind reeling. Actually, I should just replace the whole damned thing. Help!

***

Before me, William strokes his finger along the stem of the glass. I'm starting to get obsessed with his thumb trailing up the glass.

"Alright. We're going to avoid the lamest question in the world: what do you do for a living, ok?

- Okay. What are you doing in New York?

- I'm here with a colleague and friend. I followed him here for a little party that took place last night. Where I met a charming woman who abused me.

- Oh, I see. A night out with some friends, without any pretension.

- There you go, quiet evening, pizza and beers with some friends."

We burst out laughing.

"What's the deal with Masquerade? I mean... why spend so much money to entertain others?

- It's about power. The more people who want in on the party, the more people talk about it, the crazier it is, the more they talk about you. Which makes more people want to work with you. It gives you more power.

- Do you like power?"

I've got to admit I'm still thinking about Olen's video, so I would like to get his opinion. Is he cut out of the same cloth? He sits there, silently, looking at me for a minute, probably to find the right words.

"Who doesn't like it? We all want to do be able to do things.

- What would you like to do?

- To make films. To kiss you."

I smile and stare at my glass, and start to run my finger on the smooth surface. He leans a bit more on the table and tries to regain my attention:

"Do you have any hobbies?

- No.

- No?

- I like the quiet, walking in Central Park, feeding the ducks. Reading... Dancing and drinking champagne. I believe that those are the two fun things I still know how to do.

- I would have loved to see you dance.

- Yeah, I would have liked to see it too. I was so drunk. It was so...

- Liberating?

- Yes."

We laugh foolishly and talk about a bit of everything.

"Your favorite dish?

- Eggplant parmigiana. And you?

- Pizza, like any true American.

- Not very original, William.

- I keep my best ideas for my writing.

- What do you write?

- At the moment I'm working on a script. A film that hopefully will be noticed by critics. What about you? Being surrounded by books, hasn't that ever made you want to write?

- Yes, actually. I used to write. Ok so, I still try to write. I wrote short stories when I was younger, and I even worked in publishing. But I had to change jobs for various reasons. And now, I limit myself to...

- Yes?

- I limit myself to writing in my journal. This is… absolutely absurd."

I burst out laughing feeling truly ridiculous.

"It's freeing to get it all down on paper. It stops you from carrying the weight of it on your shoulders, and we'll see what comes next, if I can manage to turn it into story. You know?"

Silence. With some people, silence feels like it's filled with other thoughts. I was beginning to fill it with images of a mask and a smile, when William resumes, smiling sweetly:

"You meet some nice people at the party?

- Uh yeah ... it was nice.

- You're miles away.

- I'm prone to daydreaming.

- What do you dream about?

- That's exactly it, I never dream at night so... I guess my brain needs a rest...

- You know that sharks never sleep? Only half of their brain is active.

- Really?"

William and I are discussing anything and everything when he puts his hand on mine, I know that I must take drastic measures. He seems like a nice guy. I will not let Olen Van Cliff capture all of my thoughts in the space of a day!

"Well I think we should go.

- Yes, it's getting late..."

He stands up, wiping his hands on his jeans, and bumps against the table on his way out.

"You okay ?

- Yeah, it's because I got a haircut. A bit like cats, when you cut their whiskers, they're disoriented.

- Really???"

William let out a bark of laughter seeing me wide-eyed and grabs me by the waist when I cross the threshold of the bar.

"You're too candid, little Candice."

Little Candice? I smile, amused. William watches me a moment before leaning towards me. Perfect. This is exactly what I need. To slowly start playing in the big leagues again. A distraction. But he plants a kiss on my forehead.

"I'll call you, little Candice."

I'm speechless. Why didn't he kiss me? What does he want? I was ready and waiting for it! For once, I needed a one night stand to take my mind off things. Liza would have clapped her hands in joy. Unless I didn't read the signs properly ? Maybe he doesn't like me. Am I just not fuckable?

Olen didn't seem to hesitate.

Yes, well, Olen's a wolf on the prowl shameless and fearless.

Maybe but that's what you liked about him.

"Shut your mouth, you idiot," I told my conscience, while burrowing under my duvet.

Chapter 4

When I set foot in the five star hotel I reassure myself. Bali, with its azure skies, and the cute smiles of the locals will do me good.

"You know what Liza. This is the best idea you've ever had.

- You're welcome, hun. I'll meet you at the pool. I'm off to get my badge.

- Still, doesn't your boss have questions?

- I'm allowed to bring someone. Other people bring their other halves, for me it's my best friend. And all the better if they think I'm a lesbian.

- Why?

- I already told you I don't mix business and pleasure."

On that note, Liza presses her lips together as only Liza knows how: looking serious all the while having a slightly sulky pout. She leaves, her heels clicking on the floor toward the west wing of the hotel, to the seminar room.

I unpack my suitcase quickly so that everything's ready for tonight. Yes, I like to anticipate. And opting for a light dress, I go straight to the pool and flop down. I've got at least an hour before Liza joins me. A waiter comes over and drops a glass of champagne on the table next to me.

"A little something for you, miss."

Would you look at that. They really go all out for this seminar... I down my glass in one go without thinking twice about it. In this heat? Maybe not the best of ideas... I close my eyes and can only think about relaxing further into the soft towel under my body. Two hours later I wake up, dry mouthed. Liza joined me in a turquoise bikini, that sparkles on her beautiful ebony skin. She laughs when she sees me stretching like a cat.

"You already on champagne?

- It seemed like a good idea at the time. This hotel goes to a lot of trouble for your company.

- Uumm... I didn't get a glass of champagne.

- Really?

- No.

- Well ask!"

Liza pushes her glasses down her cute upturned nose and looks at me above them with gleaming eyes.

"My God, you must be ovulating. They're dropping like flies at your feet.

- Huh?

- Didn't you ever think that, maybe, it was sent over by a guy at the bar desperately waiting for a sign from you?"

I don't believe it. A third contender? Impossible. A quick glance at the bar assured me of the absence of any male presence. I didn't seem fuckable three days ago in William's arms. It's not at the pool bar, dripping with sweat, and a few extra pounds too many on my backside, without makeup on that I'll win the votes. I wrinkle my nose and steal Liza's magazine to feel even more insecure watching young actresses strutting around in crazy outfits, a Starbucks cup in hand.

"Alright Candice love, I've got to go. The opening conference begins in forty five minutes. Go to the beach, enjoy!

- Did I drool in my sleep?

- They could've opened a second pool under your sun lounger. But with your sunglasses on, nobody saw the whites of your eyes."

I turn onto my stomach, grumbling.

"All's good, hardly any damage done to my dignity then.

- No, not your dignity. Your desirability, on the other hand... But some guys like a bit of drool."

She whipped her towel on my ass. I can't help the shrill cry that passes my lips, one that could wake the dead. She turns around and adds,

"Okay so, when I'm done where do you want to go?

- I know a great place, don't worry. A small local restaurant.

- No funny business? I can't afford to get diarrhea during the seminar ok?"

I get up with the gracefulness of a cat, smiling softly.

"Liza, we're so different. Only you could get the turista and still keep your dignity.

- I said no funny business, ok?"

Liza wags her finger in a threatening way before we go our separate ways at the bar. The waiter gave me a friendly smile.

"Tell me, about the glass of champagne... Who sent it over?

- Ah. He left, miss. I'm sorry."

I was so frustrated. I would have liked to use him to put my charms to the test. You don't know how to practice your charms Candice. Your charms are at the bottom of a closet between two g-strings bought two years ago and garters that date back to Halloween. I push the gate open and soon my feet sink into the sand. The sand has a perfect texture and leaves behind a light powder on your feet. There's no one around. I find a sheltered spot behind a palm tree where I can lay out my stuff. The surf of the turquoise ocean cleanses my saturated brain. I laugh thinking of Liza always so confident, except in the bathroom. And getting an idea, I unhook my bra and take it off, right here, on the beach, for the first time in my life. After all. Why not. Liza would be proud. Yep. That thought doesn't stop me from quickening my pace to submerge myself in the water as quickly as possible. My hair isn't quite long enough to completely cover my chest. Imagine the incredible feeling of floating in waters that are at the perfect temperature. Just cool enough to give you delicious shivers and absolutely no limits between the water and the sky. I completely melt in this wonderful water and forget the rest of the world. Even sharks? Yes, Candice, even sharks. I don't know for how long I stay like that before a male voice shakes me from my thoughts:

"Hello."

I shake myself off like a crazed poodle... and discover Olen Van Cliff positively beaming when I spit out all the salt water in the ocean.

"Are you crazy!

- Do you want me to get you another glass of champagne to help you calm down?"

I look at him, astounded, when a breeze reminds me I'm going topless. I sink into the water suddenly stammering something between a "thank you" and an "excuse me."

"Why are you apologizing?"

He immerses himself in turn right up to his lips. Did he recognize me? Impossible. I note the slight sweat forming millions of pearls adorning the outline of his lips. His glowing skin. And suddenly I can see why the rich widow of his first film got seduced on a boat in the middle of the Mediterranean. Does he have these little beads of sweat collecting at the small of his back when he makes love? Candice shut up, concentrate. What's he even doing here? A blonde sylph throws herself on him laughing.

"Olen babe, you talk too much!"

I can't help but raise a quizzical eyebrow and move away.

"Not so fast!

- You seem very busy."

She must be twenty at the very most, and is trying to climb on his back. Olen gently pushes her away and taking both her hands in his says:

"I'm coming Jenny."

The girl pouts and splashes him before declaring forfeit.

"Do you ever manage to be alone?

- I have a feeling that your question has more than one meaning...

- Only a feeling?

- I'm busy pursuing a brazen woman who wouldn't even give me her name.

- Brazen?

- Everything about you is brazen."

Olen rakes his gaze down my body, and slowly bats his eyelashes.

I realize that, while I was hypnotized by his blue eyes, he had moved much closer.

"Thanks for the glass of champagne. That was very nice of you.

- It was my pleasure."

When I feel his finger grazing my belly button and slowly make its way back up, I grab his hand, with a defying look. Eyes still fixed on me he whispers:

"You're not running away this time?

- No, I choose to fight back."

I place my hand in the middle of his chest. His heart skips a small beat. What's gotten into you Candice? His nostrils flare, his breathing quickening and when I pull his chest hair with a jerk, his lips part slightly and he takes in a shaky breath.

"Be careful Mr Van Cliff. I'm here on holiday.

- I know.

- What?

- You came with Liza Cole who got the invitation to the Masquerade party.

- You... you followed us?"

He looks both surprised and playful.

"You think you're worth it?"

What game is he playing? Blood rushes to my cheeks, and I administer a well-deserved slap. Olen blinks in shock, and shakes his head as if to wake up. I leave him standing there to get out of the water as fast and as gracefully as I possibly can, praying he hadn't noticed my cellulite and that he wouldn't follow me.

I hurry to recover my bathing suit from where I left it on a branch. I feel eyes on me, and a sidelong glance confirms that I've piqued the interest of his group of friends. Why is he here? Could he have followed me? Of course Candice, you idiot. He's too busy with skawking enamored models. I choose disdainful intransigence, pulling my shirt on and retrieving my old copy of "Pride and Prejudice". However, a few minutes putting up with the giggling gets on my last nerve and I get up to leave, readjusting my sunglasses, and trying to pretend I can't hear them.

I feel a shiver run down my spine while regaining the hotel. Can I feel his eyes following me? Well, at any rate, no one here's paying attention to me.

Here I am, back in my idyllic room: I think it's the honeymoon suite. I don't know how Liza managed to get this room. The curtains, the aroma, the view... everything's just perfect. She's still not back from her conference... Perhaps this is the perfect time for a bath...

I draw the curtains, turning on a lamp in the living room that glows with a dim light. I light the candles in the bathroom and step out of my clothes. The enormous full-length mirror reflects its ruthless portrait: pretty skinny, brunette, fairly long hair, and slightly arched eyebrows that give me a smug look, on top of having a small mouth. I gave up on doing anything with my hair, and just let it grow out, and change color according to the sun. An ordinary girl, with ordinary looks. I contemplate my nails. They've grown nicely since the beginning of the week, but that's normal. Peeling off labels isn't an activity that makes for fabulous nails. Yes, the kind of girl that nobody does a double take of on the street. But in any case, I don't believe the stories in magazines that would have you think they would pounce on anything that moves as long as it's an active and rather pretty woman. I shrug and adorn a contemptuous pout worthy of Scarlett O'Hara while slipping into the shower to turn on the hot water. Liza almost had a go at me this morning:

"Why are you so conscientious? We're in a fucking five-star hotel in Indonesia, with expenses covered by my boss and you, you're just being pretentious on behalf of the environment!" She cried out.

"I don't need so many luxuries Liza!" I tried to protest in vain.

Liza, the tyrant, shook her head puffing out a breath of air. She was beautiful but she was behaving like a chauvinistic male. That's exactly what earned her such a great position in a big marketing company.

"We never have enough luxuries hun!" She shouted.

I lose track of time listening to Liza Ekdahl sing Salvatore Poe in her syrupy voice. Alright. I have to confess. I don't need all this, but I could get used to it. The image of Botticelli's *Birth of Venus* :

that's what crossed my mind. Yes, it truly was a Venusian emerging from the waves that I met... and as for me, simple mortal, I really must have looked foolish topless, and stuttering!

After a couple of songs, I feel the need to move. I get out of the tub, looking on sadly as the water drains away. One bath in ten years, Liza was right, I had to stop beating myself up!

I slip on a purple evening dress made from bamboo fabric. It looked like a beach dress, but I loved its light purple color too much to let the sea salt destroy it and the fabric's as soft as silk. Only less expensive. I pour myself a glass of Chinon rosé, and go to sit on the balcony to admire the sunset. The first notes of Lisa Ekdahl's "Daybreak" could be heard. Yes, everything was perfect in my perfect little world. That's what luxury stands for. Doing what I want when I want to.

Suddenly, Olen's deep voice resounds from the neighbouring balcony amongst female laughter and laughter in general!

Chapter 5

"Guess who I met at the reception!" Liza shouts, coming back like a rampaging elephant.

I jump out of my skin, nearly knocking my glass over and cover her mouth with my hand.

Olen's harem falls silent. Suddenly the guests, Olen included burst out laughing. Liza then looks at me bewildered. She gets it when I point to the balcony on our left, mouthing Olen's name to her. Then Liza starts laughing in a way that sounds fake and taking me by the hand, she drags me along with her. I find myself in front of Olen's door, while Liza knocks, eyes shining.

"Liza! I'm not wearing any underwear!" I whisper panicked.

"All the better!" the little vixen whispers back.

She looks at me, frowning, and literally rips my hair tie out. I cry out in pain:

"What the hell!!?"

That's when Olen chooses to open the door. He's to die for. How can he have such perfect skin and shirts that suit him so well? Perfectly natural. Looking good is a full time job. I think I glimpse a smile gracing his lips when he lays eyes on me. I blush immediately, and undertake to conscientiously push back every little hair that falls in front of my ear. And to say that I slapped him earlier in the water. He doesn't seem to hold it against me. Liza smiles widely,

"I'm sorry but I'm one of your biggest fans and I couldn't not come to say hi!

- Thank you...

- I hope you don't mind ?"

Olen took his time before grinning. That smile. A wolf's smile. Suddenly I feel the need to leave. Otherwise he might get his claws into me. Looking to escape from Liza's grip, who senses that I'm about to cop out. She knows me all too well.

"No not at all! Want to come in? Olen asks, opening the door wide.

- Oh thank you so much!"

And while Liza gives a general good evening to the audience in a singing voice, using her innate charm, I advance, and find myself looking defiantly at the wolf while entering his den where his other victims are shrieking.

Liza grabs me by the shoulders to introduce me to the twins with long blond hair raving about my insufferable best friend's dress. And I naturally slip into the conversation. It takes a few seconds for it to hit me. Before me is the sylph, Jenny, from earlier.

"My God, the hotel's yoga teacher is great. Do you do yoga, Candice?

- Uh… I've never tried. But I have yoga pants."

Subject of the coy smile of my audience, I feel compelled to justify myself and give an explanation.

"I mean they're perfect for staying at home or doing... some cleaning. Ahem."

Liza laughs out loud while nice-blonde number one looks at me with a mocking pout: apparently wearing yoga pants without doing any yoga was banned in Hollywood. Or, maybe, you just didn't admit to it in public. Damn it! We were in the depths of Indonesia. Who cares about this stuff? Liza brings the conversation to the delicious cocktails at the bar while nice-blonde-number-one, aka Jenny Jump-on-Olen-in-the-water has no desire to let it go. She looks at me insistently:

"You want to be an actress?

- Ha, not at all.

- Oh really?"

No honey. I'm not looking to profit from Olen's celebrity to advance my career. I have too much pride for that. But you're ready to literally be part of a harem to glean a bit of his celebrity, his lifestyle and his money.

"No. Too many sacrifices.

- What do you mean?

- Well, since you're not the only one beating the pavement, you're going to have a hard time finding any contracts, so no dough, no health insurance, no nights out, no love life, no nice clothes, no amazing trips... to say the least a lack of stability regarding everything. For at least a decade. And on top of that a feeling of loneliness. Your career, if it takes off, can end after just one movie because it didn't work out. And to be bossed around by self-centered idiots who are actually under orders of marketing teams, and not answering to the desire to create, no thanks."

Jenny was slack-jawed in a matter of seconds. Suddenly, I pity Jenny. Candice, what do you know about her? Maybe, she didn't have parents to pay for college, and this is one of the few options she had.

"That and it takes real talent to make it in the industry. No, I don't have enough courage for that. But I admire those who do! Maybe that's what talent is... courage!"

Jenny's smile finds its way back to her face. That's all she took out from my speech. Great.

I turn to tell Liza that I'm off: I'm going to create a diplomatic incident with my clumsiness. But my face crashes into Olen's warm chest, he grabs me by the waist and hands me a glass of champagne. I instinctively squeeze my thighs together. My eyes have got to be as big as saucers. He smiles and I meekly let myself be led towards the balcony. I capitulated even before the battle began, as if hypnotized by the mere touch of his hand around my waist. He says calmly without looking at me:

"You have beautiful eyes." I feel my bare thighs turn to jelly.

It's been awhile since someone's paid me a compliment. What an idiot I'm being, he must say stuff like that all the time, to all the girls who hang around him.

"Just so you know, if you keep doing that thing with your eyelashes I won't be held accountable for my actions, Candice.

- How do you know my name?"

I could feel the conversation slipping dangerously.

"Your friend.

- But of course."

He turns towards me, his face close to mine. He's only a few inches from my body, his skin stretched over taut muscles, and his predatory smile begins to emerge. Part of me would love to press myself up against his chest and succumb. Just to let go for once in my life... one last time. He whispers softly. Too softly,

"You're not drinking?"

Right. Is he being a player, trying to get me into bed by making me drink or something?!

However, taking a sip of the sparkling rosé, I realize how defensive I've been. He might only want to get to know me. I must be an intriguing distraction... compared to... I look through the bay windows: the guests giggle eyeing my dress.

Olen then opens a gate to the left, and invites me to follow him. A private access to the beach! I honestly smile at him for the first time and then follow him, much to my surprise. The moon's high and gently bathes the path between the dunes in a soft glow. Olen comes down the stairs right behind me. Special thanks to my intuition for making me wash my hair with rose oil. Suddenly, arriving on the sand, Olen grabs me by the waist and holds me against him. My heart speeds up to a pace akin to light speed.

"Not so fast."

His touch has got my adrenaline pumping from my toes right upto the tips of my hair.

"It's slippery around here. I already found myself in a predicament."

And he takes the lead, putting his hands in his pockets, and I wonder if he's not going to start whistling his way down the small dune.

"Do you do this often?"

He slowly turns with a deceptively innocent look.

"Being in a predicament?

- Inviting strangers into your room ..."

Oh I'm sure you've had lots of entanglements with young single women that have been hypnotized by your sexual magnetism!

"My life is full of strangers. You're not very talkative.

- It's just... People must be constantly asking you lots of questions. I would feel like I was making you rehearse your interviews.

- You're nothing like a journalist."

Nor a model! Yet, for someone who spends her time sitting, I was rather slim. I push back my long brown hair.

"Are you a student ?"

I giggle at that. Surely, I'm a little too old.

"I'll give you a hint. I like books. Do you ?

- Yes. Steinbeck's my personal favorite."

I remain silent. It was a rather sophisticated choice: Salinger, a classic from high school, or Stephen King would have been less surprising. I wonder, truly interested,

"And why's that?

- The truthfulness.

- Strange for an actor."

Fortunately, it's dark because I blush after having uttered those words out loud. He doesn't respond, I'm pretty proud of myself for that. I managed to shock Olen Van Cliff. I chuckle internally. We walk in silence for a while, watching the waves that have become a phosphorescent blue.

"It's the bioluminescent plankton. It lights up under stress and the pressure. He explains.

- It's beautiful."

The sea shimmers a bewitching blue, and the waves roll like huge magic carpets of a thousand diamonds. The air was mild, fresh.

"What's your favorite novel?"

I would have liked to impress him with a clever response, but the only book that came to mind was the two books I had flicked through this afternoon…

"*Pride and Prejudice*, of course. *Nana* by Emile Zola".

And I turn on my heel.

"Are you tired?

- After that answer, I suppose you either have me all figured out, or you find me boring. I'd rather take the initiative.

- Do you often initiate things?

I don't answer and focus on my hair that's refusing to stay tucked behind my ear, due to the wind full of sea spray, stubbornly keeping my gaze straight ahead.

"I find you refreshing.

- So, now I'm a refreshment.

- I would say a very good vintage cognac disguised as a half sweet, half sharp fruit juice. A bit like a cactus. I've actually come to enjoy cactus juice for some time now. Apparently it's very good for your health."

He stops and looks deeply into my eyes. They were an incredible translucent blue. I'm hanging onto his every word, looking deep into his sparkling eyes. They can easily have you under his spell, but they show no emotion, only total control of his body and his expressions.

"You work in a library?

- Sorry to disappoint, I work in a bookshop. And I'm sorry but I'm not going to sleep with you tonight. What am I saying? I'm not sorry. Doesn't matter, you should find someone to share your bed in that harem of yours. There you have it. Bookseller. I'm very boring.

- Do you always judge people by their job?

- What about you? Do you always judge people on their looks?

- You didn't answer.

- Neither did you."

We stare each other down for a brief moment, then his mouth stretches into a thin smile and he bursts out laughing, head thrown back to the sky.

"Why did you become a bookseller?

- Well, I wanted to write but... It's complicated. I needed a job to put bread on the table, and books, that's the best company you could ask for.

- Wow that, that hurts." He said, feigning being wounded.

I start to laugh wholeheartedly. Here, away from his army of sylphs who all look alike, everything seems so easy with him. Everything seems like a game: no rules, no losers.

"I think nothing can hurt you, Mr Van Cliff.

- You really believe that?

- Being a star, is like being a superhero. What problems could you possibly have in common with us mortal men?

- You're ruthless. Here I thought you were shy.

- I'm not shy." I say a little too drily. I mean honestly, what does he think I am, a teenage girl? I quickly add. "Just a little wild. I like watching people.

- Me too." I turn to look at him, and see a shy smile half-hidden by his aquiline nose. My God that shirt left half open... I'm not sure if I want to scratch down his chest or send him packing to teach him some manners. I go for a polite smile.

"Are you on holiday?

- Yes, Liza's here for a seminar with her company, and she hates traveling alone.

- How long are you here for ?"

He seems to think about it for a moment. I think I'll never get tired of his handsome profile. Almost Greek-looking actually... I could slap myself for these thoughts and I answer in a falsetto voice.

"I leave tomorrow night.

- Would you like to stay?

- Yes. No... It's impossible anyway.

- Why? Anything's possible, if you want it enough." He says, laughing.

"In your world, maybe. Not in mine. And it's time for me to return to my world, my safe haven."

I add to fill the lull in the conversation:

"I appreciate your career choices.

- Oh really?

- Yes you've convinced Hollywood to bet on you while you were frankly set out to have a career as an inconsistent boy toy. Hats off to you.

- Thanks.

- You didn't step on anyone's toes, at least not in the public's eye and you imposed your style. You're far from the peacock with no brains I thought you'd be.

- I was right to invite you both in," He says, laughing.

I join him in his laughter.

"It's strange meeting a woman who doesn't wonder what it feels like to be the most eligible bachelor in Hollywood!

- The most eligible bachelor ? Honestly, I thought you'd show up dead from an overdose surrounded by a sea of prostitutes after a rocky career."

He suppresses a gasp. Well done Candice, you shut him up. It must make for a change from all those people who must kiss his ass all day long. I continue:

"I thought fame was going to kill you, Mr. Van Cliff.

- Celebrity turns you into a juicy piece of meat to some people.

- Well, now you know what it's like being a woman making her way through a throng of drooling men.

- Drooling doesn't necessarily show a lack of respect, you know.

- Oh really?

- Some men know how to show respect while admiring feminine beauty."

He turns to me and looks me up and down, stressing his words. I burst out laughing. Does that really work on women?

"Some men are eternal teenagers.

- Teenagers?

- Yes, I don't believe the line that men are unfaithful pigs. I think it's just that... they're eternal teenagers.

- I'm not that kind of man.

- And what kind of man are you?

- The kind that likes to hunt for pleasure... and not to hurt.

- That's textbook child behaviour, I dare say: he doesn't think he'll break his toy and so he doesn't mind mistreating it a bit. Well, back to adulthood."

We were back at the entrance to the hotel. No way I'm going back through his harem and their amazed gazes. I abruptly stick my hand out for him to shake:

"Wow. Really?

- What "really "?

- You're going to leave me just like that?"

I'm taken aback. What was he expecting ? That I wouldn't be able to keep my hands off him ? Alright, I'm dying to get my hands on him, honestly. I smile at him.

"Yes. Just like that. Thank you Mr Van Cliff for a lovely evening.

- Fine. Good night, Candice. See you soon, maybe."

Olen gently shakes my hand, smirking. If I hadn't made the first move, would he have tried to kiss me? I shiver feeling the warmth of his hand in mine, and for a split second, it's as if I could feel his entire body against mine, I open my mouth to apologize. After all, who am I to judge his lifestyle? But I can only look down at his hand holding mine. And I turn on my heel. Before the hotel doors open for me, I catch his reflection, he's still looking at me with his hands in his pockets: I thought I could distinguish a glint in his blue hooded eyes, like someone lying in wait, preparing a ruse which he is the only one to know the secret of.

Chapter 6

Liza spreads newspapers on the coffee table screaming.

"It's crazy right?? You've been dubbed Olen Van Cliff's official girlfriend!"

I nervously smooth my thick chocolate brown hair with the palm of my hand. I can't bring myself to touch the magazines strewn across the table.

"That's impossible, that can't be me."

And yet it is: it was, in fact, me in those coarse-grain pictures. The moonlight that seemed so beautiful to me, and the moment that was so precious ... It was all an illusion. Or were the magazines the illusion? I see the world as black and white: grey? No thanks. I feel contaminated. Violated.

"Please... Liza..."

My oldest friend opens her mouth to say:

"Oh sorry. I thought you'd get a kick out of it."

I drink my tea, scowling curled up in the corner of the taupe slightly threadbare couch.

"You had a good time, right?

- Yeah, it was nice."

It's true, it had been awhile since I last flirted. Three years actually. And I couldn't stand somebody sullying his image. And violating my privacy. I was going to become the rival of millions of women around the world whose opinion doesn't matter. Without meaning to and without any legitimacy.

"If I see Olen again, what's going to happen? Will everyone be watching us? Will I have to play a kind of public role? The silent and enamored girlfriend counting her blessings?"

I shook my head, annoyed.

"Why do you always take everything so seriously, Candice?

- I don't know, I can't help it."

Liza looked at me suspiciously.

"Well would you look at that, you've got it bad haven't you?

- Absolutely not! We only talked for a few minutes."

Liza points to Olen's face.

"Didn't need to talk much apparently..."

Olen was smoldering at me while I was fiddling with my hair. I don't know what to say. I stand up suddenly,

"Right it's not everything but I have a real job!

- Marketing project manager is a real job!

- Bossing people around is second nature to you, dear Liza!"

And I flee from the bombardment of pillows that are headed my way from across the room. Liza retorts with "little bitch" while slamming the door to the apartment. The life of a bookseller, suited me well. No contingencies, no trouble. Open the metal shutter, disarm the alarm, turn on the computer, check stock, take a look at yesterday's best sellers, the weekly best sellers... Jeffrey's Corner was a small local bookstore. But the big brands were literally devouring the market and the Internet wasn't helping any as Jeffrey often points out. We managed to boost sales a bit by inviting authors for readings and autographs. We were hanging in there, but I preferred to be in touch with the readers: I felt like I was recommending a journey and not a simple object. And the good thing is that I work alone. Often alone. I had very little to answer for with Jeffrey, the boss, and I even know how to deal with Niels, who would eventually get over it. Besides Jeffrey left me a message: he's going to be out for the rest of the week. Right. I was drinking my chocolate macchiato at the Starbucks on the corner watching the passersby. A nice job, a nice roommate, a nice lifestyle … You've landed on your feet kiddo! There's not much missing in this cozy little nest I've made. Just something to keep me warm at night other than Mr Pilou, the giant teddy bear that my parents gave me for my fifth birthday to help me be more social. And who still has a place of honor in my room at almost 30 years old! I never dared to tell my parents that I hated teddies. What a stupid idea for a gift. Only good for collecting dust, unnecessary and cumbersome. The greatest gift I got recently was a steam cooker. It's the modern woman's best friend. That and the epilator, can't forget that one. I pulled out my phone to check my email, probably already swarmed with ads. When I browsed through the senders' list my heart stopped. An Olen980 left me a message. I read the short missive, incredulous. Once. Then a second time.

"Hi ! Let's forget what happened and leave it there. It was nice. Please don't reply to this message. Good luck. Olen."

I leaned back in my chair laughing nervously at the absurdity of existence. Nothing goes as planned.

***

Liza conscientiously applied my lipstick. She takes a final look at the makeup tutorial that appears on her screen. Michelle Phan made up as Angelina Jolie was just stunning.

"That woman has incredible eyes!

- Michelle?

- Angelina.

- Everything she has is incredible: her career, her gene pool... people like that aren't normal."

Liza looked at me kindly.

"Are you sure you want to go out Candice? It's a weeknight, it's not like you.

- After everything I've been through this morning, I need a drink. Ok, that's enough, let's go!"

And without a glance at the end result in the mirror, I grab my bag and go. Curiosity, lust and seduction: wolves with over shined shoes made in China were taking root in the line forming in front of the club. Liza takes me by the hand, puts on her best smile worthy of the glory years of Sharon Stone for the bouncers' benefit, and we're in in a flash. The cozy atmosphere of the restaurant Tao DownTown and its false oriental splendor gave way to the club and its blaring music. I briefly wonder while sipping on my drink if David Rockwell's giant Buddha that overlooks the room is plastic or some sort of porcelain. It watches us, its smile as vacant as my gaze after two Pama Sutra cocktails. Vodka, iced grapefruit and grenadine aren't enough. I don't want to hear my heart beat anymore. The loud music and decor that fit Liza like a glove is just what I need tonight. I call the bartender over to order a third with Liza yelling to make herself heard,

"There's so many people it's crazy! All for the birthday of a reality TV starlet!"

I don't acknowledge her and order a Royal Rickshaw. My eyes then meet those of Becky Parks, who renamed herself Becky Sparks. After a reality show as shallow as the next, she made a sex tape with a soulless hunk from a radio talent show, which had her making the headlines for several months. Her miscarriage and her tendency to party were the secret behind her success. Determined to prolong her career in the public eye, she claimed to have changed: all in all she had her skirts lengthened and grew her hair out. Pseudo-celebrities are all alike, forgotten only to be replaced by another face every month, even worse, criticized by the press ... I open my mouth to speak after a sip, but Liza has her arms around a guy's neck, a brunet with a big nose and a shirt with asymmetrical stripes, letting him whisper something in her ear, giggling. Would you look at that! She had to be under a lot of pressure at work to do something like that. I start to snigger when I see the short brunet making himself slightly taller by standing on tiptoes to talk to Liza who was perched on her stool. Gratuitously mean... and simply delicious. Suddenly, Becky Sparks is in front of me, batting her eyelashes at an alarming rate.

"Oh my God, you're Olen's fiancée! How is he?"

I sober up real fast, looking her over from head to toe. Do they know each other? Olen Van Cliff's known for not having a type: brunette, blonde... whatever... but in this case I'm actually shocked. Becky and her arms inflated with palm oil filled cakes, the ubiquitous teeth... with Olen? A cheap and reinvented version of Britney Spears?

"I saw the pictures taken in Indonesia. It must be magical. I have to appear in the next music video for a singer. I'm his muse. I met Olen once. He's so... Oh my God!"

There was no stopping Becky who was spouting out her new exciting life in her Texan accent, so hyped up. I probably don't seem the smartest with my dumbfounded look because she takes me by the hand and in a confidential tone, she adds:

"Us, the people who weren't born in this world, we know what it's like. It's hard, but you have to find a way to fit in. Oh, by the way!"

Quick as a flash, she grabs her phone and takes a selfie of us pulling me in by the neck. I catch a glimpse of my bewildered face stuck to her swollen one and in a split second, she's gone, waving her hand to go shake her derrière on the dance floor in her theatrically tight-fit dress. Liza looks at me, finally alone, eyebrows raised. I quip,

"Well, where's Romeo gotten to?

- Oh Romeo! Wherefore art thou Romeo? She shouts bringing her hand to her forehead and arching her back on the stool.

- Because his mother had rubbish taste!"

We start laughing hysterically. We look like two fifteen year old girls, but damn does it feel good.

"Oh Candice, we've finally got you back! Olen needed to come into your life for you to let go! I knew the guy would do you some good!

- Liza. I haven't shown you his email yet.

- Okay, go ahead, it can't be that bad... You're so proud and sensitive you probably just misunderstood, that's all!"

I thrust my phone under her nose. Her eyes widen.

"I can't see anything! I've had too much to drink! Read it to me!"

I shout as loud as I can, after finishing my drink.

"Hi! Let's forget what happened, leave it there. It was nice. Please don't reply to this message. Good luck. Olen.

- What? Candice, I can't hear you!

- Hi! Let's forget what happened, leave it there. It was nice. Please don't reply to this message. Good luck. Olen." I screamed.

Liza looked at me like a deer caught in the headlights. She snatches the phone from my grasp and brings it closer to her face. Obviously, that's when the music stops.

"WHAT AN ASSHOLE !!!!!!"

Liza shot up from her stool, her gold Balmain dress riding up to the top of her thighs.

The whole room looks at us taken aback in a deafening silence. The DJ plays the traditional Happy Birthday and a giant cake is brought out. I think back to Leslie Caron emerging from the birthday cake before a bewildered Gene Kelly in Singing in the Rain. There had always been starlets, and Becky with her fake bun was going to get crushed at that game. Not everyone can become the next Marilyn Monroe. How could I be jealous of a girl I just met? Why was I even jealous!? Liza shakes her head sitting back down.

"Who does he think he is? He'd be lucky to have you on his arm! It would make a change from the bitches he...

- Look, I don't care!

- But he caught your eye, didn't he?

- Maybe a bit but don't worry. I'm not made of glass.

- I'm sorry, Candice ... I didn't think he'd be like that, the cad.

- Cad? It takes four drinks for you to stop swearing?

- It's just..."

Liza takes my hands in hers, and holds them tight. Tears come to her eyes.

"It's just ... I haven't seen you so carefree in a long time.

- Listen, it'll change."

And in a moment of genius, I order a bottle of champagne, Moet & Chandon, Imperial for two. Tomorrow, I'll send a heartfelt tirade to Olen. I was going to paint a picture worse than those poor photos that were as shiny as Becky Sparks' forehead.

**

It was cold in the forest. I looked at my basket that I suddenly found rather shabby with only a jam jar in the bottom. I looked at my wrists. Well that's funny. The skin there was white again, smooth and silky. No scars. I should have at least have some after the chase in the forest. I've been running in the woods for a while now. Everything was clawing at my skin. Suddenly, my red cape gets caught in the sharp branches of a tree that sprang from the ground, there, right next to me. I run faster, while a wolf howls at the moon. A large white bed appears, there in the middle of the cottage. Hypnotized by the whiteness of the sheets, I take off my cape and spread it out on the bed, before I slip between the crisp sheets. The shadows move around the bed. I close my eyes: the shadow joins me and hovers over me. It stings. It's heavy above me. Arms suffocating me. Blue sparkling eyes have me glued to the spot and I get lost in those eyes. A frog appears on the chest of drawers and whispers "Young beautiful girls, nice girls, don't do well listening to all kinds of people."

Wow. I haven't had a hangover since... college. Holy shit. It's half past six. I have exactly twenty minutes to take a shower, look like a human being and a decent woman on top of that, I've got to run to the other end of the block, open the library and check the stock.

It's Tuesday, and I have a feeling this week's going to be hard. Liza's already gone, and I didn't hear a thing despite my two alarm clocks. I manage the feat of finding my clothes in mere seconds, and slipping my sneakers on, I sprint out of the house. Poor me, I had no idea the magnitude of the crappy week I was in for. When I get to the library, a huge truck is parked out front. I understand immediately and start to shout,

"Hey !! Stop!"

I'm aware that I look like a scruffy teenager

"Miss Candice Evans?

- Yes ?! What are you doing ? Where's Mr Jeffrey ? And Niels?

- Here's your box Miss, with your stuff. The bookstore's closing. I don't know the details.

- But... that's impossible, Mr Jeffrey hasn't said anything to me.

- I don't know the details miss. Mr Jeffrey's inside."

Box in hand, I rush into the bookshop. The beautiful wood paneled walls, glossy beeswaxed shelves, the blackboard and the cushions for childrens' storytime... how can it all just disappear?

"Ah Candice!"

Mr Jeffrey appears to have aged ten years.

"My dear I thought I'd fight till the end, but it's over. The bank isn't coming through.

- But... it wasn't that bad! We were doing pretty well, weren't we?!

- Not well enough. I had... complications, my wife's health. And... It was either the bookstore or the house... Everything got out of control this past week." He said ruefully.

I bite my lip. I knew Mrs. Jeffrey had problems, and therefore content myself in giving the poor man's arm a squeeze.

"But... you're going to be alright?

- Yes .. I have a brother in a sawmill. He'll get me a job, a handyman of sorts! At my age, no one here will employ me. I'm leaving New York, Candice ... I'm sorry. I couldn't bring myself to tell you."

Mr Jeffrey belongs to an older generation of men who couldn't admit defeat. This was a sore loss. I could tell by his look of despair.

"Don't stay here. Come with me."

I take him by the arm, box in hand. Glancing back at the truck, my heart sank at the sight of books carelessly piled in boxes.

"What are you going to do Candice?"

Mr. Jeffrey's question hits me. After all, these past few years I prioritised my job. What was I going to do, me who, by now, only loved reading and drinking hot chocolate while joking around with people, moved by the smell of paper and the comfort of an old leather couch?

"I'm young. I'll bounce back. Waitress or cleaning lady... you know. It doesn't scare me.

- I admire your generation Candice. You're... stronger.

- I wouldn't say that Mr Jeffrey. I think we're well aware that the world can be ruthless at times, and that life can sometimes be sweet."

He stops me at the street corner.

"Listen, I'll send your resume to all my contacts. With no exception! You're bound to find something!

- Thank you... Good luck Mr Jeffrey."

I hug him for the first time since we met. He looks at me from under his big bushy eyebrows, taking me by the arm and turns away with a sigh, his head tucked into his shoulders.

The sun's shining. I decide to take my time walking home to give myself time to think. Disheveled by my run, I adjust my box under my arm when a text from Liza makes me jump. I wiggle around to grab my phone from my back pocket.

"Honey, you're all over the internet."

Okay. Fine, more pictures of me in Indonesia... I amble up to our reassuring and cozy apartment, and dropping my box on the floor, I go to make myself a hot chocolate. The world will keep going despite a few pictures after all. I can't stop thinking about Olen and his magnetic blue eyes, but I have to be realistic. We're just too different. His free-spirit and his carelessness are good for me, beyond his aura as conquerer of the opposite sexe. As much as he annoys me, I'm drawn to him, I envy his freedom, as unattainable as it seems to someone like me. And I mean, he's probably in Los Angeles by now. I sit at the computer. How do you look yourself up on the internet? I'm not a celebrity, so my name won't do any good. I type in Olen's name, all the while feeling ill at ease. That's weird. Before, he only took on the role of a fantasy, insignificant. Now he's a human being, flesh and bone. And here I am, scanning through pictures of him: he's mercilessly perfect. Chin devoid of scruff, a strong jawline, a distant and piercing look. He knows how to electrify crowds with his personality as well as his phenomenal talent. But is he a good person? I'm incapable of answering that. This man is a paradox: the king of parties, king of Hollywood, and someone who keeps his family close, secretive, born to be an actor and thrive at the top. I lay eyes on him, superb in his snug blue shirt and slightly disheveled hair. In the midst of his flock of admirers with his usual smirk, he seems invincible. But even as the object of all that attention... I'm under the impression he seems lonely. Maybe he throws all these parties with more and more models in the most exclusive places... because that's all he has. At almost thirty, he balances filming and parties, he works like a mad man according to Liza. Yes but... things aren't always what they seem. Why would women be the only ones waiting for true love? You can talk, you don't get attached easily either... I click on the latest news.

"Olen Van Cliff our favorite womanizer has struck again. Over a hundred and twenty models were at his last party. Special occasion? No way! The most coveted bachelor in Hollywood takes advantage of the absence of his mysterious new girlfriend to rediscover his party boy habits in New York. Unless she didn't manage to hold onto him? The story that was off to such a good start in the torrid heat of Indonesia was only a holiday fling! But who knows? The mysterious young woman is unknown to the media. Has she got a trick up her sleeve? Nancy O'Brian keeps you in the loop XoXo!"

So he's in New York. And apparently has forgotten all about me. See, it was just an entertaining adventure for him. He's NOT ATTRACTED TO YOU. Get that into your thick skull, Candice. I sigh, realizing that the Olen Van Cliff mystery will never be solved by any woman. I jump upon seeing the following news thread, which includes a video.

"Exclusive!!! Our correspondent was at Becky Sparks' birthday party. We finally have answers to all your questions about Olen Van Cliff, the handsomest man in American cinema (well still alive) and his mysterious girlfriend. Our exclusive video sheds some light on the matter. They broke up by email! Is Olen Van Cliff, the famous actor, really behind the break up? What happened? Maybe she didn't want to make their relationship public? Can the rift caused by different lifestyles really be overcome by love? Or has Candice had enough of Olen's lifestyle always surrounded by models that are younger and surely fresher? What would you have done if you were in her shoes? Do you have what it takes to click on the link? The identity of the woman remains unknown. If you have any information, be sure to tweet ☺ Nancy O'Brian keeps you posted XoXo!"

The video ends with Liza standing up abruptly and swearing in the surrounding silence. A little bit more and you could see her underwear. I'd forgotten. Liza only rarely wears underwear. I watch the video again, biting my nails. You can distinctly hear me shout out Olen's email. I reread the article. Damn it, they know my name, they're going to find me. Who told them? The face of blonde number one comes to mind. I go on to see myself pursued, while wearing that horrible orange jumpsuit that Harrison Ford had on for the filming of *Fugitive*. Will I have to hide in a dumpster to escape the paparazzi? For God's sake, Candice, stop being so paranoid. You've got TOO MUCH imagination. My fingers are shaking. I still manage to click on the link to the video. I need to know. Facing the camera, I scream showing my phone to Liza, filmed from the back. Damn it! I didn't see a thing last night. How did someone manage to film me? Someone with a phone maybe? Or a cameraman from Becky's team? What a little bitch... By getting her name in an article about Olen, it's as if she made it into his inner circle. If it was, I had underestimated her. They know my name, they've got my face on camera. Damn it! I look at the number of views on Youtube: three million. In less than ten hours... I jump seeing my phone vibrate. Unknown number. Does he... maybe he wants to apologize for all the fuss? I pick up and feel my hair stand on end at the voice.

Chapter 7

"Candice Hello, Nancy O'Brian here! We don't know each other, I work for the magazine..."

I immediately hang up.

There you go. Disaster struck. The week has just begun and I'm convinced that it can't get worse. The phone vibrates again. Unknown number. Damn. What do I do? Should I answer? I pick up praying that it's one of Mr Jeffrey's contacts:

"Hello?

- Hello Ryan from Gossippies website, what do you have to say about..."

I hang up immediately. Who gave out my phone number? How did they find me?

The phone doesn't stop ringing all morning, and I take refuge in my room to sort stuff out. I would have liked to send out resumes, but I'm too afraid to come across those damned pictures or a picture of me. That's the thing about the Internet: there's so many ads and links that even if you don't want the latest news, the news will find a way into your life, into your inbox. At noon, I send Liza an email to keep her informed:

"Hi! The bookstore shut down, here's my resume in the attachment, can you proofread it, and tell me what you think please? Tons of calls from journalists, I deleted my Facebook profile, see you tonight. People almost saw your ass on the video. You should wear underwear from time to time. See you later."

I go to clear my head and decide to take a walk through Central Park. I sit on a bench to drink my hot chocolate, watching afternoon joggers. Well, kiddo, you've survived worse. My biggest fault is my introverted side. I like people, but networking, that's Liza's domain. I mistakenly prioritized my day to day comfort without worrying about the future. The publishing market is mobbed by tons of freshly graduated trainees who work for almost nothing. Young and fresh trainees. Stop, that's enough, you're twenty-six that's not old!

"No, but I feel old." I say out loud.

When I return to the apartment, my phone has thirty-five missed calls. My voicemail is full. I delete the messages from lousy reporters and read Liza's response.

"More detailed with the interests' section. No underwear, ever: I refuse to have a pantyline across my ass. It's the ultimate fashion faux-pas."

That makes me laugh. The phone vibrates showing a number I don't recognise. I pick up, ready to fight those damned reporters.

"Candice it's Olen."

I freeze, butt glued to my stool. I don't know what comes over me, but I get up and start rushing through words at full speed,

"Alright listen, Olen I-think-I'm-the-bomb! I didn't ask for all this. So you can keep your life filled with Jaguars, Ferraris and models galore, and I'll keep my peaceful life as a stuck up bookseller. And sorry if you think I'm not good enough for you, but that's fine by me, got it? Bye!"

And I hang up. He better not hold it against me. I mean, honestly! My phone vibrates again.

"WHAT ?!

- I never sent that email Candice."

It knocks the wind out of me.

"And I'm sorry for all this unwanted attention.

- But... who sent it then?

- Someone who doesn't want to see me with you apparently. Listen, don't worry about the press, carry on with your peaceful life as a bookseller. I really envy you for that at the moment."

He said that with so much tenderness, and an inflection to his tone that literally makes me melt.

"Oh... Really? Uh I mean, okay. Do you think I should change number?

- Do as you see fit, but journalists are vultures. They never give up on anything.

- Okay..."

I'm pensive for a moment, not knowing what to say.

"Candice?

- Yes?

- I enjoyed our walk on the beach. The pictures don't do you justice.

- It's a shame you can't see the plankton."

What an idiot. What was I thinking? Why did I say something like that?

"Liza insisted on showing me. I... I don't know how you can stand it. The constant public attention.

- You get used to it. He told me flatly.

- Listen, I've got to go, Olen. Thanks for calling.

- Go to lunch with me.

- Sorry?

- Lunch.

- Okay… Fine."

I cautiously tell him to meet me in my favorite pizzeria near the bookstore, Saturday. Maybe his phone's been tapped... You idiot you're being paranoid. When I hang up, I bite my bottom lip. I'm dying to see him again, to get lost in his blue eyes, and feel his muscular arms. Or his chest, just to feel his taut muscle. Does he have this effect on all women? Of course. They all try to touch him. I go back to my room to look at my reflection. Right. Hair bleached by the sun: get another henna. Ass: looking pretty good, I only ate fruit in Indonesia and Liza's new alkaline diet is working a little,

I've got to admit. Eyebrows: I took advantage of the spa at the hotel to get waxed. Alright. Just need to find the right outfit. I frantically push the hangers out of the way in search of inspiration. No way I'm going shopping after I just got fired. Maybe I can get something from Liza's wardrobe? I abandon my search, a little depressed. How do you impress a guy who dates women dressed in Chanel or Michael Kors? That's when Liza comes back, with a bottle of Viognier to celebrate my new life.

"You're not unemployed, you're just turning a new leaf in your life. That's all! It's a sign I'm sure!

- Liza, you're brilliant."

I down my glass in one go. My phone buzzes while she's busy unpacking maki: it's a Facebook message.

"You know what really bugs me when we get to thirty?

- Don't tell me: white hair?

- Youtube shows you pregnancy test ads before every video.

- You know white hair is due to lack of keratin. You should eat seaweed, that's what the Japanese do."

I grab my phone mechanically and check Facebook.

"What do you think Olen's sushi tastes like?" Liza jokes.

My eyes are still glued to the screen in disbelief.

"Hi, I'm Olen's wife. I think we need to have a little chat. Can we meet up? I completely understand if you don't want to, but I think we should. I'll be honest, and I hope you will too. Clarissa."

In shock, I don't say anything, and smile meekly.

"I don't feel too great Liza, I'm going to hit the hay.

- Seriously? I have to eat all these maki by myself!"

I'm nauseous, and get up with difficulty.

"It must be the wine... I'm going to bed."

Mr Pilou is looking at me blankly tonight while I burrow under the quilt. Why stubbornly dream that life's like a beautiful movie when it's actually more like a rotten Sunday afternoon TV movie?

***

With my back resting comfortably against the seat in my favorite bar, I browse LinkedIn looking for interesting publishers. I spent an hour uploading my resume to every website I could think of... Come on, don't give up hope! My eyes drift to the door every five minutes. Is that her? No. The brunette goes to sit down with a couple. I force my gaze back to my computer screen. Nothing forced you to meet her. You don't have to feel guilty. You didn't know! Still I need to know. I need to see this woman so that I can move on. To always associate her face with Olen's. It will be more effective than any book on how to deal with a failed relationship. Someone looks at me. Tall, blonde, thin, dressed all in white. She has a scarf around her hair. She smiles at me sweetly and sits opposite me. Grace Kelly would have looked like a brat next to such a goddess. And I don't even dare sit up, with my jeans and my old sneakers, probably looking frightened.

"Hi Candice.

- Hello Clarissa."

We remain silent a moment. That's what you'd call beating around the bush.

"I'm sorry about this whole affair. But I needed to know.

- Listen, if it makes you feel any better, nothing happened with Olen.

- Really?

- We only spoke at a party. I was on holiday... Anyway. I assure you, I won't see him again. I'm not into married men."

Her face relaxes as she let's go of the breath she was holding. I then notice how tired she looks. Is it Olen's crazy parties that worry her so much?

"I'm sorry, but... I've never seen you on the red carpet... I mean... Nobody knows Olen's married. How did you manage to keep it a secret? It's crazy.

- Olen and I have been married for eight years. And we've got some problems in our marriage. Fame doesn't make it any easier.

- I guess not.

- I decided to devote myself to my husband, giving up on my career. I wanted children, but ... Olen doesn't see it that way. He did everything in his power to keep our marriage a secret. He knows how to be... very persuasive."

I can feel my annoyance bubbling under the surface: why does it not surprise me? Persuasive? What does that even mean?

"Olen's a very talented actor, and he knows how to surround himself with the right people. And how to control his environment. He could have been a great businessman."

Staring into space, I realize that apart from a few vague career elements, I don't know much about him. His smile, his profile, his shimmering eyes... I shake my head. Stop. Those are forbidden thoughts now.

"Thank you for meeting me. I have one last thing to ask.

- I'm listening...

- For forgiveness.

- What?

-I'm the one who sent that email... I... I was desperate. I just wanted to save my marriage.

-Don't worry, of course I forgive you."

And it was true. I understood. Being as beautiful as her and to be neglected by her husband for the sake of little nymphs ... I can't imagine her pain and daily humiliation. I close my computer, and get up.

"Good luck Clarissa.

- Thanks, Candice. You too."

I made my decision, not only will I not go to lunch with Olen, but I won't tell him. For the first time in my life, I want to hurt someone. Obviously, it won't be much: a mere dent in his oversized ego, but it's better than nothing. Given what's left of mine, I don't have much to lose.

Chapter 8

"Yes grandma, so the positive thing is that I'll probably be able to come over for the New Year. Now that I've lost my job. Ha ha ha! Yes, always look for the silver lining, see I've taken after you, even if it's just a bit. Ha ha! Love you Grandma!"

After a week of unemployment, and no response to any of my resumes, I'm at a dead end. I need to find something. I'm not prejudiced about certain jobs, but I really want to continue in an area that I know. I stop by Jo's restaurant, our childhood friend who has a family run Indian restaurant, to enjoy a tasty and spicy dish which she alone has the secret to. Jo's busying herself behind the bar emptying the small dishwasher especially for glasses. With her big seven month pregnant belly, it's funny to see her waddle and try to busy herself. Jo doesn't accept the fragility brought on by pregnancy.

"What are you going to do?

- I don't know.

- Ok I'll find you a job. Assistant, waitress, anything!

- No don't. It's sweet, but I don't want you to pull strings for me.

- And what about babysitting?"

I swallow the lump in my throat. I'm afraid of babysitting. It's too much responsibility for me. Besides, the only time I held a baby it was Jo's. Believing that I had milk, he bit my breast.

"You'll bounce back Candice. Faster than you think. You're young, no kids, single, mobile and overqualified... Of course you're going to find something. You should enjoy these few weeks holiday."

Is it Jo's Indian side that allows her to always see things from another perspective? Probably. I go home and throw myself on the couch, putting down the tupperware Jo filled with lamb and eggplant. Liza has already eaten,

"Babysitting? Can you imagine... Screaming all over the place, yogurt in your hair.

- Okay enough. Well... um... I don't want to work in your company. But I don't mind you putting the word out for me.

- Don't worry, you practically won't even need to sit through an interview.

- Why do you say that?"

Liza looks at me out of the corner of her eye:

"Because you don't like talking about yourself. You know how to sell anything you're passionate about, but when it's about you... You're like a closed book. You know, I picture the person having an orgasm during the interview. Puts it into perspective, just like that."

I have a coughing fit, reeling from this revelation. Liza takes a deep breath, proud of herself while looking at me. She pulls out her phone and starts frantically typing away an array of messages. I come back thirty minutes later, after doing the dishes and taking a shower, she's still at it. Liza has an impressive amount of contacts.

"Well, I've found something in the meantime. You start this weekend. It's a catering job. So you make sandwiches and deliver them.

- Where?

- Depends, they've got customers all over New York.

- Alright, fine. As long as there's no small talk involved..."

I down my glass of wine in one go.

"How's Jo?

- She was queasy. She says it's her stomach.

- Well being pregnant, that's not surprising.

- Rubbish Liza! That has nothing to do with it. Digestion and the baby are two completely different things.

- You sure?

- Uh... no."

We're speechless, thinking that perhaps we should know the answer. First of all, because we're supposed to be educated and intelligent women, and second of all, because being of age to marry and procreate, we should know this stuff.

"It's weird.

- What?"

Liza turns on the stove.

"To see everyone get on with life, and ending up at square one.

- You're not at square one, Candice. You're starting a new chapter in your life. That's how you should see it.

- I know.

- Before, girls were married at twenty-five and already had a kid under each arm. Look at me, I'm twenty-eight and still nothing. Just a job, and my health. But you know what, Candice, that's a lot in this world!"

I'm about to tell her that some people seem to have it all when the lights go out. Liza lets out a shrill cry while I stiffen.

"The power went out, obviously.

- You think? Didn't you tell me that your last boyfriend was a bit weird? You think he memorized the code for the door downstairs?

- God, don't, just don't say that."

By her tone, I can tell that Liza's afraid. I jump to my feet to rummage through the drawer and retrieve a box of candles.

"Well, can you find them? Goddamnit, I hate the dark."

Liza despite being smart and confident, and sending all the suit and ties of the city into a frenzy with her brazen black beauty, is still a woman who panics when confronted with a broken toilet flush. Not unlike me.

She pressed repeatedly on the circuit breaker.

"Hey you maniac, give it a rest! We need to call an electrician."

She looks at me, biting her lip.

"Yeah I know, emergency electrician, we'll have to cough up, but we're two women in New York.

- We can't live without electricity, okay? How are you going to dry your hair tomorrow?"

Liza types away on her phone for a while and calls someone.

I go into my room, dragging my feet and face-plant onto the bed The atmosphere has changed in the apartment. The candles give it a romantic vibe. A cocoon with soft orange hues. I block out a song by Louis Armstrong with his velvety voice, one that comes back to haunt me. I'm lucky to have such a roommate. Liza can do everything: assistant, entrepreneur, cook... ok I'm a better cook, but Olen should have set his sights on her. I don't know how to get over a break-up in a few days.

I fall asleep thinking that I might need a certificate of fitness for employment to deliver sandwiches. I wake with a start:

"Six hundred dollars? Damn if I'd have known, I would have been an electrician, not gone to Columbia!"

I get up staggering, feeling a little guilty about leaving Liza alone with the guy. If I know her at all, she's probably already crucified him with a fork.

"The whole circuit needs to be replaced. Those are the prices. But if you don't want my services tonight, fine by me. Just know it will cost you more in the end than the deal I'm prepared to give you."

The man with the square jaw and light eyes patiently puts away his tools with his big hands.

Liza looks at him defiantly.

"You should be a negotiator."

She takes out her checkbook, raising her turned-up nose. He smiles sweetly at her.

"No ma'am, I'm fine as an electrician."

Liza gasps.

"Is it an interesting job?

- Yes ma'am, we meet all kinds of interesting people. What have you decided?"

Liza hands him her business card and the debonair giant pops it in his jacket with a smile.

"So, is it ma'am or miss?

- Miss.

- Okay Miss Cole, I'll call you to set a date for the intervention asap. I'll deal with it personally.

- What there's more of you?

- Yes miss, I have ten employees.

- I really should have been an electrician."

Liza said with a hint of admiration. I clear the table and do the dishes while she sees the electrician out.

"Damn it, I had to call the only gay electrician in New York.

- What makes you say that?

- Why do you think I got out my blouse with the button missing?

- Oh really. It didn't work?

- No. Nothing worked. Not even a small gesture. I mean honestly! And "we meet all kinds of interesting people"... What did he mean by that?

- You met the only man in New York that won't have Liza Cole wrap him around her little finger. But he was cute, right?

- What?

- Come on, I know you love guys with light eyes. And I saw you staring at his ass.

- It's a reflex."

I take her in my arms laughing and bid her goodnight. In front of my window once again, I pick up my journal to blow off some steam. Dr Tran would give me a death glare from above his glasses, it's been days since I last wrote. Right. What can I tarnish this white page with? Obviously, I want to write about Olen. The warm Indonesian waters. My hand on his chest. Liar… Anger floods through my veins. No, I need to put an end to this. Where did I leave it last time? Ah yes. Dad warned me.

His phone's bombarded with messages. Probably his agent. Danny, my light in the darkness, is leaving soon to go on tour. I got my black stockings out for the occasion.

"I'm so happy for you, babe."

I go to sit on his lap, and snake my arms around his neck. It's time. It's the perfect moment for the next step. I'm ready. I gulp.

"You had something to tell me.

- Yes… I'm happy with you. I love you Danny.

- You say that to all of them.

- You know I'm not really a seductrice. No, I don't tell them all that. I love you. Believe me."

He strokes my cheek.

"With you, I can be myself. What about you? Do you love me Danny?

- How can you not love Candice Evans?

- That's not what I want to hear.

- You have everything. A great family, a good job…

- Yeah I know. I have the perfect life. But that's superficial. Looks can be deceiving. Something's missing. And I found you. I love you. I'm… I'm being honest."

He doesn't answer, he kisses me with a smile on his face. A quick peck.

"Marry me Danny.

- What?

- Marry me. Let's have kids.

- Candice, we've only been together a year.

- When you're in love, nothing else matters."

He looks at his feet now, as if he were uncomfortable, and lets go of my waist, putting his hands on his thigh instead. His phone buzzes.

"I know you love me. And you'll make an amazing mother.

- And that's not enough to marry me?

- We'll talk about it later, ok?"

I feel like someone put a dagger through my heart. I jump up.

"Coward, are you afraid of admitting your feelings or something?

- And here we go, proud Candice making an appearance.

- Are you serious right now?

- I'm not a serious kind of guy. Candice, I'm a jazzman, a nomad, and you're a Manhattan princess.

- I don't see how that makes us incompatible.

- I do. You'll see, our paths will go separate ways naturally.

- But it can work! I can make it work! Mad love is always an impossible love. We have it all, you're the only one who doesn't see a future!"

He doesn't respond, annoyed he grabs his phone that started buzzing again. I snatch it out of his hands to tell his agent to get lost, it's Christmas in two days. But what I see is a picture of a woman in lingerie with a message that finishes breaking my heart and has rage bubbling up inside me:

"Danny baby, I miss you."

Danny stands up looking at me, suddenly very pale.

"I can explain. It's not what you think."

I tighten my grip on the phone, ready to crush it in my hands. Liar. He takes a step forward. I take one back and look at him, still shaky.

"You put so much effort into making us work, Candice, that you didn't see that I'd changed.

- Was anything real? Or was it all just a game to you?

- Love is a game… One that I don't like to lose."

I process this shocking revelation, feeling a knot forming in my throat. Danny, the clumsy man hiding behind his shyness was in fact a manipulator. How did I not see it?

"Would you have lost with me?

- I would have lost my freedom.

- I never wanted to make you feel trapped, Danny. All I wanted, was to be by your side, to love you, seeing you happy made me happy.

- I'm sorry.

- I don't care. Screw you Danny. I've had enough of your puppy dog look, the one that looks like he doesn't know what he wants. Why did you flirt with me then? Was it the thrill of seducing Candice Evans, the person who scared the crap out of the guys in accounts? Just to leave me afterwards?"

Suddenly he looks rattled.

"Don't say that, that's not how it happened.

- And then, when you got me, that you got an agent, and your audience of bimbos, that was it, it wasn't as thrilling anymore and you needed someone else?"

He was about to answer, but I slap him with everything I've got. He stands there in shock. I just want to tear his handsome face to shreds. I gather my things, and storm out of the apartment. Outside, I tighten my coat around my thighs and hail a cab to the airport. It doesn't matter if I have to fork out a hell of a lot for the ticket, I'm going to my parents' tonight. A young couple passes me by: Christmas the season of proposals. The bite of the cold on my thighs barely covered by my nylon stockings reminds me of the searing disillusion I've just fallen victim to. Danny, the manipulator, Danny the opportunist … who'd have thought? Was I that blind and stupid? And the godforsaken Christmas was finally here, Danny bombarding me with messages since morning.

"Listen, can we talk?"

"I believed in us. All I wanted was to be by your side. I was there for you for over a year and you screwed it all up."

"I'm sorry if I hurt you."

"Go to hell. You'll need more than that to break Candice Evans."

"I'm coming to see you, we're not going to spend Christmas fighting."

"Don't you dare come. Go see one of your fans who has no idea what a loser you are."

"I'm already at the airport, I get in tonight. Please, come and pick me up."

Who's to blame? Me, who refused to go and pick him up? Danny, who contacted my folks directly? Or my parents, too kind and helpful? The other driver, who hadn't slept in over 48 hours and crashed into them?

***

"Is it possible to ever find your place in this world?"

Doctor Tran's watching me over his glasses while sticking a needle in my arm. I asked for the hard version, so he does it forcefully and fast making me shudder.

"Yes, it's possible.

- Really?

- Yes. When you know who you are, what you want, where you want to be.

It's actually as simple as that.

- But people change.

- You've forgotten. But deep down you know what you want.

- Yes. It's true that at five years old, I already knew what I wanted to do... but it's my love life that's complicated.

- What did you dream of as a child?

- Well I was brought up on Disney, so obviously…"

He looks at me smiling.

"So obviously?

- Well Prince Charming, clearly.

- Ah there it is. The myth of Prince Charming…" He sighs.

"You don't have a problem. It's just that you would have been happier twenty years ago.

- Yes, that's it. I feel like Captain America right now, always a step behind, with an old school education.

- Who?

- Captain America... You're joking... You don't know who that is... ?"

The Doctor laughed heartily.

"I'm joking. Of course I know who he is.

- Go on then, make fun of me... Liza says I act like I'm from a different time.

- You're going to have to bring her down, you're friend, Liza".

I burst out laughing. I can just picture a conversation between Liza and the Dr Tran. Not sure Liza would get the last word.

"You're going to find him, you're Prince Charming. There are people like you, who don't like channel-hopping. Who like simplicity, sharing, and who hold trust dear.

- Someone told me that soul mates are like Prince Charming.

- Who cares about what people say. Dreams are beautiful. If we didn't have that... What do we have? It's what lifts us up. Santa Claus isn't only presents. It helps children to grow.

- You're not like other doctors.

- You're not like other patients.

- That's the best compliment I've got in months.

- Come on. Out."

He hands me the medical certificate with a smile on his face.

"Good luck on the new job. Change is good. Don't worry too much about your future. It's not easy in the beginning, but maybe it's a crossroad.

- Here's hoping it's not a u-turn with nausea added to the mix.

- Life is change. Skin renews every day, can you imagine? Why couldn't we change jobs, life, friends, and horizons?"

Reaching the ground floor of the building, I find an out of breath delivery guy:

"Thank God, you're second floor apartment B, right?

- Yes."

The young delivery guy lifts the enormous bouquet of daffodils.

"Go on, I'll follow you, these are for you."

I've got the urge to tell him to throw them in the trash, but Liza will probably like them. I climb the stairs, heavily, and after having signed the receipt I put them in my roommate slash best friend's room. I've always hated daffodils. I know it's mean, but I find they look stupid, seemingly always seconds from drooping. I shut the door to Liza's bedroom as fast as I can to not have to look at them a second longer, so they don't remind me of Olen.

Chapter 9

I straighten my hair one last time, the logo of *Le Délicieux* on the black uniform: a knife crossed with a whisk. It's very grandiose for a catering company, but so be it. Staying at home twiddling my thumbs is out of the question. You've got to earn your bread as Grandma says.

"Showtime!"

Brittany shoves a tray of petit fours in my hands. I follow the wave of girls clicking their heels and spreading throughout the guests who have just finished clapping after a speech on research for cancer. It's a fancy charity gala. I thought only kids and teenagers could scoff down food at such a staggering rate. But I was wrong. There's also elderly people, with or without dentures. They stand in front of the buffet like a school of piranhas. I see a venerable older woman with white hair open her Louis Vuitton bag to stuff petit fours in it. I watch her speechless, when Brittany whispers in my ear:

"Oh yeah. Wait till you see what it's like in retirement homes. They go at it like bunnies, it's crazy!

- What do you mean?

- I worked New Year's in one of those places. Talking about that, stay far away from that guy, over there, the one with the walking stick that has a silver pommel. That's George, he always tries to get it between your legs, every time.

- Oh my God…

- Oh my God.

- What?

- Olen Van Cliff."

My heart jumps out of my chest to end up on the chandelier somewhere. I slowly look behind me, hardly daring to believe it. Or maybe I'm afraid of believing it.

"What's he doing here?"

Olen pushes his way through the crowd to get to me.

"Oh no, he's coming this way."

I take a step back but Brittany grips my arm, eyes bright with excitement.

"My panties are so wet, if I throw them in the air they'd stay stuck to the ceiling."

Olen is on me within seconds, looking furious.

"So, what about lunch?

- Whenever you want." Brittany answers.

I ignore her and sending him a death glare, I bark at him:

"A certain Clarissa had a few interesting things to say, and I suddenly I wasn't all that hungry."

Brittany mutters, hypnotised by Olen:

- I love you."

Olen gently takes her hand, and kissing it, asks her nicely:

"Thank you. Do you know somewhere quiet, where I can torture Candice who hasn't been very nice to me?"

Before I can protest, Brittany jumps up and down and answers giggling:

"Oh sure, the changing rooms.

- Thank you, dear angel."

Brittany leaves smiling with a dreamy look on her face.

"You really are a jackass."

Everybody turns to look at us, bewildered. Olen grabs me by the arm, dropping my tray of petit fours on the closest table, he drags me to the changing rooms and pins me against the wall.

"A jackass?

- Yes a jackass.

- Anything else?

- An arrogant douche who thinks that everyone will throw themselves at his feet, especially women and… and…

- And?

- And…"

My gaze is lost on his lips that stretch into a diabolical smile. Olen Van Cliff's smile. Bastard. He knows the effect it has on me. He leans forward so that I can feel his breath on the crook of my neck. I painfully swallow the lump in my throat. I can see the muscles in his face relax. He wants to make sure I still like him.

"Thank you for the flowers…

- The flowers?"

What an idiot! Naive. Stupid. Romantic idiot.

"Candice? Is everything alright?"

William West looks at me worriedly from behind Olen. And when the latter turns around I see his jaw clench.

"Yeah. Um... Mr Van Cliff and I were finished."

I look pointedly at Olen slipping far away from him, and I lace my arm around William's to rejoin the rest of the team.

"You got here early, but just in the nick of time.

- If he laid a hand on you without your consent…"

I elude the subject so I don't have to answer the question about my consent.

"It's ok. I had it. Right… See you later?

- I'll hang out in a corner and admire you from afar."

I smile and glance towards the changing rooms in spite of myself, but Olen doesn't reappear. I rush towards the kitchen and grab a tray of champagne glasses to avoid Brittany. But she's too busy watching the entrance and probably Olen. I flit through the guests, miraculously avoiding George with the crazy cane and finish my service only ten minutes late. I want to make up for lost time spent with Olen. When I take off my vest to shove it in my bag, Brittany drags me by the arm.

"You did a good job Candice. Reactive and amicable.

- Thanks.

- Tell me… How do you know Olen Van Cliff?

- Oh… an unfortunate series of events.

- What? Unfortunate?

- Listen… He's probably a fabulous actor, but in real life it's a whole other story.

- Oh?! So you know him well then??"

I bite my lip. Judging by the intonation of her voice, I get the feeling she's never going to let up.

"No not at all. That's just it, I feel like he's the kind of person that doesn't let people get to know him… although he has his charms.

- He didn't even notice me.

- Oh believe me he did. He wouldn't have kissed your hand otherwise.

- I love his manners. A true gentleman."

I laugh internally at that. He's married and flirts without restraint.

"See you Brittany!

-Yeah, I'll call you tomorrow with the rest of the planning."

When I get out of there, I take in a deep breath. Yes. Olen Van Cliff's a complicated man to get to know and I want something simple. Really? Is that really what you want Candice? I feel a warm hand stroke my back. William whispers in my ear:

"Come on, little Candice. Your turn to be served."

We walk in silence for two blocks, before reaching a bar with black opaque curtains and a cozy atmosphere. I'm so tired that I don't order an alcoholic drink. A simple fruit juice to keep a clear head.

"I was surprised you called. It's been a while.

- Sorry, I... I had to sort something out with someone, professionally speaking. So, I preferred to focus on that.

- I've had a few complicated days over the last few weeks myself.

- So... what were you and Olen talking about? William asks me nonchalantly.

- Oh... not much. I thought he sent me flowers, that he was a gentleman. But no. I was wrong about him.

- I'm glad you saw his true colors. Olen knows how to fool the world like nobody else. A fine actor.

- But... aren't you two friends?

- I think the way we looked at each other didn't go unnoticed. Well no, we're not friends anymore. I told you I was working on the script for my first film, didn't I?

- Yes.

- It's with him that I had to sort out some professional differences. That jerk bought the rights but he's refusing to produce the movie.

- What?

- Olen doesn't like to share the limelight. He's telling everyone that he bought the rights out of pity for me, that the script was crap. Can you believe it?"

I'm dumbfounded. Olen... What a manipulator!

"That means that even in five years, when my script's available again, nobody's going to want it.

- Shit, William, I'm sorry.

- It's not your fault. Just, don't let his pretty face fool you.

- I had a feeling he was a bit... sure of himself and... he always knows how to make things to his advantage. But...

- He's the most capricious star there is."

I choose to change the subject when we get to the restaurant. It's so unexpected. I can picture Olen taking off his mask and showing his true face: a ruthless businessman prepared to crush other people, a ladies man, to who friendship depends on his best interest... We talk about old jazz, thai food, how Facebook has become an addiction, Australia and its weird animals.

"Alright, I'm shattered. I'm going to head home."

William takes my hand.

"I'm sorry you lost your job."

Here we go.

"If there's anything I can do to help… don't hesitate. I don't think I'll be able to do much at the moment, but I'll do my best." He chuckles.

"Thanks."

I get up and grab my coat. He helps me put it on, and lets his hands gently brush my shoulders. Without meaning to I stiffen. He immediately removes his hands, and we leave in silence because I simply don't have it in me to make small talk. I hail a taxi and William takes me by the waist to turn me around. He delicately cups my cheeks and kisses me. I gently push him away.

"There's something not right…

- It's him isn't it?"

I look down to avoid his gaze. Yes. Olen has insinuated himself, like sand, in every confine of my mind.

"There's just that something missing between us. You know the spark.

- Yeah, I get it."

William looks heartbroken, and grinds his teeth, looking at the floor in turn.

"Last time… If you'd kissed me … maybe it could have worked out.

- I guess some people move faster than others."

I bite my lip.

"I guess the timing wasn't right."

And laying my hand on his shoulder, I look at him one last time before I clamber into the taxi. I don't turn around, no regrets. Yep. Olen consumes me. But since when? Since Masquerade? Bali? I feel a lump form in my throat. I'm cursed. I couldn't choose a better way to punish myself. I'm nearly sobbing when I slam the door to the apartment. Liza's on the couch, and is biting her nails while looking at the screen of her cell.

"So how did it go, hun?

- Olen showed up at the charity gala, and then William got there. I thought they were going to fight. I don't feel anything for William, even though he's charming, and he writes scripts, we could be compatible, right? Goddamnit, how did Olen find me? It's too late now, I'm doomed!

- I… I was the one who told him."

I flinch, my brain trying to catch up.

"WHAT????

- The flowers we got two days ago… I thought they were from him, like you did. I told him when you left, that you'd be at that gala tonight. At the time, I thought it was a good idea.

- But then…

- It was Jake. You know the electrician… he just called me. The flowers were from him."

That's when I throw myself on the couch and let my purse fall to the ground.

"Yeah. Jake… invited me to dinner.

- To dinner?

- Well yeah."

I snicker when I see Liza's lost kitten look.

"Well go then!

- You think?

- Wait a minute. You, who's always up for an adventure, for anything, anytime… you're having doubts?

- It's just that...

- What? He's cute. He's nice. He proved it.

- He's… white.

- So what?!

- What will people say?"

I take her hand.

"Liza, I think that I'm rubbing off on you. You need to take action. I'm begging you. For all those good women who end up with egocentric jerks, and spoilt capricious actors!

- Well, put like that… how did it go at work?

- Good, but my boss saw me with Olen and was beside herself with joy. I don't think she's going to drop it. Starting tomorrow, I'm looking for something else.

- Crap, sorry Candice.

- It's only the second job I lose in two months. It's fine!"

I bring her in for a hug.

"Goodnight gold-hearted Liza!

- Goodnight stubborn ass."

Chapter 10

"Call me back, please."

"Candice… I've got so much to tell you, so much to explain. Things aren't like they seem, you know."

"Right. You're not calling me back. Are you mad at me? You know I love the way you pout when you're sulking. I bet you've still got the same face as when you were a kid. Did you sulk for this long when you were a kid? Call me back and you won't sulk anymore."

"God you're stubborn! If I meet your parents one day I'll ask to see pictures of you as a kid, when you were sulking. Why don't you want to hear what I've got to say? I'm sorry I made you lose your second job. I want to make it up to you, whatever it takes. But please, call me back, answer, send me a text, I don't do this often… but, I'm begging you. There you have it. I'm begging you."

After the sixth time, I don't listen to Olen's messages anymore. He knows how to use everything in his arsenal: anger, compassion, tenderness, good-natured ribbing… I don't know by what unknown force I'm stopping myself from answering and yelling at him:

"Ask your wife bonehead! Get a good look at yourself in the mirror you shameless carbuncle!"

With every wave of anger I dive back into my job search. But one Saturday morning, I realize that it's over. The phone has stopped ringing. I hear myself say out loud:

"Finally…" But I don't mean it. I'm waiting. Candice, stop, will you make up your mind already?

Thankfully, I start my new job. The great thing about this job is that I can work in jeans and sneakers. I dream of Ava Gardner or Audrey Hepburn's class, but I like dressing like a retarded teen. It's comforting. The funny thing is that I didn't think I had so many hidden talents. I can have the patience of an angel. Because, yes, you'd have guessed, I became a tutor.

"Pfff… I don't get it. What's this guys' problem?

- That guy is Shakespeare and he's one of the greatest playwrights and poets of all time. He simply writes the using the terminology of his time. Come on, tell me what you know about him.

- Well he couldn't have been that good because he became a farmer."

My blood boils and my hands tighten into fists with the urge to strangle him. I shut my eyes. Keep calm Candice. Don't slap this little pretentious jerk. His parents pay you a small fortune to give him litterature lessons. When I open my eyes, Jason is staring at me unashamedly.

"Listen carefully bonehead, I got my A levels without Google and made friends without Facebook, so I'm not going to stop until you get your diploma, got it?"

The brat nods, wide-eyed.

"Ok. So, things can go smoothly just as well as they can go badly between us.

- Is that a threat? I'm going to tell my parents.

- Exactly. Your parents are on my side. Get that into your thick skull."

Jason's about to say something, but he must sense that I'm just about ready to explode because he shuts his mouth straight away.

"Well, he wrote 37 productions, including *Antony and Cleopatra, Coriolanus, Hamlet, Macbeth, Romeo and Juliet, Othello, Julius Caesar …*"

I take a deep breath, and Jason keeps a low profile until the end of the lesson.

"You see, it's actually really interesting, right?

- Sure."

And Jason runs to the TV to watch a horror movie. I'm off to catch my bus for my last lesson of the day. It's my favorite one, actually. Sharon's a shy young lady of sixteen, who has a lot of potential, but self-conscious about everything. She opens the door while hiding her forehead:

"Is everything alright?"

She moves her hand to reveal a huge zit.

"Oh. So you couldn't resist some chocolate cookies?

- No. A cheesecake. I tried to resist but it was too good.

- You don't have to justify yourself Sharon. Don't worry about it. A bit of vinegar and the swelling will go down.

- They call me pizza face at school.

- If you can get through high school, you can get through anything. You're a fighter Sharon."

The young girl adjusts her oversized sweater and sits down:

"How did you do it?

- Do what?

- Become so strong?

- I don't feel strong.

- It seems like nothing can get to you.

- That's not true. Everything gets to me as much as it does you. It's just that I don't show it. But everything gets to me. And I keep doing what I need to do. Getting up in the morning, getting ready to take on the rest of the world, and going to work.

- Life's crap.

- What makes you say that?

- So when do you go after your dreams? If you're too busy doing what's got to be done?"

Way to go, Candice. You wanted to play big sister, giving her advice and now what?

"Maybe you need to be the one to figure it out. A way to combine both. Do what's got to be done and pursuing your dreams.

- What was your dream?

- Come on Sharon, let's work.

- Tell me, please. Then we'll work, promise.

- You'd make a great negotiator you know.

- Please. I need inspiration.

- Writing. I always wanted to be a writer.

- And why didn't you do it?

- Maybe I'm not as strong as you Sharon," I reply, winking at her.

"And you… gave up on your dream?

- I don't know. No. I write a bit, when I have the time. I think it's still there, in the back of my head. Alright! Let's get to work! What did you choose from the list?

- *Address unknown* by Kathrine Kressmann Taylor.

- OK. What can you tell me about the book?"

Sharon launches into a full speed explanation of what she understood of the epistolary novel, and I feel my chest swell with pride.

"You've gotten better. Your answers are more structured, have you noticed?

-Yes. It's as if my brain wanted to delve deep into the process of writing in itself.

- Do you know that what you're learning to do, could very well be useful in a lot of careers. You aren't just learning stuff about literature, are you?

- No I'm learning to develop ideas.

- Good."

I'm so proud and give a satisfied smile. I'm lucky to have students like Sharon who love to learn. I nag her for half an hour about the other works we've already studied, to test her memory. The last few minutes fly by.

"Um, tell me, if you write something, you'd let me read it, right?

- I love your way of asking that. A question turned into an affirmative. Didn't I tell you, you'd make a good negotiator?"

Sharon bursts out laughing... and continues in a conspiratorial tone.

"Tell me… did you have a boyfriend in high school?

- Why?

- Does it hurt? You know the first time.

- Um… well… do some yoga, I think that could help."

I put my hand on her shoulder:

"See you next week!"

Sharon was smiling from ear to ear. Is it at the thought of losing her virginity or is it her love for learning? I rather think about something else while walking to the apartment. I'm the first one home. I open a bottle of wine and hit play on a Diana Krall playlist while preparing maki. I feel light, more and more so, when I suddenly hear the tone indicating I have a new email. Not able to resist my curiosity, I discover a very moved email from Eleanor, Sharon's mom.

"Sharon just told me that she wants to take up yoga: you're a great influence... I have no doubt that, aside from her literature classes, the benefits are going to be huge and lasting. Thank you Candice!"

Ahem. Well done Candice. Note to self: talk to Sharon about condoms. I shift from foot to foot in the middle of the lounge for a bit, my plate overflowing with maki. I throw myself on the couch, gaze empty, miles away. Sharon's right. It's a drag having to choose. I gulp down my glass of wine and go through to my room. I know I didn't get rid of everything when I had to sell my parents' house. I root out a box from under my bed and open it. A pile of diaries and loose sheets of lined paper that smell like my high school years. I have a sudden urge to read what I wrote in my spare time. Is it as bad as I think? Probably worse than that Candice!

Conscience, shut up. Tonight's a small reprieve. Eating another maki, a big glass of wine in hand, I delve back into the chapter of my life that I never really finished. I laugh when I come upon an old manuscript of erotic poems. It wasn't bad. It's actually pretty… inspiring judging by the warmth pooling in the pit of my stomach. I put it aside for Liza. She's going to love it! But three glasses of wine later, Liza still hasn't come home. No messages, no note, no call. I'm worried. It's not like her.

I carry on going through the different manuscripts snickering at some of the pitches scribbled hastily in notebooks. A young student discovers her science teacher's a cannibal and has just formed a sect. A family of vampires that have moved to Kentucky, believing they could fly under the radar. A doctor, crying the loss of his wife who passed away, decides to take a road trip around a country that has never been explored: death. Where did I get it from?

I think back to Liza. Normally, I'd get a note at the very least. And all of a sudden, it hits me. Could she have gone out with Jake?

Chapter 11

When I wake from my restless sleep filled with dreams heavily inspired by my poems, Liza's already left, a note waiting for me on the kitchen side, proof that she came home safe and sound, at least. The apartment seems empty all of a sudden. I send her a text.

"So? Sushi night tonight? Or have you been building a bunker somewhere over the last few days?"

I get an answer almost immediately.

"Sorry, hen! Too much work, barely got time to stop!"

What's with all the mystery? She's gone out a lot lately: without getting changed. Otherwise her bed would be covered in clothes. No news from Olen. Nor of William. I have dinner with Jo and her husband every tuesday night.

A gossip website called me unstable because, apparently, I change job every other day. A part from that, I'm under the impression that the media's starting to get tired. There's a guy who hides behind a car with his cell when I go to buy some tea from the street corner, sometimes. Hell, who even cares about that?? If it were toilet paper, it could be juicy, but tea? Unless he's expecting that Olen will come and hang out in front of my place. I choose to ignore him. I refuse to wear sunglasses, I'd feel as if they'd won and I'd be playing into their hands. Then again, there's only the one guy, and I don't think he's a professional. Someone from the neighborhood who recognized me and decided to earn some pocket money by selling a few photos. So, that means my address is still private. All my classes being in the afternoon, I laze around the flat, until today. The day when I come across that binder that I still haven't put back under my bed. I reopen the notepad that's already been started like my innocence and never completed like my adolescence, and I say :

"Becky Sparks wasn't the prettiest girl in high school. But the one that had buck teeth in her yearbook picture. The eager beaver, literally and figuratively. Was it fascination? Or the fear of this creature that made her pairs crown her prom queen? How did she manage to turn the survival system of a private catholic school into a mission for world domination?"

I snicker remembering Becky's empty stare.

Olen comes back to haunt me a few seconds, like a wave, then his face disappears when I replace it with Becky's. I write all morning: thoughts, bits of dialogue, prompts. All this has no rhyme nor reason, but it helps me blow off some steam. In the evening, Jo prods me.

"Look at you… you're… glowing.

- Really?

- Did you meet somebody?

- No, I'm working on a little project.

- And?

- Olen? I still think about him. But I haven't heard from him in three weeks.

- Do you go out?

- Without Liza it's hard. I have a hard time hanging out in a bar on my own.

- So basically, apart from spotty teenagers in the afternoon and us, you don't see anybody?

- Said like that, of course it sucks.

- What time do you get dressed?

- What do you mean by that?

- When Ilan sits in his PJs composing music until I force him to go out, I feel like it's the beginning of the end of our relationship."

He looks slightly offended at that.

"You like seeing me in pyjamas. It's my boyish charm.

- I like seeing you naked.

- OK! I really don't want you to finish that sentence Jo!

- Try Tinder.

- Come on. I'm not desperate, alright?

- Stop it, dating sites aren't for desperate people!

- Actually, you're considered out of touch if you've never been on a dating site," Ilan, her husband, adds.

"Alright. I'll think about it."

I play around with my phone to download the app without them noticing. I still have too much pride to admit it, but they're right... Suddenly, I get an email.

"Hello, we saw your profile, would you be interested in a job with our production company? Please call us tomorrow morning to set up a meeting."

"What's up?

- I... this is so out of the blue. I just got a message from a guy who works in a production company... and he wants to meet up with me.

- What goes around, comes around you dope! It's from the goddamn baraka who's saying: "alright, you've been through enough fucking crap, now it's time to fucking enjoy".

- Jo can be rude when she's happy if you hadn't noticed," her husband tells me looking stoical.

"I can't imagine what it's like when she has an orgasm then."

They both look at me, shocked. Then Ilan puts his arm around my shoulders, laughing and tussles my hair:

"That's great. You're getting back to your old self!

- Right, well I'm not going to stay out too late.

- Set up a Tinder account. Don't get too caught up with work again!

- Promise!

- Candice, have faith in life.

- I try."

****

"Hello! This is Candice Evans, I got your email.

- Candice! That's great! When are you available to meet with us?

- Well... I know this might seem a bit bold but I... this morning?

- What? Are you out front?

- Ha ha! No, but I can be. I hope I don't come off desperate but such an opportunity. It's just... Wow.

- Well come on down then!"

As you've probably guessed, I'm already dressed and I practically fly to catch a bus.

"Come on, admit it, you were already out front when you called, right?" Paul joked.

"I'll admit it, I've been camping outside the shop across the street.

- Ha ha! I like a good sense of humor! Ok Candice, tell me about yourself.

- I have a literature degree from Columbia. I've worked in editing, I read the manuscripts, took notes, and I organized the meetings and the readings for the authors near the end.

- Why did you leave?

- For personal reasons that took a few years to clear up. And that's why a simple job as a bookseller was good enough for me.

- Why?

- I had enough of a lot of things. The responsibilities, the stress, the people who were relying on me. Of being the one everyone relied on. When you're strong all the time, people lean on you. And it's exhausting.

- Alright. I completely understand that. Does that mean you don't want anymore responsibilities?

-No! Well, what I mean is, things are better now. The library I worked at closed for financial reasons. So, it made me realize how much I've missed that feeling.

- What feeling?

- Being able to contribute. Feeling useful.

- Do you know why I called you?

- No.

- I have an assistant proofreader job. The pay won't be any better than when you were selling books, but you can make an impression here. And you will be of use.

- You're going to pay me to proofread projects and give my opinion on scripts?

- Yes. Said like that, it sounds more glamorous, that's for sure!

- Well yes, definitely. Ok.

- Ok?

- Yes ok!

- Alright then, I'm just going to need some information to finish setting up the contract and … you can take a few days to think it over.

- No no. What I mean is, it's yes. It's funny… I… Well, someone recently told me to start writing again, so I told myself it's the right time. It's not a coincidence.

- No, indeed… See you Monday, 8 o'clock then."

***

I bound into the lobby of Colors, the company where Liza works, with a bounce in my step. I come to a sudden halt in front of the perfectly manicured blonde who's looking at me down her nose from behind the reception:

"I've come to see Liza Cole. Tell her it's Candice."

The blonde narrows her eyes, looks at my shoes with an air of disgust and picks up her phone as if she was doing me a favor.

"Miss Cole, there's a Candice here to see you. Oh…"

I'm getting impatient and run to the elevator rushing inside before blondie can stop me. I open the door to her office, nearly ripping it of its hinges, only to discover Liza back-arched on her desk, a blue and yellow skater dress on ... and Jake's head between her thighs.

"Oh wow... Um are you even allowed to do that here?!"

Liza has already hurried to shut the door and Jake is getting dressed, jumping up and down on one leg trying to get his jeans on.

"Do you realize people can see you from outside?"

Jake blushes, ears going pink and picks up his bag.

"See you later babe."

He puts his hand out for me to shake before changing his mind. I say, chuckling:

"Don't take this the wrong way, but I know where that hand was a second ago, so I'm going to pass.

- Oh right, of course. Well, bye!

- I'll see you soon I'm sure!"

Liza sits down remaining quiet, not looking at me. She pretends to rearrange the papers that are scattered on her desk and smooths out her dress.

"You could have knocked, jeez!

- Sorry, I was so happy, I wanted to share the good news with you.

- Oh my God! Olen called back? Did he explain everything? Did he dump his wife?"

Liza jumped up from her chair, eyes shining with excitement, and is about to take my hands in hers. But I put my hands up in the air.

"Um, I'm going to tell you the same thing I told Jake.

- Oh right. Sorry. So, is it Olen?

- No, I found a job as a proofreader for a production company.

- Oh, but… Oh yeah that's great!

- What, that's it?

- No! You're an intelligent woman. I didn't doubt for a second that you'd get what you wanted.

- Thank you. But you know what, I don't remember applying. Did you give them my resume?

- I sent your resume out to so many people... Honey, your love life is what you really need to work on.

- Yeah, I know. I've done it, I'm on Tinder.

- Great! We better mark the calendar for next year!

- Right… and Jake?

- Well you know... it's going ok.

- Liza, are you blushing?

- Blacks don't blush!

- Liza Cole, you never avoid looking somebody in the eye so... something's going on.

- Yeah, something's going on.

- And is it going well?

- Damn well!"

That makes me laugh.

"Right, don't you have a job to get to?

- What? Are you throwing me out?

- I'm getting behind on the new ad campaign.

- The cell phone?

- Julianne Moore isn't available.

- Try Meryl Streep… or Jane Fonda!

- Jane would be cool. Go on, out!"

Liza might as well dress in a 50's mobster costume with a big cigar between her teeth. She harshly slaps my ass while opening the door wide. There's a brunet busy at the copy machine in the hallway, his jaw hits the floor.

"What are you looking at?" Liza barks.

Jeez. I feel sorry for the person who's ever dared to hassle or persecute Liza at work. I slowly make my way back downstairs while playing around on Tinder. It's simple and strange all at once. My afternoon classes go by and I spend the rest of my minutes calling parents to warn them that starting Monday I'll be out of the game. Shannon has a voice full of excitement when I tell her about my new job.

"You've done what needed to be done, now go and do what makes you happy!"

I barely have the time to sit in front of my laptop to jot down a few notes on Becky Sparks, who is decidedly too great of a source of inspiration, when I get an email from Paul.

"You'll find attached a project which I'd like you to have a look at for Monday. Meeting at 2pm with the co producer."

The document is twenty-six pages of character descriptions, and intrigue development... It's full of good ideas and I start making notes on the characters that could be more defined. The problem is that the project's real hook is on the tenth line before the end of the file.

Right, I've got to work on my diplomacy to tell him that it's only natural that his project's being thrown on the pile. As far as a baptism of fire goes, we'll see if you've got what it takes, Candice. What if I screw up? What if Paul fires me? I've already left my students in the rearview mirror! Crap!!

Chapter 12

"All right, well… Welcome! Here's your copy of the contract, that you keep, and we'll keep a copy here. Did you get what I sent you Thursday night?

- Yes.

- And have you got anything to say?

- Yes."

I was holding my breath. Paul smiles widely at me and tells me energetically:

"Great! I'll let you go over this folder with all our past projects, the three current ones… If you have any questions, I'm in the office next door."

I look around: Forget the glamour of the big classy Hollywood offices with a designer table and the latest coffee machine. Owl productions is made up of two rooms that serve as offices overloaded with files, binders, VHS and DVDs. The only place that's truly amazing is the conference room where coffee stains have been embedded on the surfaces for what seems like forever. Note to self: make this office fit for Steven Spielberg. I review the projects. Owl productions is a fairly new production company. Five years in the making, suffice it to say, my job is anything but permanent. I flick through Paul's emails over the last six months.

It's incredible the amount of projects launched to finally have so little of them be produced.... and sold.

A project catches my eye: a spy thriller with a volunteer in an non-governmental organization opposed to an American agent: starting off as antagonists, in the end they form an allegiance to overthrow the dictator of that country in the Middle-East. That country in the Middle East reminds me of the very real dictatorship in Kyrgyzstan, where Kefir Ben Ousour imposes a reign of terror. Anyway, it was rejected by all the studios. Too close to the truth to be financed?

I have a quick look at the company's Facebook page. My God. Paul really isn't good at this. But, come to think of it, it's probably a lack of time. Just then, my phone vibrates;

"Hi! I'm waiting for you in front of the Chinese place."

I grab my bag on my way out and poke my head through the door. Paul looks up and quickly takes off his glasses, blushing. I didn't realize he wore glasses.

"Um, Paul, I'm going to eat out: do you want me to bring you anything?

- No, that won't be necessary, thanks."

I run out of the building: is this what being happy is like? Whatever the case, I feel alive. And when I meet up with Alec, I think to myself that this week is going to be absolutely great. Alec is tall, blond, messy hair, and whistles with his hands in his pockets, looking at the menu displayed out front of the Chinese restaurant. I tap on his right shoulder while standing to his left. He spins to his right, just as I anticipated and I grab his left arm.

"Oh! Hi!

- Hi!

- It's been ages since anyone's tried that on me!

- Yeah, I love messing around.

- You hungry?

- Yes!

- Ok, how much time do you have?" he asks me while holding the door.

- A short hour. It's my first day."

The waiter in a black shirt is in front of us in a flash and asks us to follow him, showing us to a table by the window.

"So, how's it going?

- Good. I get the feeling my boss can't do everything on his own and has trouble dealing with the day to day management side of things.

- You're going to make yourself essential, I'm sure of it.

- I hope so. It's been a while since I haven't done something I like, something that makes you want to get out of bed in the morning.

- I know, I completely understand! I managed to get myself out of a sad and bleak life, trapped in an office.

- And what did you used to do?

- I worked in a restaurant. Might as well say you don't have a life."

The waiter hands us two laminated menus and I take some time to check out the surrounding decor. All Chinese restaurants look alike, don't you think? Be it in the States or in Europe. You'll always get that old outdated charm, and that goddamn aquarium containing fish with frayed tails. Not forgetting the friendliness of the waiter, all part of the package with the never-ending plastified menus: Chinese dishes, Vietnamese, Cambodian… everything, you'll find absolutely everything. The waiter has come back to our table without making a sound, small pad in hand. We order two bo buns.

"And what do you do? It was quite the mystery on your Tinder profile.

- I own a diving club in Mexico. I started it about two years ago with my brother.

- How's that working for you?

- Really great! I round up all the stressed out execs from over here."

We both laugh and we talk about unexpected yet necessary career transitions for our generation. And my lunch hour flies by. It's nice, I feel refreshed and at ease.

"Alright, well, I'm going to have to head back."

Alec walks me to the street corner. I don't feel like having Paul see me with him.

"Did you enjoy yourself?

- Yeah, it was really great."

Alec smiles shyly and without warning, grabs me by the waist and tilts his head to kiss me. I let myself be lead as he brings his lips to mine. He has thin lips and closes his eyes at the last second, just how I like it. I relax in his arms, breathing in his cologne. When I feel his hands stroke down my waist to my hips, I push him away gently. When I open my eyes again, I see a figure walk into Owl Productions in my peripheral vision.

"Crap.

- Really? That's not what I was expecting.

- No crap, I think my boss saw us.

- Thank God! At least, that way, he won't bother you.

- No, he seems like a decent guy. It's just that I like keeping my personal life… personal.

- I see."

Alec has his hands back in his pockets.

"Alright then … I'll call you.

- Yes. I'd love that."

We go our separate ways between two shy smiles and I grip my hand bag to keep my hands busy, which all of a sudden seem to hang awkwardly. I didn't plan pockets on this skirt. I step into my office like a whirlwind and notice that Paul's door is shut.

"Weird. I thought he already got back."

True to my word, I hurry into the conference room: I start with the table. Goodbye crumbs and stains, in less than five minutes it's spotless. I dig out an old vacuum cleaner that, by some miracle, still works. It makes a huge racket and it's missing a wheel. I'm crouched under the table to reach the last of the crumbs when I jump out of my skin seeing a shoe pressing the off button.

"Paul! I didn't hear you."

But when I stand up and turn around, I'm face to face with Olen Van Cliff. Jaw clenched, an undecipherable expression. My heart literally bounds out of my chest to go to him but I swallow the lump in my throat instead:

"O...O… O…

- I love it when your mouth does that."

I blink. My brain is trying to shout some unknown information to me that just doesn't make it past my last mental barrier.

"What are you doing here?

- I was admiring the nicest ass on the planet up until now."

I tighten my grip on the vacuum cleaner and narrow my eyes:

"Now, I think I'm going to have to fight for my life leaning against the vacuum cleaner's handle.

- What are you doing here?

- I'm here for the meeting.

- You... You're the co-producer?

- Yes."

I swallow. What does this mean? I feel trapped like a rat. Paul risks poking his head around the door frame.

" I... are you ready?"

I put the vacuum cleaner away and making my way past Paul I tell him:

"I'll go get my notes."

I can't help but slam the door to my office violently. I grab my tiny pocket mirror to flatten the hair of my tight bun. The reflection shows me a Candice with a hard and merciless look in her eyes. I check that all the buttons on my shirt are done up.

"You organic carbuncle... You'll see what Candice Evans is capable of. The lioness is going to enter the arena and shred you to bits."

It used to crack my mom up when I made up insults.

"Chicken defecation." I say while looking for my notes.

If you've ever had chickens, you'll know it's not a pretty sight. I mutter while stepping out into the hallway:

"Sheep stew vomit."

Chewed and attacked by gastric acid, sheep stew isn't a pretty sight either. In two strides I'm in the conference room. I still have to stay professional because maybe Paul doesn't know what's going on. Has he known Olen for long? Was it Olen who gave him my application? Does he know about the whole story between us? How did Olen know I worked here? Just looking at him, my rage comes back full force and I have to restrain myself from throwing the file at him. But Olen surprises me by speaking up in a firm voice to explain the project with rigor and passion. I listen to him with interest, presenting the idea that came to him a year ago.

"It's a great idea, but twenty-six pages is much too long for a first pitch.

- The project has already been pitched to a studio, they're actually waiting for a substantial development.

- Indeed, but I think the writing can be shortened and more to the point.

- I'm sorry Miss Evans, but I didn't go to Columbia," he says scowling.

"Nor finishing school from what I can see."

Olen goes tomato red. I clearly got under his skin. Paul watches us as if he were watching a tennis match.

"I'll go and make some tea." he states jumping up and running towards the kettle.

"The characters are really good except for the researcher.

- Writing a character is complex. There aren't any good or bad people, Miss Evans, there are just bad choices. I hope you realize that."

The conversation is slipping dangerously. I get a grip staying unmovable:

"True and this character has made some interesting choices, I'd say. However, I think he should be just as developed as the main character. After all, he's the antagonist.

- Absolutely, the complete opposite of the main character.

- Exactly, his exact opposite…

- And yet, they have a lot in common, when you draw a parallel."

Olen and I look at each other in silence for a while, each of us on opposite sides of the table. Yes. We're so different. Our respective fields, our life choices, our values.

"And what do you think of the last part of the pitch?

- I'd say that the fact that it was inserted at the end of the pitch is going to reveal your utter unprofessionalism."

Olen grows pale and I immediately regret my cruelty. But there you go, all the sadness resurfaced, and I need to see him suffer as much as I've suffered. I just destroyed him, plunging a dagger into his ego and I hope into his heart.

"But I find the idea of a live scavenger hunt absolutely great. Particularly for a TV show project about a lost treasure."

Olen's eyes light up.

" Yes, they did that for Batman the dark knight.

- Yes I know. But never for a TV show. That's what will reel in the studios, M Van Cliff. All these transmedia devices disseminating clues on Youtube, blogs, social media, I think it's a great idea but all that needs to be on the first page of the pitch."

I think I can detect gratitude in his eyes. He lets out a deep sigh.

"Would you be willing to revise the project with me?"

Paul, who had sat back down in silence, watches me without a word. Here we are. The moment of truth. Do I have it in me to stay professional? My job's on the line. Heads or tails.

"Yes. I'll send you a revised document tomorrow with my personal notes on the characters, if you'd like.

- That would be perfect. Thank you."

Paul nods with a sigh and takes over:

"Right, well let's go over the financial aspect. You thought of Glenn Close for the lead?

- Yeah, I mentioned it to her. She'd be interested.

- Great, but I'm going to need to plan a big check just for her.

- We're going to need a guy who can hold his own to work with her.

- Duchovny?

- Forget it, X Files is going to be renewed.

- Shit."

I leave them to discuss the finances which allows me to observe them at my leisure. How the hell did they meet? Olen never went to college. At a party? Paul reminds me more of the protagonist in The 40 year-old virgin. But there's something about him, he's gentle yet direct, it seems to put Olen at ease because I've rarely seen him so relaxed. He starts laughing and I can see his adorable dimples again and the lines that are starting to surface at the corner of his eyes. I want to slap myself because Olen caught me looking.

"Right, I think we should wait for Candice's version to launch this more officially.

- Yes, I'm going to start right away."

Paul and I get up but Olen whispers:

"Just a moment Candice."

Chapter 13

I look to Paul, who gives me a slight smile: reassuring or encouraging, I can't tell. He leaves the room hastily and shuts the door behind him. I'm still standing, staring at the doorknob. A glance at Olen and I rush to the door.

"No!"

He had it all planned, pouncing on me like a cat, he spins me and presses me against the wall.

"Hold on, I just want to talk.

- And say what?

- Things aren't what they seem.

- Indeed. I thought you were an arrogant Hollywood jerk, then I thought that maybe you were one of the good ones. But no. You really are a lying jerk of a player without shame.

- I don't have a ring.

- That confirms what I said.

- I'm still slightly married to Clarissa but we don't live together anymore."

I blink.

"Why?

- We were young. I wasn't thinking when Clarissa came to me with the idea of getting married.

- Do you still love her?

- No."

He answered straight away with such a look of honesty that I believe him immediately.

"Then why are you still married?

- She's ill Candice. Really ill.

- Meaning?

- She has breast cancer."

Ouch. I think back to her hair, too shiny to be natural, her eyebrows that were drawn on and how tired she looked. I feel stupid all of a sudden.

"I'm waiting for her to finish her treatment before I make her sign the divorce papers.

- But how? Does anyone know?

- Very few people do. But it won't be long before the press get a hold of the story. I didn't make Clarissa sign a confidentiality contract.

- I see.

- And since a certain sexy little bookseller, the media are passionate about my personal life."

I feel my jaw drop when I look at him and drown in his blue eyes. I take a deep breath at his words. I can't help but examine his chest with some rebellious hairs peeking out from under his shirt. Olen lets go of my waist and puts both his hands on the wall, one on each side of my head. But I don't give in yet. I tear my gaze from his chest and look at him defiantly. We'll see who Olen Van cliff really is now. What excuse is he going to come up with?

"What about William West?"

Olen straightens up, eyes narrowed. I can feel the anger coming off every inch of his skin in waves, and it seems as if he's slightly taller.

"William West?

- Apparently, you ruined his career.

- You still seeing that jerk?

- What's it to you?

- He derailed his project all by himself, the idiot.

- From what he tells me, you put the first nail in the coffin.

- I should have nailed him with my fist to the face when I had the chance.

- I can't believe it! How can you be so impulsive?

- I bought the rights to his script, but he decided to change everything last minute. Being all high and mighty, he felt that I didn't respect his talent as a writer enough. And he is not a team player.

- Couldn't it be that you felt threatened by his talent?

- What? I surround myself with the best Candice! And I pay them well. That's how you become an actor recognized by his peers. Not by opening your big mouth every chance you get like he does."

I waver. What if I was wrong about William? It's true that it wasn't very professional to unload all his problems on a first date.

"William refused to bring the modifications that we asked of him. He wanted to play the tortured artist whose work is untouchable. Too bad, that doesn't work here, in America."

Olen grabs me by the waist and, suddenly, pulls me towards him.

"Alright, enough about that pitiful jerk."

He grips my hair, pulling my head back.

"Who's that idiot you were kissing earlier?

- It's … You saw us?

- Yeah, I saw him throw himself at you.

- I'm definitely not going to tell you who he is.

- I don't dive a damn about who he is, I don't want him to touch you anymore.

- I'm not your plaything, Olen.

- You owe me a lunch.

- I didn't ask you to choose between me and your harem of models now, did I?

- The sparks between you and me.

- You're just looking to get fireworks in bed, aren't you ?! Men!

- I prefer cinder under the ash, slowly catching fire… when I least expect it."

I'm rooted to the spot, his hands tangled in my bun which has come undone. He runs his lips along my face. I feel butterflies in my stomach, and my breathing becoming shallow. I whisper:

"Be careful, you could get burned.

- What I would give to see that and to make fire course through your veins."

I bite my lip to repress the desire that's starting to chip at my good resolutions.

"I think the problem is, you're confused. You want to, but you're afraid to jump. Or maybe it's something else.

- Don't try to psychoanalyse me."

I look away.

"Why is it that everytime I try to talk, you shut me out?

- Because, that's just the way I am… I… It's hard for me to express my feelings.

- You have feelings for me?

- I… I…"

I feel the prickle of tears.

"Candice, do you have feelings for me?

- God, why do you think I'm trying to run from this?"

Olen blinks in surprise and gently strokes my cheek.

"Can I kiss you?"

Of course, I'm dying to. I nod shyly and when he brings his lips to mine, I feel all the tension in my body fly away. He holds me tight, and strokes my tongue with his.

"Why don't you let anybody close, why don't you let anybody in?

- I could ask you the same thing, Olen.

- Tell me."

I stare him down angrily:

- Letting others get to know you, is giving them the tools they need to hurt you.

- Candice I swear, I only want to make you feel good."

I see a glint in his eye. He comes closer whereas I manage to free myself and hold up my hands.

"Not here.

- Yes here. That's what makes it fun."

I struggle but he already has me held tight against him.

"The more you struggle, the more excited I get."

He crashes his mouth to mine. I throw my head back, with a defiant look, and I slap him. He marks a pause, processing what happened, head still to the side from the impact. What's he going to do? His hold doesn't loosen. He looks at me, and brings me even closer, wrapping his arms around me, and kisses me again with force. Tense with anger. The anger of feeling my resistance fail me, and of admitting that he's made a breakthrough where no one else has managed to in years.

I bite his lower lip as it's getting too close for comfort. He leans back, shocked, and runs his tongue over his lips. I'm left breathless, cheeks burning, eyes alight with rage. He leans down again, and kisses me once more, searching for my tongue, now enveloping me completely in both his arms. He presses my body against his member. I resist a moment longer, but my body which is burning with passion is the first to lay down arms. My panting practically turns into a whimper. He then cups my face in his hands to look at me.

"I'm sorry. Did I hurt you?"

I bury my head against his chest whilst my whole body trembles. He rocks me in his arms for a while, but his scent awakens my senses. The scent that's purely male, the smell of perspiration emanating from him mixed with the smell of his cologne. His scent and his alone. I take it in, eyes closed, like a drug. I take in a deep breath, nose pressed to his chest.

I move back slightly, but he grabs my hair, forcing me to lean my head back, he kisses me passionately, without mercy. I answer his call and his hands make their way to the top of my thighs, stroking the curve of my ass, and pulls on the elastic of my underwear with his thumbs. I groan while stroking his tongue with mine faster still. I lose it when he lifts me from the ground, pressing me to his crotch setting fire to my body. I take advantage of this and stroke his member through the fabric. He lets out a moan. And slowly, he lays me down on the desk.

"Olen.

- I've missed you.

- You barely know me.

- Hm, true."

I push him away gently.

"I'm sorry, I got carried away, but I'm saying no.

- Your body's saying yes.

- My body says yes to a muffin as well and yet it's better to resist.

- You want to make me work for it, is that it?

- I'm not manipulating you Olen but I'm the type of person who likes to take it slow.

- Like a tortoise?

- A hedgehog."

Olen steps back, running a hand through his hair while looking at me from behind it.

"That's right, how could I forget, my little cactus. Right... what if you came to my birthday party?

- It's your birthday??

- Tomorrow. I'm having it at the Mandala club.

- Where's that?

- I'll send someone to get you.

- I don't need someone to come and get me.

- I'll send someone to get you, end of."

I put my hands on my hips shooting daggers at him.

"And you know where I live?

- See you tomorrow," He states with a diabolical smile.

He pulls me to him, kisses me on the forehead and opens the door.

"Wait a minute."

He spins around, alert. I stare at the carpet, because there's one last aspect that's running through my mind and I need to clarify it. A doubt. A horrible doubt that, this time, has me doubting myself.

"How do you and Paul know each other?"

He shuts the door silently and leans against it.

"Paul was a production assistant on a film, we met on set.

- And… how come you're still friends?

- He told me about his plans, that he wanted to become a producer, so…"

He pauses, choosing his words carefully. So, he perfectly understood what I was getting at.

"So?

- So, I invested a small amount in his company in the beginning with my first paycheck so that he could launch his project. I told you, I like to invest.

- And how did he find my resume then?"

He takes a deep breath.

"Promise me, you'll keep the job.

- I can't make any promises.

- Then I won't tell you.

- I knew it. You were the one who… who got me the job?"

I clench my fists with all my strength.

"Promise me, you'll keep the job. At least until you find something better."

I put my hands on my hips and say through clenched teeth:

"Fine.

- Yes, I told Paul about you.

- I can't believe it!

- Come on! You deserve this job, and anyway, I don't know anyone who got a job in this line of work without a good word from someone. So get off your high horse, right now.

- You know, I've been to university, and I want to get recognition for my capacities, not because I know the right people.

- But you are capable, Candice. Paul found your resume on a professional site, he looked you up, I swear. I told him about you, that's it. If he hired you, that's because you can get the job done. So stop being so prideful."

He comes closer, carefully taking me by the shoulders.

"And now, we're counting on you to help us develop projects. We need you, to… to stand up to me and make me be more professional."

I stare at his tie and slowly run my finger along it. I look up, and say while fisting his tie:

"You look good in a suit, M Van Cliff."

His pupils dilate, and he traces my lips with his thumb.

"Your skin against mine would suit me better, Candice."

And after a quick peck on the lips, I let him go, my skin still alight.

Chapter 14

I'm so anxious that I didn't sleep at all last night and I crashed the company's Facebook page. Thankfully, I triumphantly finished my report on the script and Paul seems to be thrilled with me. We diligently avoided mentioning Olen and yesterday's meeting. And now, I'm on the phone pacing in my room, the living room and Liza's bedroom.

"Liza, please help me!

- What's going on? Haven't you left yet?

- No… I don't know what to wear!

- What's the name of the restaurant?

- Uh… that's the thing, it's not at a restaurant, it's a club…

- A club??"

I hear the disapproval in Liza's voice.

"It's his birthday. He invited me, that's nice of him, right?

- Sure, I mean, he didn't exactly put a lot of thought into it. You haven't seen each other in a month and he's taking you to a club?

- Our last conversation was pretty rocky, so maybe he thought something fun would be nice. Less tense, you know?

- And who's going to be there?

- His friends, I guess…

- Right, 2007 Lanvin dress.

- How the hell do you want me to recognize a Lanvin dress from the 2007 collection in everything you have?

- Try the tags.

- Oh. Right. That's a good idea."

I push the hangers aside as fast as I can to find said dress.

"Is it the one that goes down to your knees or the short one?

- What do you think?" Liza asks, maliciously.

"Obviously… Isn't it a bit too short?

- No, absolutely not. Come on! Put on some nice heels and don't forget, comfortable for dancing and bring him back tonight, by the scruff of his neck if you have to. I want to see your bed destroyed with feathers flying around like in *Twilight*, got it?

- Of course, I'm going to let out my inner Edward Cullen.

- Ha ha! Tell me how it went tomorrow!

- See you tomorrow Liza! Thanks!

I hang up and rush into the bathroom. An hour later, perched on vertiginous yet comfortable heels, I have a hard time recognizing myself in the mirror. I pull my hair up into a ponytail which accentuates my figure all the more. It's really short.

"Olen's going to have a heart attack."

I pull the fabric down to cover my thighs, which has the flesh popping out from the low neckline, and I can practically hear Liza saying:

"It's never too short, hen."

The bell rings: I run to the window, not believing it.

"Already???"

The chauffeur is waiting, hat firmly secured on his head, in front of a black limousine. I grab my clutch and make my way downstairs, slowly. It would be incredibly stupid to get a sprained ankle now. I bend down to get into the car, but change my mind when I feel a cool draft slip through my thighs. I turn around and try to sit down delicately while smiling at the driver in what I hope is an elegant fashion.

"Are you a friend of Olen's?"

I jump when I lay eyes on my travel companion: a tall blonde creature with colorful streaks in her hair, judging me with crossed arms while typing away on her phone with her right hand. I recognize Glossie Free, the most high profile model at the time.

"Uh yeah…"

She blinks slowly and suddenly stops chewing her gum. Has she recognized me? I think so because the atmosphere changes and she looks back at her phone with a face three feet long. I try to strike up a conversation:

" What about you?

- Yes. An old friend."

Right. So, Olen stays friends with blonde models with never-ending legs for a long time, then. I'm fuming, out of jealousy and resentment. Does he know how to surround himself with anything but beautiful women? What has he got up his sleeve? Breathe Candice. He really has a gift of getting on my nerves. Sat next to this blonde goddess who's thigh is roughly the size of my arm, I can't help but feel ridiculous and like my clothes are too tight. The ride is spent in a tense and deafening silence. The limousine stops in front of the club and Glossie gets out without a second glance in my direction. Stunned, I watch her as she stands up and transforms in front of the bouncers into an enthusiastic and innocent little girl, kissing each of their cheeks in turn as a greeting while laughing. I didn't hear her give them her name. So is that the secret behind a model's super power? A bit of little girl attitude combined with "I couldn't care less about you but I'll be cool cause you're going to be useful to me in the meantime".

Glossie Free has already disappeared into the club whereas I'm barely getting out of the limousine on unsteady legs, I pull my skirt down to cover my knees and I see that I blew it with the bouncer in a matter of seconds.

"Miss Evans for M Van Cliff."

He nods and steps out of the way looking elsewhere. I make my way through the hyped up crowd, young people for the most part. All of a sudden, two hands are on my shoulders and I feel myself being pushed forward. When I turn, I can just about make out Olen's blue eyes, head lowered and wearing a Lakers cap. After a few feet, I feel his body wrap around mine in all its warmth. His hands go to my hips and his nose comes to tickle along my neck then behind my ear as he says:

"I love your dress."

I turn around, so that we can be face to face, and the corners of his mouth, stretching in a Cheshire cat smile, makes me melt. He pulls me to him, leaving no space between us and I can feel his desire against my stomach.

"I love everything about you."

When he crashes his lips to mine, I relax into the kiss, closing my eyes. His kisses are anything but shy, polite, tentative. They set me on fire, desire pooling in the pit of my stomach while his tongue gives me no respite. He abruptly let's go of me and takes me by the hand, pulling me towards the stairs that are barred off by a chain and a security guard. A quick glance at the mezzanine reveals a small group of people at the balustrade, watching me. The rest of the pack, I suppose. We make our way there, and while climbing the stairs, Olen's gaze follows a pretty woman pushing her hair back behind her ear while making her way down. I hate that, and he must feel it because he turns around and sees my blank expression:

"A work of art deserves an admiring gaze, don't you think?

- Not when I'm here.

- Yes you're here, and you're the one in my arms."

He makes his point and takes me into his arms, kissing my neck.

"You'll see, I'm not letting you go anywhere tonight, you're going to beg me to let you go."

I calm down slightly, and try to manage an enthusiastic smile when approaching the small group:

"Candice, this is Tony, Max, Dennis, and John. Old friends."

Max is a small brunet with blue eyes who keeps pulling on his t-shirt to hide his curves, while holding a beer in his other hand, I can only guess, to give an impression of composure. He smiles shyly at me while awkwardly extending a hand for me to shake:

"Hi Candice.

- You were in The Best of the West, right?

- Yeah, I was."

His face lights up with pride.

"It was a good movie.

- Thanks."

I've never seen it but I want to give him a compliment, seeing as he's being so nice to me. He's the same kind of guy as Paul. Harmless, nice and not very comfortable in his own skin, but solid as a rock. I'm reassured by this second meeting with Olen's entourage. We'll see about the others. He's shifting his weight from foot to foot and it hits me. A part from an ad for chips, Max has been languishing on a cable TV show and a few secondary roles alongside Olen.

"I'm Tony."

Because he's got brown hair and dark eyes he wants to seem Latino by wearing Italian clothes. I think I've seen him in music videos before: the singer of the lot then? He kisses my hand which makes me guffaw.

"Do you know Amore mio?

- Um yes… I've heard it…"

I stop talking because I realize the last time I heard it I was in high school … I give it another go with a guess:

"You've also worked with Olen, right?

- Yeah! We've been a part of the same group of friends for ages! But music is more my thing!"

I'm surprised, Olen never talks about his friends, not even in interviews. I've noticed, after a few times watching that the young actor that used to proudly talk to the journalists transformed into a fearsome diplomat who never let's the topic escape his control. From a young arrogant jerk he turned into a true pro at handling the press. Dennis and John wave from behind the others shouting a quick "Hi", then go and sit on the red armchairs and talk in hushed tones. Are they actors too? Does Olen deliberately surround himself with average looking celebrities? He sends me a slightly embarrassed sideways glance when silence befalls the group and he calls the waiters over.

"Sit down."

He points to the velvet chairs, where Dennis and John are looking at us, not in a hostile way, but for some reason I still feel uncomfortable.

"Here, let me introduce you to John a bit better, I've known him since high school."

John's blank expression suddenly becomes warmer. Another shy person? Olen sits next to me, placing his hands behind my back, spread out on the back of the seat in an attempt at nonchalance, but I still sense his barely perceptible nervousness.

"John's in business now. He's probably the only one who isn't going to turn up dead in a motel in a pool of blood and drugs."

They all burst out laughing. I try to crack a smile but… what a sordid joke. I hope it's ironic or maybe humor in an attempt to ward off bad luck!

"What do you do John?

- I have an internet business. I started off as an actor, and after a first big hit, I invested in my company with my cousin. It helped me make a break.

- Cool. I've always admired people who give entrepreneurship a go.

- Thanks, it means no holidays for a few years, but it's worth it."

I can't make Dennis out, that's until Olen introduces him properly. He then leans forward to shake my hand.

"Dennis is my shield, my assistant, my knight in shining armor, the one who's going to get me a great part, very soon.

- That's what your agent's for. I only hear whispered rumors, and report them back to you, call the people you want me to. If you were more focused as of late, you'd see the great parts that slip through your fingers.

- I've done two films back-to-back, I think I'm entitled to relax a bit."

And Olen relaxes even more into the seat to make his point. Dennis looks at him with a polite smile, too polite. And sends me a sideways glance before finishing his beer from the bottle. I shake my ponytail to get him to avert his gaze, that frankly, makes me feel uncomfortable:

"So, how old does it make you?

- Ha! Go on Olen, tell her!"

Olen fidgets beside me. The four of them are doubled over laughing, and it piqued my curiosity.

"Why won't you tell me?

- Because he can't admit it to himself! He doesn't want to age."

My eyes go as wide as saucers and I burst out laughing. Olen frowns and waves to somebody.

"He's twenty-nine.

- I'm eternal. Age doesn't count and I'll never die.

- You're getting closer to the big four-o.

- Yeah, watch it dude, you're only missing the house in New Jersey, the labrador and a little wife..." But Max elbowed John in the ribs, making him stop instantly, looking at me embarrassed, and gulps down his beer, finishing it.

"Twenty-nine?

- Yeah, do you have to say that?

- You don't look it. I would have said twenty-five, at the most."

Olen turns to face me:

"Really?

- Yes."

He doesn't want to look flattered, however, I visibly comforted him.

"Getting old is stupid. You need to stop believing the crap journalists tell you. Like, white hair and wrinkles are signs of wisdom. It's just crap to get you to take a pill. To convince you not to shoot yourself before you've finished paying the mortgage on your house."

The music suddenly stops and the acoustic to "We are the champions" can be heard. Two waiters approach us in a spray of sparks and triumphantly deposit a gigantic bucket filled with ice cubes and three bottles of Moët & Chandon. I can just see, out of the corner of my eye, the movement of the crowd getting up on tiptoes to catch a glimpse of us. Olen, as for him, is sporting a satisfied smile. The waiters busy themselves by uncorking the bottles and filling our glasses. Olen looks me in the eye while toasting with me.

"I'm glad you made it."

I feel his hand on my shoulder pulling me to him. There's just the two of us, like on the beach in Bali. He lets his index trail on my neck, then my shoulder. We look at each other in comfortable silence and that's it. I feel the walls I put up start to crumble under his caresses. A sneer interrupts us, and I discover two men leaning on the chair opposite us, watching us. Olen clears his throat and takes a quick look at the bar. Are they actors too? Hard to tell in the semi-darkness. But the first one with salt and pepper hair has decided to butt into the conversation and calls out:

"So, Olen, everything going how you want? Not too hard feeling the years settle on your shoulders?

- As long as it's not in my balls, unlike you!"

Everyone bursts out laughing whilst the waiter appears on Olen's right.

"Drinks for everyone! Jay, go on, have a glass!"

Olen stares at Jay who then sits up, and smiles in a friendly manner as he takes a sip. Applause and high-pitched shouting resonates. I understand where it's coming from when I see a flock of wiry girls with long hair appear out of nowhere to sway closer to our table. Jay and his acolyte are suddenly surrounded by Glossy

Free, Palinka and Jen. The three most high-profile models at the time. Jay shouts while giving a thumbs up to attract our attention.

"Happy birthday, Olen!!"

Olen stands up, without answering, grabs my hand and takes me to dance further away, away from the prying eyes and away from his pack. He takes me in his arms and pulls me to him.

"Why don't you want to get old?

- I want to live. Extensively. I don't care about living a long life. I would have liked to stay twenty for ever, and then die all of a sudden.

- All of a sudden?

- Yeah, poof gone. To evaporate.

- Like the little Mermaid?

- Why the little Mermaid?

- She disappears in the whitecaps of the sea in the early morning when she didn't manage to seduce the prince.

- You just tickle my balls."

I throw my head back laughing. He tightens his grip on me, takes a hold of the back of my neck:

"It's not as good as a dinner, but I'm glad you're here.

- So you've said.

- And what about you're stunning? Did I already say that?

- No, that you didn't.

- You're stunning.

- You're not so bad yourself.

- It's too much of an honor, Miss Evans.

- I'm in a magnanimous mood towards you tonight, Mr Van Cliff."

He slowly bats his eyelashes and bringing his hand down on my ass pins me against him, groaning.

"Your insolence isn't going to save you tonight, Miss Evans.

- I thought you were my knight in shining armor…

- Until I take off the armor and everything else with it.

- I still haven't completely taken off mine, M Van Cliff."

He looks at me not saying a word and tightens his hold on my back.

"Noted. It really turns me on when you call me Mr Van Cliff, you know that?"

I relax, dancing pressed against him, we sway to the beat. Inspired by the moment at hand, I whisper:

" We could get out of here, the two of us. Just the two of us. No one will notice we're gone.

- To go where?

- Far away. Wherever you want, as long as we're together!"

I'm about to kiss him tenderly when I feel a presence next to me. Palinka a twenty something Russian model let's loose shaking out her blonde hair. Olen glances at her indifferently and I bristle when she sends him a look while rubbing up against him for a few seconds.

"Happy birthday, Olen…" she whispers while resting her chin on his shoulder before swaying her hips, just what she needed to get his attention. I violently shove him away, furious, and make my way through the crowd, not looking back but I'm guessing Palinka threw herself into his arms to give him some lessons in the Russian tongue without having to be begged. And without knowing how, a flock of women are surrounding Olen, dancing with him, around him, forming an unbreachable wall. It was a vortex of which I wasn't the center, and I felt as if I was ejected like a satellite. But how does he know so many people? How does he know so many women? Suddenly someone grabs me by the waist:

"Well well well, the sexy little bookseller."

I find myself nose to nose with a fifty-year-old guy, with a reddish complexion and a menacing glint in his eye.

"Let go of me or I'll slap you!"

This huge pig has a tight grip on my arm and is sputtering all over me.

"Look here, you should talk to me better, young lady!"

I search for Olen, but he's being thrown in the air, carried by the crowd, that are taking him to the rope upto the mezzanine. I see him shout while holding his arms out:

"Who's the boss?"

The hurrays of the crowd are his only answer. He roars again, haughtily and pounding after each word to grab everyone's attention:

"Who's the boss?"

The crowd goes wild, not able to stand it anymore and urging him to continue. My scream is lost in the sea of people when the disgusting pig pulls me to him, and Olen jumps over the balustrade shouting:

"I'm the king of the world!"

Chapter 15

Suddenly, a hand takes my waist and pulls me back: I find myself behind Max, who's shielding me from the disgusting pig. He nods towards the dance floor.

"Evening, Hank! How are you? You having fun with all these pretty ladies?

- Not too bad, yeah. Olen knows how to throw a party.

- And did you get my script?

- Yeah, we'll talk about it soon Max, don't worry.

- I'm not saying I'm going to make it, but what did you think about the role of Peter? Not bad, right?

- Yeah we'll talk about it."

I watch Hank's figure turn away to clutch the waist of a young woman and gyrate with her a bit further away. I breathe out a thank you while putting a hand on Max's arm, who had watched him walk away.

"No problem."

He has a small shy smile that must make women melt, once they get to know him better.

"You want a drink? He asks me.

- Go on then!"

And here we are, side by side at the bar. I rummage around my handbag looking for my purse.

"What are you looking for?

- My credit card. It's on me! It's the least I could do."

Max shakes his head.

"No need! Olen has a deal with the manager.

- Really?

- Yeah. Free drinks and tomorrow everyone's going to be talking about the Mandala Club.

- Oh right…""

A few minutes and a bottle of caramel vodka later, Max and I are joking around like two childhood friends. Behind Max, the two men from earlier, Jay and his friend are taking digs at each other, which makes us laugh.

"It's true that men don't like intelligent women.

- Not me!

- Yeah, but you've given up! An intelligent woman is too cold. You can tell she's never gotten drunk: she doesn't have any compassion when it happens to someone else. Definitely none for a guy. They already want to punch us when we crack a lousy joke.

- Come on man, we're not going to complain, life's great!

- Especially when you have access to all this tail!

- Especially when you're young.

- Bastard!'

They move away to go and sit on dark purple couches. Max leans towards me:

"Jay's over forty now. Forty-three to be exact. The age you need to settle down if you want to hope for a shred of credibility.

- The age where you can't claim to be when you've already been.

- Exactly! The age where you can't count on a pretty face and lovestruck girls to make your career: you get replaced by younger guys, the girls grow up and don't have the time to go to the movies anymore. Being a good looking old guy is a good thing if you're a businessman. But his salt and pepper hair looks alright, doesn't it?"

I laugh, giving a nod of approval.

"He's really into defending human rights, isn't he?

- Yeah, but it doesn't stop him from hunting on his old turf.

- Do you think he's going to end up alone?

- I don't know. I just hope he won't get blindsided by a nice ass, and end up with a woman who's going to go after all his money."

He turns to me sporting a fake detached look:

"Alright, tell me, what do you think of Olen?"

I sigh.

"I really like him. A lot, Max. But he's really pigheaded.

- He really likes you too. But you're stubborn."

I burst out laughing hitting the bar with my fist. Hanks' red face pops up in front of me. Max, taken by surprise, freezes behind his bull-sized neck. I stop in my tracks.

"So, you've cut loose?"

Hank puts a hand on the small of my back, and I freeze. Max tries to get up however, he's trapped between the bar and the giant who planned his move beforehand. He clamps his hand around my arm and murmurs in my ear:

"Shall we take the private party upstairs…"

And without asking my opinion pulls me to him.

"So, Hank…"

Olen appears at his side and brutally puts his hand on his shoulder. Hank stiffens slightly, his gaze furtively wandering between Olen and me, evaluating the risk of a confrontation.

"You're not going to scare my favorite guest, are you?"

Hank clicks his tongue sniggering. Fear giving place to rage.

"I didn't scare you, did I?

- It takes more than that."

I snigger in turn. I don't like the sound of my voice, it's so unlike me.

"And we all know who here is the big bad wolf.

- You're right little red riding hood," He laughs.

I jump up but lose my balance perched on my high heels. Olen catches me mid-fall. The adrenalin mixed with the alcohol fumes courses through me and he holds me up, glowering.

"Oh my God !!! Candiiiiiiiiiiice, I'm so happy to see you again!"

A blonde tornado launches at my neck.

"Becky. Great.

- So, how's it going? So happy that you and Olen are still together.

- Thanks… But…"

I didn't have time to finish my sentence saying "the bastard is just a player who doesn't know what he wants", but she's already thrown herself into Hanks' arms, who had started going on his way looking for some other prey.

"Oh Hank, thanks for inviting me!"

A bit taken aback by this outburst, Hank lets himself be charmed by the appetizing cleavage of the little blonde. He whispers something in her ear and she starts cackling, giving an approving nod. All of a sudden, the music is too loud but I can hear Hank say to Olen in passing.

"Power has its advantages."

They both leave, heading towards some stairs in the back, that you can barely make out. The second mezzanine is plunged in darkness. Olen nods and looks at me attentively, not saying a word. I shout out:

"Thanks Max!"

Olen whispers something to him and drags me further onto the dancefloor.

"So, I'm the big bad wolf?

- Bad, that's for sure."

He takes me by the waist and tries to kiss me.

"I'm not in the mood.

- You're cute enough to eat.

- Stop. A wolf only has one mate. Do you know the Indian proverb? Choose the wolf instead of the bitch, she's more wild but more faithful.

- Interesting." He says, phlegmatic.

I blurt out coldly:

"And you're a stupid player who only knows how to mimic good manners.

- A player? That's what you think of me?"

I've made him angry. Perfect.

"What are you playing at Olen?

- What?

- These people are taking advantage of you… it's unhealthy.

- Hank is an epicurean. I'm not in a position to judge his behaviour.

- But people judge you, Olen, judge you on who you're friends with, on the company you keep.

- People like you?"

I can sense the wariness in his voice. He's looking at me defiantly. I shake my head.

"I judge what's best for me, Olen. Or what isn't. I know I don't belong in this world. You know it too.

- You belong to me.

- Not yet."

I grab a last glass of champagne, off a passing tray and empty it in one go, sending him a look full of arrogance. His nostrils flare in anger ... or desire. I don't know. I can hear blood rushing in my ears. Whoa. That was one drink too many. Somebody bumps into me while dancing, and I feel as if the ground is trying to make a ninety degree angle.

"Alright. That's enough."

And in a fraction of a second, he's thrown me over his shoulder.

"Put me down!"

He lands a spectacular spanking on my ass. I see Max, double over, pointing at me while Dennis raises his beer for my benefit. In a fit of rage I slap his ass in turn:

"Olen, put me down!"

We're already outside and he carries me for another few feet before I manage to get him to put me down. I stagger, and balance myself with the help of the wall:

"Do you know why men like beautiful women, Mr Van Cliff?

- Because beauty attracts us… Candice, you're drunk.

- For their gene pool! You say you don't want children, YET at the same time, you only need to see a blonde bimbo with genes that seem to be not so bad, for you to start following her around like a lost puppy!

- Are you done?

- Woof woof!

- Come on, I'll take you home!

- But you know what, Mr Van Cliff? It's just the packaging. It's just smoke and mirrors. "

I start screaming arms raised to the heavens:

"And you fall for it like a fifteen year old teenager! Long live Photoshoooooop! Long live airbags! Do you know some models have ribs taken out to have a slimmer waist?

- Are you going to alert the whole neighbourhood?

- Why? Have you slept with all their wives?

- That's a low blow, Candice.

- As low as my esteem for you right now, Mr Van Cliff."

We're sizing each other up, at a stalemate for a few minutes.

"You're going to end up alone, Olen. Like Jay. And I think that's sad.

- You're always alone in life, trust me."

He says it with such a somber expression. And so calm. I take a few uneasy steps but then I realize we're at the back exit of the club.

"Are you too ashamed of me to take the main exit?

- If you start throwing up, you'll appreciate not being in the headlines tomorrow."

I scowl, crossing my arms over my chest.

"Alright, let's go.

- No.

- Do you want me to do it again?

- What spank me?

- Oh, I'm definitely going to do that again, my little Candice."

He takes me by the waist and carries me in his arms. I doze off on his shoulder. Stupid player. He called me my little Candice.

Chapter 16

Sandalwood. I breathe in the perfume. It's new. It must be the candle that's on my desk. Have I ever had sheets so soft? The heat from another body at my back. Shit. Olen's watching me, smiling lazily, propped up on the pillow.

"Hello.

- Hi.

- Did you take my clothes off?

- You should be thanking me, the lines left behind on your skin by elastic aren't very nice. And it creates cellulite. The French are right. Apparently, they have beaches where you can be naked all the time.

- Naturism originated in Germany. It started in the twentieth century as a part of the free body culture. You have no shame.

- Can I get a kiss?

- You probably did more than that last night.

- Oh come on, who do you take me for Miss Evans?"

He jumps to a standing position on his bed, pulls the sheets to wrap them around himself, like a woman draping herself in her dignity. He sticks his chin out and covers his chest.

"You're making attempts on my virtue by throwing yourself in my bed. And, that, I will not tolerate.

- Alright, alright.

- No no ! I demand an apology.

- Go on then, make fun of the behaviour of another time Mr Van Cliff. They were barriers against wolves who are always hungry.

- I'm the viscountess Candice Goody two-shoes, if you please! Mind!

- Would a goody two-shoes do this?"

I arch my back, and run my nails against my breasts. I trace red stripes there. Olen stops in his tracks. He was going to find out what I was made of.

"Would a goody two-shoes do this?"

I turn onto my stomach and slide my hand down to my crotch back-arching slightly. Olen rips the sheet off the bed, watching my every move, whispering in a low tone, as if he was praying:

"Miss Evans. You surprise me more and more every day."

He kneels down and starts stroking my rear, undulating under his eyes. I turn around once again and hiding my breasts this time, I run a finger over my lips.

Olen admits in a husky voice:

"You know how to distract a man.

- So that's all I am ? A distraction?

- You're an obsession."

He lunges at me and pins me underneath him. His hardened manhood makes my mouth form an o.

"Yes Miss Evans. That's how it is. You have to face the consequences of your provocative actions."

I pant, after all these years of frustration, I implode under his caresses. I can't take anymore of his touch, push him away, only to grip him tighter. He slowly rakes his teeth against my breasts. I was expecting him to lick them but he pinches my nipple between his lips. I arch under the slow torture and Olen presses his manhood against me a bit more. A condom wrapper later and he's inside me. Olen makes love the same way he lives. There's something desperate in his eyes. I kiss his chin when he sends me to the stars to join him.

A few minutes later, my love holds me to him while breathing in, nose buried in my hair, and wraps his legs around me.

"Are you afraid I'm going to escape?

- No chance. The two exists are locked and I have two security guards."

My God, is he joking? Olen bursts out into beautiful laughter at my silence.

"My Candice…

- I love it when you call me that…

- Mistress of my dick.

- Mmh… now that's new!"

Suddenly he distances himself and with the tips of his fingers he grazes my thigh, my stomach, my breasts, my neck, my face. Surprisingly, it calms me. I drown in his eyes that are contemplating me. He goes on with his obsessive exploration and takes his time on the smooth skin of my forearm. No!! I stiffen, and try to hide my wrist but it's too late.

"What's this?"

He has a firm hold on my wrist and takes in the white lines, tracing his thumb along them. For the first time, I'm ashamed of my scars.

"I'd like nothing more than to tell you that I'll explain one day but I think I'll never be able to."

Olen watches me and bringing my hands to his lips kisses the inside of my once tortured wrists.

"Stop, I don't want your pity.

- And what about my tenderness?"

I turn my back on him to pout.

"You didn't show much tenderness earlier."

Olen plays into my hands and whispers in a playful voice.

"Dear Goody two-shoes, I'm going to cover your body in so many gentle touches, that you're going to be begging for my dick to break all the barriers of your body."

Indeed, I've never implored God as much as I did Olen in the next hour. But Olen has become my God after all…

"I'm hungry.

- Mmh.

- Do you want to go out?

- Mmh.

- It's eleven, I'm hungry. You should already be making me something to eat, naked.

- You're incorrigible Miss Evans."

He lands an expert blow to my ass.

"You're making a bad habit of this. I think my ass deserves better than that.

- I think so, too."

He rakes his nails against my skin, but I wriggle away:

"Alright that's enough. I'm really hungry.

- Last night made you demanding."

I laugh and stand up to search for my clothes.

"The problem is that there's nothing to eat in this house.

- Oh really? Why?"

I kneel down to look for my panties under the bed.

- Wait… a house? Where are we?"

I get up and find Olen sitting up, back against the pillow, hands linked behind his head, my underwear propped on his head as a hat.

"Welcome to New Jersey. The land of upper-class families with two kids and a labrador.

- Are you going to keep it?"

Aside from my underwear, I was also referring to the house. Could Olen dream of a white picket fence?

"Rent it. When you get to my age you start to invest."

I rip my underwear from atop his head:

"And why didn't you take me to your other house? The one from Masquerade?"

He looks embarrassed, and after a while spent in silence, shrugs.

"It's more peaceful here.

- Ok. Alright, is there a place where we can grab something to eat in New Jersey?

- I'll ask Kim to go out for some pancakes.

- No. Never mind. You know what, I'm just going to go…

- Oh… Alright."

He doesn't even make a move to stop me. Silence befalls us and I feel anger insinuate itself in my mind whilst I put my shoe on. Not standing it anymore, I turn around and bark:

"Are you ashamed of me?"

Olen looks at me, eyes widened in surprise. He slowly removes his hands from behind his head.

"What?

- Are you ashamed of me? What's wrong? Am I too fat to be seen with you in public? Not famous enough? What's the problem?

- Not at all, but do you have any idea what you actually want?!! You wanted your peaceful normal life, and I screwed everything up!

- Damn, screwed everything up, that's an understatement!

- Shit I wanted to make it up to you! I thought... "

He gets out of bed and paces the room while running a hand through his hair.

"What did you think in all your wisdom, Olen? That I would want to be treated like a hidden mistress?

- No! That you wanted us to live something away from the public eye. That we'd protect ourselves from now on from those crazy paparazzis!"

I'm speechless.

"I need to feed you... you become unmanageable when you're hungry, I'll remember that."

A few minutes later, here we are sitting in front of the table covered in pancakes, muffins, bacon, and potatoes, two coffees, and two orange juices.

"Are you sure you're going to eat all this?

- Positive.

- Be careful, if I have to throw food out, you'll get a dare.

- Challenge accepted. If you declare forfait before I do, you give me anything I want.

- And what do you want, Candice?

- You'll see.

- Ouch. I'm already regretting this bet."

I've already finished my pancakes, and methodically eat my muffin whilst Olen looks at the bacon pitifully.

"I really should have kept my mouth shut.

I laugh, mouth full of chocolate, at his defeated look. He's pouting:

"Do I get a consolation prize?

- Mmh… What do you want?

- You naked, now.

- I'm always naked for you Olen.

- Seriously, I've never seen you naked enough.

- Alright, fair enough. But you first."

Olen grabs his phone and the sound of "Can't get enough of your love baby" resonates between us.

"Barry White? Seriously?

- A classic. Barry White for the strip tease. Frank Sinatra for cooking and Dean Martin to dance to…

- And to make love?

- Your voice is enough for me. You sing so well when you're in my arms."

He pushes his chair back while looking at me enticingly. Crap, I have to find a secret weapon too. He gets up, does a spin, slowly swaying his hips. He runs his fingers up his stomach, lifting his shirt as he goes. Obviously, I stopped eating. Crap, he's good...

He takes off his belt cracking it in the air. At the third chorus, he's in his boxers, and is getting dangerously close. I wolf down what's left on my plate. He's not going to win that easily....

"Cheater!

- There you go. Finished!

- Mmh what am I going to do to you?"

I jump up from the stool and go round the table.

"Wait a minute! I won! Despite your admirable attempt at a distraction. I won.

- What do you want from me?

- To know... what you really think about me.

- Mmh ... Access to my most private thoughts.... But no one's allowed that."

He catches me and pins me against the work surface. I try my best to keep my gaze on his clavicle that I would love to tantalize... I force myself to keep a cool head.

"No funny business, Olen. Answer me.

- Ah. So no hanky-panky either then?

- No.

- Yes.

- No.

- Look me in the eye and say you don't want to."

I look at him defiantly.

Breathe. Take it slow. But he presses his pelvis against mine, and I can feel his erection. I set my hands on the edge of the work surface behind me and think about a joke of my own, a diversion. He beat me at my own game

"So?" he asks me gently in a playful tone. I open my mouth to answer, but nothing comes out. He catches my lips with his mouth and bringing his hands to my ass brings me closer to him still.

"You're sexy, my little Candice.

- I'm not sure you're my Olen," I blurt out sadly.

He gently cups my face with his hands and talks to me as you would a child:

"What do you mean?

- We're from two completely different worlds. I'm not sure I'm totally compatible with…"

My words are lost. With you, your friends, your lifestyle, your professional relations… Hank's face comes to mind.

"What was that pig doing at your party?

- Who? Hank?

- If Max hadn't intervened, he could have raped me.

- I was there, so you didn't have anything to worry about.

- You were there, without really being there, you were too busy with your entourage."

This time he sticks his chin out: clearly stung.

"In this business, it's part of the job description to have to mingle.

- Yes and to provide them with their lot of distractions, while you had yours.

- Don't exaggerate."

He lets me go and turns away to go and sit back down on his stool. But I'm determined to get the truth out of him.

"Is that all I am to you Olen? Really? A distraction?"

He freezes at the other end of the table.

"A small distraction between two models that served as appetizers?

- What are you talking about?"

However, I'm on a roll and this time there's no stopping me.

"Seriously Olen, why did you do it? Why were you in Bali, and why did you invite me to the party to then forget me halfway through? Because if this is just you playing cat and mouse, I'm not going to let you."

He casts his gaze down to his plate.

"So, we're not compatible?"

I'm going to try and pull all my strength together to answer in a tone that I would like to believe full of determination.

"I don't know, Olen? You... you've been with too many girls, I reckon. And I'm a woman.

- We were more compatible this morning I think," he says giving me a smile that would make anyone melt.

Quick, get out of there Candice, or he's going to pull you back in again.

"Olen, I'm scared.

- Scared of what?

- You don't see it: I don't want to suffer.

- Candice I swear, I don't ever want to hurt you.

- I want to go home.

- Are you sure?" He sits up in surprise.

"Yes, I need to go home. I've got a lot of things to do.

- Right, my chauffeur Kim will take you home."

I run to the bedroom feeling his gaze following me, and get dressed as fast as I can. When I cross the living room, Olen's outside, talking to his chauffeur in front of the 4x4 with tinted windows. I don't regret bringing it up. Only the fact that he didn't really answer my questions. Alright Candice, that's enough, otherwise you're never going to make it out. I exit the house with a falsely determined air, and opening the car door, I'm about to get in, when he catches me by the waist and looks deeply into my eyes. He takes my hand laying a gentle kiss to it.

"I saw that in an old movie... I've always wanted to do that."

I can't help but laugh. That's my Olen, eternal teenager, mischievous, insolent and charming.

"See you soon, my little Candice."

I climb into the 4x4 as he caresses my backside tenderly.

"I hope your ass appreciates the change. And send back the chariot please," he purrs.

I giggle while joking around.

"Yes, sir."

Chapter 17

When I get back, Liza's sprawled out on the couch, drinking tea.

"Hi.

- Hi."

I throw myself beside her, still in the Lanvin dress, without saying a word. Liza sits up and holds out a cup of tea that she'd made for me. And I start sobbing like a child.

"Oh God, what's he done??

- Nothing I didn't agree to. But… it's going too fast. It's been so long since I haven't felt like this. I feel happy and extremely stupid all at once.

- Happy and really stupid… Yeah, that's not a bad combination," she says, pensive while stroking my hair.

"Was he nice to you?

- Yes … Olen is nice to all women I think, and that's what annoys me. I don't know if he really likes me or if it's the idea of going out with a normal woman that's got him going."

Liza has the tact to not interrupt me between two hiccoughs.

"I feel like I'm fifteen again, and like I go insane when I'm with him…

- Do you want to seduce him?

- Well, I've already done that actually… But I want … I want it to go on. I realize that… that nothing else matters when he's here, when I'm with him. We're together… and everytime I try to escape, he brings me back to the present. And it's great. It does me good. God, are you listening to me? You'd think I was crazy!

- Not at all, hen. Listen, men like sluts, and you, you can be a killer when you want to be. And, then again, it was the perfect opportunity to get laid.

- I'm not sure that's enough for me, Liza.

- Oh what a little perv you are, Candice."

I start laughing wholeheartedly.

"I feel like I know him off by heart sometimes… and then there's other times… its as if he's shut a glass door and he's watching me from the other side. He's so free, spontaneous, carefree. You know what, I envy him. I'd like to be more like that."

I finish telling Liza about last night, from time to time having a quick glance at the re-run of *Gone with the wind*. Liza draws out her smartphone at the mention of Glossy Free.

"Her? He can't possibly find her attractive, impossible. She has a big nose and her second toe is bigger than her big toe."

I chortle.

"How on earth do you know that?

- Just need to look at the photos of her at St Barts from last summer, plus she has cellulite at twenty-two years old, can you imagine?

- Liza Cole, you're merciless. I thank God every day that I'm your friend, you need to know that."

Sat in an armchair in my red dress, as red as my lips, that's tight around my chest, I feel Olen's finger stroke along my arm, in a menacing ghost of a touch. I'm hypnotized by that touch, the delicious shiver running down my spine. I know that if I give in, I'll be caught. But I can't resist that whisper, so delicious, so tempting.

I wake up in a cold sweat, without finding sleep again. Four o'clock in the morning. Shit. After pacing in the quiet apartment for a while, I resign myself to taking a notebook and scribbling down scraps of dreams that are mixed with the scent of sandalwood, Glossy with long teeth and a masked man.

Monday, Tuesday, Wednesday. I pass my days laying on paper everything I can think of. My notebook becomes my lifeline to stop me from thinking about Olen. I know what he's playing at. He wants me to be the one to send the first text. Out of the question. The faces of Glossy Free, Becky Sparks, Hank run through my mind. A gallery of monsters that I couldn't have conjured on my own.

Thursday morning, I go out to grab a sandwich on my break when the garish front page of a magazine displayed in the street stops me in my tracks. "The secret orgies of Olen Van Cliff ". I get closer and read what's written while hiding the cover where Olen's laughing face appears. "An incredible birthday for his twenty-ninth, turns nightmare for the young Iulia Ionescu."

I rush to the office as fast as I can, throwing myself at the computer to look at Yahoo news. Liza's number displays on my phone.

"Have you seen?

- I'm reading it now.

- Olen hasn't called you back then.

- No he's too proud I guess. Like me.

- Or he's trying to extricate himself from this shitstorm."

I hang up facing the truth. Or Olen's dealing with the crisis between his lawyer and his P.R who's probably pulling their hair out. "Iulia Ionescu, twenty-one year old model (Aurora Model Agency) presses charges for being raped by Hank Wayne, the famous producer, during the birthday party of playboy Olen Van Cliff, notoriously known for his love of women and of pleasure of any kind. Olen Van Cliff is said to not have intervened despite being present, it being his party. The police are currently investigating the matter. "

For fuck's sake.

At six, there's still no comment from Olen to the presse. Article after article hits the stands, the comments on twitter are going wild, all the hate and resentment towards Hollywood coming out of the woodworks. I jump up and knock on Paul's door.

"Paul… have you heard from Olen?

- Yes, we'll have a meeting very soon. He's pretty busy at the moment.

- Paul, the two of you are friends, he listens to you, he needs to do something, a press release, anything! What's he waiting for? That the police come to arrest him in his home and that the paparazzis spread the pictures of him handcuffed or something?

- Listen, I'm happy you're slightly worried about him …

- Slightly? Paul, I'm really worried. That the media try to take pictures of me without make-up, I don't really care. I have nothing to gain from being popular… but Olen... if people believe all this… His career… He doesn't deserve this.

- Don't worry, he's well surrounded. Go home, Candice. See you tomorrow. We'll prepare my departure for Cannes. Ok?

- Ok."

I have to stay professional even if I want to yell at him. Calm down, Candice. Paul's always calm and gracious. How on earth did he make it in this business surrounded by sharks? The answer hits me, straight away. Olen protected him, guided him. Obviously.

Walking past the Chinese restaurant from my date with Alec, I have a craving for noodles. Sitting not far from me, kids of barely twenty are having dinner. The waiter sat me at a table while I await my order to go. They watch me for a while, in silence, before picking up their conversation, all the while typing away on their phones. Did they recognize me? I don't care after all. I'm here alone, pensive, looking at the dark wooden table top without really seeing it. Suddenly, inspiration strikes. I take my phone out and pretend to read a text. I call my voicemail and begin my monologue:

"Yeah, it's me… Olen? No I saw it in the street earlier."

I feel the teenagers' eyes on me.

"Mmh… Yeah… Yeah."

Out of the corner of my eye, I see a petite blonde grab her phone and put it on the edge of the table. Could she be recording me? Never mind, here goes nothing.

"No, of course he wasn't there." I draw circles on the table.

"You know the Mandala Club, there's the ground floor, the mezzanine with a private bar, and a third mezzanine. Yeah."

I can sense the teenagers febrile, they're staring at me so much.

"Basically, I saw that guy go upstairs with some girls and Olen stayed with us. And we spent the evening together, so I should know. Anyway, there's loads of witnesses, everybody that was there. Yeah. It was crazy. Alright, I have to go, I need to pick something up. Bye."

I quickly shove my phone back into my pocket, thinking that I might have overdone it.

I need to let off some steam. I watch Jessica Smith's Youtube channel. Yes, kickboxing, that will wear me out. Thirty minutes, shit. I'm drained. I leave the TV connected to the internet, while I down a bottle of water. In the shower, waiting for the noodles to heat-up in the kitchen, I realize I don't recognize myself. I've never been so impulsive. Could Olen have rubbed off on me?

When I take a seat on the couch with my bowl of noodles, I distractedly notice Nancy O'Ryan's botoxed face announce in a conspiratorial tone:

"Let's take a look at the footage!"

I freeze, spoon halfway to my mouth, seeing myself on the phone: shit, they were filming me, great!!

The audio isn't brilliant, but I can hear myself distinctly spurt out my monologue, that I thought was actually pretty well spun.

Nancy reappears.

"There you have it, we've reached the bottom of this. Will these statements be enough to exculpate Olen Van Cliff? Is he the victim of terrible rumors? Who's looking to destroy him? But, above all, could this be the making official of a relationship with a certain Candice? Who we thought dead and buried? To be continued very soon!"

Shit. He's going to kill me.

I hastily switch my phone off. Quick put it on silent. Act like a woman with a lot on her plate. You coward. I feel so stupid. How could I underestimate overly connected teens?

Obviously, Liza doesn't come home all night and I spend hours biting my nails under my covers. I've already made the front cover of the papers in only a few weeks, but this is different. I know I did something bad...

What an idiot, what an idiot, what an idiot!

I'm awoken by Liza pounding on my door. She must have forgotten her keys at Jake the electrician's who, supposedly, has no effect on her. I jump out in my shorts and t-shirt and rip open the front door.

"Shit Liza, I've messed up."

Olen's staring at me, arms crossed, leaning on the door frame. Out of panic, I immediately shut the door. What an idiot. What do you expect? That he's going to disappear? What are you going to do now?

"I'm still here."

I open straight away.

"Ha ha… It was… Um… A joke"

Silence.

"Sorry, I'm an idiot, I didn't think."

He slowly unfolds his arms and pressing his hand on each side of the door frame, he rakes his gaze up my long legs poking through my shorts that had lost their shape, my belly-button that peeks out from under my shirt. He smiles and arches a brow.

"Can I come in?

- Um, sure."

I try to escape so that I can throw on a dressing gown, but he catches me by the waist, and burying his nose in my hair, whispers:

"So, like that, you didn't do it on purpose, hmm?

- You're not mad?"

I can't believe I'm seeing him so affectionate. I thought he was going to kill me. What's he playing at?

"So, you didn't think? It still seemed like a very well thought out speech.

- Are you mad?"

He's still holding me tightly against his chest.

"You would have made a pitiful actress."

This time around, I'm offended:

"Now, wait a minute you…"

I don't get the chance to finish my sentence that he's already groping my ass fully in his hands, lifting my shorts and says through clenched teeth:

"I'm very very unhappy."

He takes me to the kitchen, lays me down on my stomach over the counter top, so cold against my skin, griping my hair.

Chapter 18

"How can you make it up to me? Mmmmh?"

His whispers and the fingers of his other hand that were grazing my back, my ass and my thighs were causing an irresistible shiver to course down my neck. He let's go of my hands and puts them on the countertop on each side of my head.

"Spread your legs."

I arch my back a bit more spreading my legs wide. He presses a hand to my clit through my underwear while I moan.

"My little Candice, you're already all wet."

With his other hand, he pulls down my shorts, and my underwear in one go. Shit. What if Liza walked in? However, I can't manage any words when he grabs a handful of my ass cheeks to separate them even more. I can hear his sharp intake of breath behind me and I scream as he bites my neck, entering me in one thrust. I think I hear someone on the stairs. Quick, I try to concentrate on the feeling, but Olen pulls out, last second, turning me around.

"Your bedroom?"

Surprised, I nod towards the left. He picks me up in his arms, and in a few strides we're on my bed, completely naked.

I don't hear Liza come in. I have to admit, I let loose… to be forgiven. His body scorches mine in a delicious way.

"Go on, show me."

It's my turn to torture him… I look at him tenderly, pausing. Laying back, arms crossed, resting on the pillows, Olen looks at me blissfully whereas I'm standing above him, back to him. He lazily extends his hand to touch me without reaching his goal.

I bend down slightly to reveal the treasure between my legs. I hear him exhale loudly, breathing raggedly. And I lower myself slowly until I take his hardened member inside me while clenching around him. I feel him arch beneath me, and it nearly makes me want to finish him off through the pleasure of my to and fros. However, I'm not done. I take his shaft and stroke it through my folds, drawing a circle around my clit. I then take only the tip in, flexing my pelvic muscles. I pull away rapidly, straighten up to look around and with a voice barely above a whisper ask:

"Do you like what I've done with the place?

- Are you kidding me?! Get back here!"

And he catches me by the hips trying to make me lose my balance. I fall over laughing.

"Little minx" he rasps through clenched teeth, pinching my nipples.

I hover over his tip, resuming my sweet torture. I ride Olen, and when he's nearly there, slow the pace. I let him penetrate me more and more deeply until I finally hear him breathe out my name, head thrown back and clutching the pillows.

He's begging me, eyes half-closed, an expression of painful pleasure on his face. And when I'm also squirming, I deliver us to the waves of pleasure that have us shivering to the tips of our hair.

Lying peacefully, I breathe in his perfume that's like a drug, a mix of sandalwood, and something else.

"Verveine maybe…" I say out loud.

"Mmh?

- No, nothing. I like your cologne, that's all."

He delicately kisses my hair, just over my temple.

"You're the best."

I wince. That's a strange thing to say to a woman just after having made love to her.

"Out of all your other conquests?

- Uh… You're overestimating me on my number of conquests.

- Don't underestimate yourself to avoid the discussion.

- Look here, you…"

He pins me under his slender and toned body, gazing down at me:

"Who did something stupid and needs to keep a low profile?"

I blush, biting my lip.

"So low that you could even kiss me down there and take me into your mouth."

I wiggle my shoulders to try and break free.

"I'm not part of your small entourage for who your wish is their command.

- Oh really?"

He has that playful look about him again, the one that makes me melt, in more ways than one. I'm flustered and furious. Furious, that he's breaking through my defences and all the walls I've put up.

"Well, I need to get dressed. I have a normal job.

- A normal job, normal life, abnormal guy."

Standing in front of the bed, I stop in my tracks while putting my underwear back on, and I try to adopt a smug and detached look throwing over my shoulder:

"So, you're my guy now? Meaning we're together?"

Olen looks at me, stretched out on his stomach, chin resting on both his hands.

"You said so yourself, not sure we're compatible."

What's he playing at? Does he want me to beg. Pesky little hotshot. I turn away and go to the bathroom closing the door halfway.

"Then again, you'd have to do things normally for you to be my guy."

I sense that I've piqued his interest and out of the corner of my eye, I see that he's now looking at me.

"Meaning?"

I lazily apply make-up in my bathroom and gently let out:

"Like grabbing a coffee, going to the movies, walking through Central Park. A proper first date, you know, in all its picturesque and precious banality."

I sigh.

"But for most normal people, that equates to boring.

- Yeah out in public, right?"

He said that in such a dreamy and forlorn way. Olen reverts to lying on his back, and is looking at the ceiling absentmindedly, hands linked beneath his head. I try to stay calm while applying mascara.

"So, if you were my guy, this is what it would be like? Dates on the sly here, or better yet at the hotel... like a prostitute?"

Olen blinks, astonished.

"I've already told you, I'm only trying to protect you! Protect what we have!

- Yeah right..."

This time he gets up opening the door abruptly.

"Do you know what it's like going out at 2a.m and to be run after by fifteen girls in heat?

- That must be quite the memory.

- To get used pads as a declaration of love?

- Oh um...

- To know that you're being followed, for thirty long minutes in a mall and not knowing if it's just for the sake of it, or if you're actually in real danger because some crazy potentially wants to throw acid on you?

- I have to admit, I didn't think of that.

- The tabloids... that's nothing compared to "normal" people Candice. Those are the crazy, frustrated, obsessed people, those who go through your trash to find something of yours as a keepsake. I want to protect you from all that, ok?"

I cast my eyes down to the ground pitifully, whereas he puts both his hands on my shoulders, and starts to stroke through the fabric.

"The day we appear in public together, it's over. We've made it official, and that means that you're fair game. Your personal life and all its details sold to the highest bidder."

I swallow. I never imagined what was going on behind the scenes.

"That bad?

- Do you remember how Lady Di died?

- Yeah, you're right. Wait a second… How do you know about Lady Di?

- Well what?

- Well you're a guy! I don't believe it, are you a fan of Lady Di?

- No my mother is."

I jump on the occasion, and gently snake my arms around his waist. And looking at him from under my lashes I say:

"You see, normal people have pizza night at home, they talk about their childhood, their parents…"

Olen stares at my hair, not saying a word. I take note of his jaw clenching. Oh shit. What did I say?

"I could maybe have a barbecue this weekend.

- At your house in Jersey?

- Yes. However, I can't guarantee normal food.

- Why's that?

- Max is trying to lose weight, and got it into his head to become a vegetarian. So, it will probably be vegetable skewers.

- Is there going to be a lot of people?

- No only my close friends."

I kiss the tip of his nose.

"Are you happy?

- Mm yes.

- I'm entitled to more than a kiss on the nose then, I think.

- If you're good until this weekend.

- Good?

- Yes good.

- That, my dear little Candice, is something I've never been."

He grips my blouse and brutally rips it open, buttons flying everywhere.

"Hey! What's wrong with y…"

He hikes up my skirt, and groans while ripping my lacy thong. A fraction of a second later I have my legs wrapped around his waist, mewling once again under his strokes. We fall onto the bed when orgasm hits us.

"My God, Olen that was…

- Come on, up!

- What?

- Go to work!

- And what I'm I going to wear Mr sexy beast?"

Malicious, he gets up still naked, and opens the doors to my tiny closet.

"Right… my little bookworm, we'll soon do something about that."

I grab some old jeans and a t-shirt.

"Oh no you don't!

- Yes I will! Serves you right, maybe this way you won't be tempted to rip it off!

- Mmmh… we'll see.

- Shut the door on your way out."

I pick my bag up as I walk past, and without further ado, I'm off to Paul and the planning of the festival.

Friday, 11 a.m, Olen and I flirt over the phone.

"Do you miss me?

- I don't know, maybe.

- Do you miss your blouse?

- Yes and my lingerie too, believe it or not.

- I'm sorry.

- No, you're not.

- Sorry. I experience things in an overwhelming way and I need to express it.

- Or, you're a huge pain in the ass.

- What are you wearing?

- Well, an old pair of jeans and another blouse that managed to survive a raving lunatic of a perv.

- Oh you little minx. Is it the light green one?

- Yes…

- With the mother-of-pearl buttons?

- Yes, now, hang up.

- Will you wear it to the barbecue tomorrow?

- I'm hanging up now.

- And what if I suspended you from the rail of the shower curtain next time?

- You better, Mr Van Cliff."

Chapter 19

Olen opens the door in a hurry and undresses me with his eyes. I'm wearing a purple flowery dress, my light green blouse knotted around my waist and pumps.

"Did you walk here?

- Yes for the last block. I didn't want the taxi driver to see where I got out."

Olen looks at me with a small satisfied smirk. I put my hands on my hips and stick my chin out in pride:

"See, I'm a fast learner.

- Good. Come in."

He looks me up and down and I can see that he appreciates my dress.

"Ready?"

I nod with a smile. He links his fingers with mine. That small contact alone is enough to make me all hot and bothered. Obviously, he notices. And, obviously, he seizes the opportunity to steal a kiss in the living room. He opens the bay windows and takes the lead, all the while never letting go of my hand.

"Right guys! Do you remember Candice?"

Max is there and gets up first taking me into his arms, warmly.

"Hi!

- Hey Max! How are you?

- Yeah, I'm good. "

He seems happy that I recognized him. Dennis makes his way forward and extends his hand.

"Hi! Dennis.

- Yeah I know, we met at the party remember?

- Yes, I do."

He still has that cold and dubious air about him. He must be thinking what the hell's Olen doing with her when he could have any model he wants? That, or he hates me for what I did? I detect a small condescending smirk directed at my pumps. I realize I'm the only girl there, a part from Laurene who seems close to Tony, the latter clarifies right away:

"She's my cousin, we're not together.

- And his assistant.

- Wow, that's great!

- Wow, I just make sure he has enough tp because, where the fridge is concerned, his mother still fills that up for him.

- It's only normal, you're the one that empties it!

- Yeah sure I do!

- I don't have the time to cook with the new album of Dancing with the stars.

- It's mainly because you forgot where all the saucepans are.

- I can't help it, mom's cooking is the best.

- And he doesn't get why he's not married.

- God forbid.

- You're right, I pity your future wife.

- Right, you just need to look on Wikipedia to find out about us, but you Candice, what do you do for a living?"

They fall quiet. I'm sitting on the armrest holding my juice between my fingers.

"Well, you know, nothing special. I mean, just a normal life. I used to be a bookseller, after that a waitress, then a tutor, and now I'm an assistant, I develop projects for a production company."

I don't detect a change in their expressions. Olen was kind enough not to say anything. Laurene seemed very enthusiastic about my case:

"That's funny, you're a true literature lover, that's for sure!

- Yeah, I think that sums me up pretty well.

- Have you already written anything? Like a novel?"

I turn bright red thinking about my book of erotic poems that I wrote in college. The first thing that pops to mind is that novel I developed in my teenage years.

"Um I started a novel a few years back but I've never had the time or the courage to tackle it…

- Oh really? And what's it about?

- It's a mix between *The Lord of the Rings* and *Star Wars…*"

Max's head shoots up, and John's staring at me, hooked.

"Really? But like medieval?

- Of course not Star Wars is futuristic!" John intervenes, elbowing him in the ribs.

"*The Lord of the Rings*, is heroic fantasy.

- Yeah, let's just say it's a fantasy.

- Well…," I was going to have to explain myself a bit more.

"No because fantasy is the irruption of the unrealistic in a realistic day-to-day life whereas heroic fantasy is clearly a purely imaginary world. And futuristic is…," Dennis clarifies.

"Alright, alright! We get it *Star Wars* is futuristic!

- Yeah, now let her finish!" Tony says.

Olen gets up to tend to the barbecue. I take a deep breath: alright, I'm going to have to get them hooked or they're going to be merciless.

"Well, it's about a little girl whose born in a forest, protected by some sort of magical dome.

- Like in Stephen King's *the Dome*?

- Um yes. Well maybe, I haven't read it.

- Who cares? There's magical domes in a lot of other stories…"

I burst out laughing seeing them bicker. I feel like Wendy surrounded by the lost boys. My Peter Pan's coming, with two hot dogs in hand. He hands me one and collapses onto the couch taking me by the waist, making me fall into his lap.

"Ok, so?

- So?

- So…"

Focus, Candice. Olen's hands gently roam my back.

"So, she grew up in a priestly caste and they discover over the period of her training that she's very gifted in the magical arts. Not only gifted, but it's practically… innate."

They look at me wide-eyed.

"So as she grows up, the priests who wanted to use her as a tool in their resistance against the outside world, at the time transformed by technology and the science cult, start to wonder…"

I mark a pause.

"Is she really on their side?"

Silence falls.

"Wow… not bad… ," Laurene says as if awestruck.

"Definitely, you need to write it," Olen says excitedly while pinching my waist.

"Alright, I'll do it when you start cooking, Olen."

He scowls.

"I can't cook, but you, you can write, you have imagination.

- That's true, however you can't do it with a snap of your fingers, people think it's easy to write a novel, that it comes easily but that chapter, I rewrote it probably fifteen times."

He watches me in dubious silence.

"Ultimately, it's like you actors, sometimes you need to do the scene five times to get the right intonation, or that little something extra that will make it a wrap."

I don't want to come of snobbish. I'm already being nerdy with my literature-filled past.

"Max, you know what I'm talking about, you wrote a script, didn't you? You talked to Hank Wayne about it at Olen's party.

- Yeah I know what you mean," Max looks all excited that I bought up his project.

I get comfy against Olen, watching Max tell his story. The doorbell rings. Olen sits up, brows furrowed in surprise.

"Were you expecting anyone else?

- No."

Olen barely has time to reach the bay windows that somebody appears in the doorway in front of him. He stops in his tracks.

"Hi, my little piggies!"

Clarissa!

She has a bandana on her head and an old pair of jeans. Why do I suddenly feel out of place in my dress? God damnit, what's she doing here? Olen looks completely in shock. But Clarissa has already sized me up .

Awkward silence.

Dennis is looking at me askance. What are they expecting? A catfight? Clarissa produces a huge yellow and pink squirt gun.

"That's what I thought. That you were bored out of your minds without me and that I needed to get the party started."

She makes her way towards us and throws a bag full of squirt guns on the floor. The lost boys look at Olen guiltily. Who will be the first one to break? Clarissa takes a step forward and before he could stop it, she gets up on tip toes and kisses the corner of his mouth all the while watching me out of the corner of her eye.

You little two legged carbuncle. Give it a rest, Candice, she's got cancer, come on.

"Plus, your wife didn't want to miss your birthday.

- Clarissa…"

Max making the most of the distraction, bent over the squirt guns, launching the hostilities. Traitor.

I'm seething. I'm this close to grabbing my stuff and leaving. No, stop it, that would mean she wins. I get closer and grab a squirt gun. The lost boys watch me bright-eyed.

"Alright, let the battle begin. Olen, Max, you're on my team. Who's with me?"

Clarissa suddenly stiffens, a spark of anger in her eye and cheeks as crimson as her bandana. In an instant, Dennis has joined her team, as have John and Tony. Laurene joins mine. Did John go with Clarissa out of friendship for Dennis? Tony hesitated for a long time before shrugging his shoulders and, remorsefully, going towards Clarissa.

We all scurry away to fill up our squirt guns, and to hide behind the hedge. I threw my pumps behind the couch, and I don't care if people can see my underwear if it means I can bring Clarissa down, once and for all. The latter shoots first even though I had a clear shot: I'm blinded by a sticky liquid. Hold on... what a bitch! I'm covered in red. Tomato juice!

Max and Olen start sniggering. As for me, my rage has taken over. I slowly make my way towards Clarissa who's smirking triumphantly. I whisper to her:

"Piece of advice. Run fast. Because if I catch you, I'll smash your skull, cancer or not."

Her smile fades.

"And I'll drink the juice from it, you vermin."

Dumbfounded, she looks at Olen who then walks over.

"Clarissa I'll take you back, you must be tired."

No! She does not get to be the poor little victim, out of the question!

"I think Dennis can put away the squirt guns and take Clarissa back. I need a hand, Olen… to get changed."

Olen hesitates. Moment of truth. Olen turns to Clarissa. No!! He takes her by the hand, putting the other one on her back, and accompanies her to the bay windows.

"Thanks for coming, Clarissa."

He shoots Dennis a glance and he rushes towards them.

"I'll take care of you, Clarissa."

What a relief. I can breathe again. I relax my shoulders. Olen turns to me.

"Where can I get changed?

- Follow me."

He gently takes my hand and pulls me towards the stairs.

"Happy?

- Relieved."

He watches me without saying a word and I see Clarissa behind him, eyes red whispering to Dennis. What's she still doing here? I'm positive he was the one to invite her. You can smell the troublemaker from miles away. While going upstairs, I sense Olen's gaze on my lower back. I'm surprised I can't feel his hands on me yet. Probably because she's still here. Once in the bedroom, I turn around.

"Has the divorce been made final?"

Olen eludes the question walking towards his closet.

"I don't have much to offer you. Even a t-shirt would be too big."

I rid myself of my wet clothes and throw them in a heap on the laundry basket.

"I'm going to take a shower."

I turn away biting my lip. That's when I realize: I've slept with a married man. Shit. I'll never forgive myself. They're separated, Candice. And what if, deep down, he didn't really want the divorce? Why is he staying with her officially? Well, it's not really official, nobody knows about it apparently. It's when I'm in the shower that I notice he's followed me.

"Olen, I understand that you don't want to be the bad guy who dumps his wife when she's got cancer. But it's not good either. Divorce her.

- For you?"

I turn around looking up into his face.

"For her, and for you. You need to free yourselves, and from what I saw she's not doing so bad.

- The last chemo worked."

I hear the pain in his voice. Communal life creates an permanent tattoo in us and forms a bond nearly impossible to break. I start to lather my hair. For the first time, I thank God for Olen's luxurious lifestyle. He thought of everything, and a luxurious shampoo that smells minty and delicious makes my anger melt away. My ideas becoming clearer.

When I feel Olen's hands on my back, I smile. The heat of his body against mine appeases and relaxes me. I turn around and snake my arms around his neck while he plays with my hair, shampoo still in it.

" What are you doing?

- You have incredible hair, you know that?

- Really?

- You're a little gnome."

I look at myself in the mirror and discover my hair standing straight up on my head through the magic of shampoo. We both burst out laughing. I nestle against him and let the water run over my hair to straighten it out. I close my eyes, lulled by the splash of water, and press myself against him even more when I feel his hands settle themselves on the small of my back. The water's abruptly shut off.

"Come on, the others are going to wonder what we're up to.

- I think they've got a pretty good idea."

When I go back into the bedroom, Olen's already dressed and is looking through his closet where all his clothes are hanging up. I notice a bowl on his dresser containing mints. That gives me an idea.

"Right what are you going to wear…

- I have an idea…"

I hook my fingers in his belt and pull him to me.

"What? My jeans?"

I ignore his answer and kneeling down, I pop the button. Then the other one.

"You're full of surprises.

- You have no idea."

And biting my lip, I push him onto the bed with a defiant look while I finish removing his jeans. I pull his t-shirt off with one hand and send it flying across the room. His chest on the edge of the bed, Olen's head hanging off it. It makes orgasms stronger. I read that in an article on tantric sex. He links his hands behind his neck, and watches me take a mint into my mouth. He's intrigued and doesn't care one bit about what's happening downstairs. Perfect, Mr Van Cliff. I plan on keeping your undivided attention on me for a long, long time. I take a seat next to him, and after looking into his eyes for a minute, I let my gaze drift over his torso, and to his shaft. I bite down on the sweet noisily, making him tense up even more. I bend down and the menthol liquor runs down the tip of his manhood. I blow on it and I can sense he's trying not to make a noise, while I take him in my mouth. And once I have taken him in completely I slowly blow out all the air in my lungs. He tenses up on the bed under my warm breath that makes him shiver. I then pinch the skin at the base of his penis, to make him tense further still. And when I lick the tip of his cock, now uncovered, he tilts his head back, tangling his hand in my hair. I feel a few drops of his nectar leak from his manhood and sense he's reached his limit. I run my tongue along his slit. Exploring it, blowing on it, sucking. He's on the verge of falling over the edge when I alternate between sucking and blowing on his slit. Olen whimpers my name, and catching me by the shoulders brings me towards him, empaling me without warning. It's my turn to abandon myself to his expert movements, we claw at each others backsides, hips, while reaching ultimate pleasure together.

A few minutes later, he's looking at me, bent down, bemused, and I let him contemplate my buttocks while putting on his jeans which I crudely turn up at the bottom. They're a bit too big, but they're low on my hips, just like I pictured. Olen's watching me, dumbfounded, without saying a word.

"Can I?"

And without awaiting his answer, I open the doors to his closet and pick out a blue shirt.

"Be my guest, you impudent little thing," He answers.

"Can you call me a cab?"

I knot the shirt at my waist and turn back the sleeves. It's utterly too big for me but it only serves to bring out the slenderness of my waist and arms.

"No, Kim will take you home.

- Thanks."

I open the door to make my way downstairs. I hear him jump out of bed to follow me, dressed in his boxers and a t-shirt that he hurriedly threw on. We descend in silence, ending up in the living room where the guys are slouched in front of the TV. As they see us they stop sipping their beers, jaws dropping.

"Right boys… Until next time."

I see Clarissa doubled over on a stool in the corner, face becoming red… in anger?

What does it matter now? I retrieve my pumps which someone had put next to the door. Olen, still in his boxers and t-shirt, opens the door for me. I turn around, grab his hand, and put the back of my hand to his lips. I did it so suddenly that his eyes widen in surprise.

"M Van Cliff…, I'll see you soon.

- See you soon…, my little Candice."

I leave the house, joining Kim who holds the door open for me. Check mate.

I get into the car without a backward glance, but I'm triumphant. I feel like I'm floating even though I'm sitting down. I look out of the tinted windows, pensive. Now, I've really put Clarissa in her place. A few minutes later, at the red light, I realize something's not right. Actually, quite the opposite. We've been going around in circles for the last fifteen minutes.

"Kim, what's going on?"

He looks at me in the rearview mirror.

"We're being followed."

Chapter 20

I turn and see a motorbike speeding towards us on my left, with a gopro on the handle bars and a passenger armed with a camera. My heart's racing. They suddenly accelerate, to come level with the window, although it's tinted.

"I didn't want to worry you, Miss Evans. I didn't manage to shake them off, normally, they get bored pretty fast.

- They must think it's Olen. When they see who gets out of the car, they'll be less interested.

- Do you want me to drop you off at your place, Miss Evans? Or do you have another address?

- I'll call a friend, we're going to show them around New Jersey awhile longer.

- Very well. Wise choice."

I call Jo, trying to remain calm.

"Jo, can I come to the restaurant please? I need a hideout right now, I don't know where to go.

- Ok."

I find her response strange, unusually terse and detached.

"You alright?

- Yes, I'm at the doctors for my stomach. We'll talk about it later. Nagee will let you in, she's there.

- Can I use the back exit?

- Sure," Jo answers.

Kim drops me off in the alley where the bins are. I bound towards the door that Nagee, Jo's sister, opens hurriedly.

"Wow! What the hell?"

Nagee's mouth falls open in surprise when she sees the paparazzis come to a halt at the end of the street. She abruptly shuts the door while I put my bag down, a little out of breath. We listen out, in silence to the sound of scooters circling the block. I say to lighten the mood:

"You'd think we were in the stainless steel kitchen from *Jurassic Park...*"

Nagee smiles at me and in the glaring light of the restaurant's kitchen, her teeth seem even whiter compared to her ebony indian skin.

"I'm going up, I'm looking after the baby. Jo and Ilan won't be long. If you need anything, give me a yell. Help yourself to anything, ok? Like always."

I sit and worry in the restaurant, being careful not to turn the lights on. And me, who selfishly only thought about not being photographed, when Jo could have a cancer. It's a bit strange what's going on with her stomach. I didn't dare ask Nagee if she knew anything. I take a seat at the bar, a glass of water in front of me, and I don't dare move. Ilan comes back first, and puts his hand on my shoulder, smiling.

"Everything ok?

- Um, yeah, everything's ok."

Jo's insulting a photographer in Hindi and comes in, displeased. I observe my friend, worried. Hopefully, my world doesn't get blown to dust. Please let her be ok.

"Jo, are you ok?"

Ilan bursts out laughing.

"That's enough out of you." And Jo enters the kitchen in a huff while shaking her black locks.

"Um, Ilan, care to explain?"

I can hear Jo yelling from the kitchen:

"Don't you dare tell her Ilan, you hear me???

- I hear you, but you know what the doctor said."

I go to grab some plates on the countertop and set the table in silence, giving Ilan, who hasn't stopped laughing, the puppy dog look. At least, it can't be that serious. Jo sits at the table and sets a bottle of lemonade down. Ilan whispers:

"That's a great idea honey, all that sparkling water.

- Go check on the lamb and its eggplant sauce.

- Alright, what's going on?"

Ilan turns to face me and crosses his fingers over his empty plate, suddenly serious.

" Jo's... not farting. That's the problem. That's why her stomach is bloated.

- What?

- Stop!!!!! It's inappropriate to talk to you about it, plus we're eating!"

I can't help but laugh uncontrollably.

"Are you angry because you're the only one here that's embarrassed?

- No because the doctor should never have said that with you there!

- Jo, I'm your husband. I want you to be ok, woman. It's alright to fart. Our son feels free to."

Jo holds back a laugh.

"There you go, let it out, and we'll record a family cd!"

I burst out laughing, soon to be joined by Jo and Ilan. He takes a hold of her chin and kisses her tenderly on the forehead.

That's what a "normal" life looks like. That's what I want with Olen. Could Olen give it to me? Could I give it to him?

Ilan gets down from the table and shouts from the kitchen:

"And I know you go number two in the toilet, too."

Jo turns bright red while screaming.

"Would you be quiet! And bring back that blasted lamb! And go and check on our son, I want to talk to Candice alone.

- Yes ma'am."

We're eating rather hurriedly, when I get a text from Liza.

"So?

- So it's messy. I don't understand how they got my home address. They're in front of the apartment. And if they have my home address, they have the address of the production company. Paul's going to be terribly uncomfortable.

- You did good, coming here.

- Yes. But the situation is completely out of my control.

- And this… situation, as you like to call it, what about the rest, how is it?

- It's… good. Uncontrollable."

Ilan looks at me wide-eyed picking a bit of lamb out of his teeth with the tip of his fingernail.

"Ok, now it's becoming a bit too existential for me. I'm going to check on our son and tell Nagee that she can go."

He kisses Jo tenderly while stroking her hair, and disappears.

"So. Tell me, how's it going?

- I guess Liza told you?

- Well, I haven't seen her much lately but I get a few texts.

- This guy… he drives me crazy. He's got it all, he's insolent, he's got women throwing themselves at his feet, he's playful… I have a hard time figuring him out sometimes. And then, the next moment, he's just gentle. So gentle.

- Gentle?

- Gentle.

- Good with women, you mean?

- Yes.

- They must all be throwing themselves at him the actresses, the assistants, the make-up artists, the models…" Jo states in a disapproving tone while stroking her belly. I answer sadly, eyes cast down on my plate:

"All of them.

- What sluts.

- No Jo, it's the men that can be true sluts. Them, I can understand. Actually, I'm surprised at their self-control.

- What do you mean?

- Well, when he walks into a room, it seems like they're patiently waiting their turn. There they are, watching him out of the corner of their eyes. It's like dogs wagging their tail.

- Candice, the abrasive returns."

We opened a couple of beers that we drink from the bottle.

"He takes on the role of the star who's absolutely adorable with women and plays hard to get all at once.

- Please, as if men were hard to get, bullshit!

- I think… all guys have that, you know, the need to play the field: to be the kid that bangs his toy on the table thinking "let's see if this one can take it" and he brags about it afterwards….

- Like all men!

- So that women fall at his feet...

- Like all men!

- And I wonder if he wants to be happy… or to feel like he has power over people.

- Well now. And this is the guy you've got a thing for?

- Yes. Yes and no. Because sometimes, it feels like… he's a kid Jo. There's something about him that makes me sad. That breaks my heart. A kid begging for affection.

- Listen, maybe men stay little boys all their lives. But deep down, they like bitches, and you… you can be a killer when you want to be.

- What makes you say that?

- Danny told me how you two met, you know.

- Really?

- Yes you pulled a face at him in a meeting, and you sent him to make copies for you by pretending to be the boss.

- Yes that's right, I did that. I thought that it was the fact that I wanted to be a headhunter that seduced him.

- No it's your confidence. It gives people the impression that... you're the goddess of sex.

- Thanks, no pressure then.

- So, be a sex goddess. You can't lie when you fuck. He can't lie in that moment. Your body speaks for you.

- Yes that's why vaginas have lips!

- Oh Candice, you blow my mind."

The two of us start laughing, and I notice that the noise of the scooters has disappeared which allows me to escape in the dark and go home.

The next morning, a group of people armed with cameras each more sophisticated than the last, smoking, making fun of each other, from time to time glancing at the entrance to the building. This time, they're professionals, no doubt about it. A whole other story from the guy of a few weeks ago, with his pitiful smartphone keeping an eye out for me from behind a car. I'm seething:

"How did they manage to find me?

- Do you want me to go down?

- And do what Liza? It's freedom of expression.

- Yeah right, freedom when it serves the financiers."

I turn to set eyes on her ebony skin. She never talked about having to fight to make it in her line of work. I met her and Jo in college during our first year. Jo got pregnant soon after and took over the family restaurant, and Liza, pragmatic Liza, quickly understood that chances were she wouldn't be able to put much food on the table with a degree in literature. She notices me watching and shrugs her shoulders.

"Don't worry about me, I'll wipe the floor with them if they get too close."

I remain pensive, tea in hand, looking out the window. How did they do it and why now? Why not just after Bali? Or right after the scandal at the club? Eight o'clock. Crap. Right, no other choice, Paul's waiting for me.

I slip into Olen's jeans as if they could shield me, brush my hair, miraculously find a pair of sunglasses, a ballcap. A glance in the mirror: Candice you look absolutely ri-di-cu-lous.

I go down the stairs, heart beating frenetically. You have two minutes to run to the bus stop, to get in and go to the office. The bus arrives at eight seventeen. It's currently twelve past eight. A minute too long spent at the bus stop and I'm going to get cornered by the photographers. I keep an eye out. Eight fifteen, I jump into action. I don't look back and run as fast as I can. The bus stops right in it's allocated space. I rush in and shout to the driver:

"Start the bus! Quick!"

He looks at me, taken aback.

"Do you think you're in a TV show or something? Validate your ticket and pipe down!"

I sit near the middle of the bus, pulling my cap down, eyes cast down, blushing from the embarrassment. I count the stops in my mind, while the driver stares at me in the rearview mirror. I get ready to jump out when ... Shit! Three paparazzis are waiting in front of number 1618 Broadway... Shoot, what other choice do I have? I get out on the other side of the street and watch them. The production company doesn't have an emergency exit. I'm at an impasse, so close. I cross the road and with hands shoved in my pockets, eyes fixed on the ground, I make my way through the crowd. There's a deafening silence when I get there, and the clicking noise of febrile cameras when I pass by.

"Candice, how are you feeling this morning? What does it feel like, being called a homewrecker?"

I suddenly feel my blood boil.

"What?"

I realize that I gave them exactly what they wanted. Me, red in the face, mouth in a grimace, looking like a crazy person with sunglasses, my sweatshirt and a misshapen pair of jeans. But I'm in shock.

"A homewrecker, or an adventuress in search of fame. What do you like the least?"

I stay frozen. Clarissa, that snake. I quickly turn away and burst into the office, whereas they block the way. How can they be allowed to do this? I go to knock on Paul's door. He pushes his glasses back on his head with a small smile:

"Hi Paul, sorry I'm late, give me a minute, I'm coming.

- Very well."

I thank Olen for this job. If Olen wasn't Paul's friend, he might not be as comprehensive. I sit at my desk. I already have a message from Olen.

"How you holding up?"

I type out my answer, sighing:

"Ask me that again at the end of the week. Right now, it's off to a flying start.

- We can see each other before then though, right?

- I don't know, I'm going to have to find a bunker for tonight.

- Taken care of.

- What do you mean taken care of?

- The divorce, I asked for divorce. I called my lawyer last night when you left."

My heart leaps. Olen calls and I pick up straight away.

"Clarissa came clean. She had a P.I start following you, and the people close to you, two weeks ago. That's how the paps knew where you lived.

- I see. And yesterday afternoon enraged her so much that she told them everything, and set them on me. And, now, they know everything about me.

- That's it. Listen, it'll die down. Stay the way you are. And whatever you do, don't get angry, ever. Never, you hear me? That's what they want. For you to push them, just a bit, so they can sue you.

- So basically, it's just going to be apartment-work-work-apartment for the rest of the week?

- Yes. Don't say anything, don't make any comments. Smile politely and don't let your emotions show. You've got this, Candice.

- Right.

- I'm sorry. This is exactly what I wanted to avoid.

- All this because Liza wanted to take me to Masquerade.

- Do you regret meeting me?

- No… no, not at all.

- Are you happy to have met me?

- Yes. You're a breath of fresh air.

- Oh really? A breath of fresh air?

- I mean … I realize how narrow horizons were … for me.

- They seemed narrow to me too, I can confirm that, but that's alright with me.

- Oh; Olen!!

- While we're on the subject…"

He lowers his voice like a cat that's about to purr.

"When do I get to admire your ass in my jeans?

- Come and get it.

- Get a bag ready for this weekend."

I sit up straight.

"Why?

- I want to take you somewhere. So pack my jeans, obviously, and something for cold nights.

- I'm going to get you.

- Mmmh, my little Candice.

- My Olen."

I hear his breathing become shallow.

"I'll pick you up Friday, straight after work.

- We're not taking your driver?

- No, just the two of us.

- I like it.

- Alright, have a nice day, see you Friday.

- Ok.

- Come on, hang up.

- You first.

- No you.

- My Olen. See you Friday."

The week passes by, filled with phone calls, faxes, meetings, sandwiches, ubers. I gave up on the bus. However, I took great delight in wearing Olen's jeans all week long, like a war flag for Clarissa's benefit. You wanted to provoke me, Missy, you'll see these jeans on ME all week in the press. Olen whispers over the phone:

"Can you bring the black dress that you wore the night of Masquerade?

- I was wearing purple.

- No black. The dress with thin straps.

- Are you trying to tell me you're a clothes fetishist?

- Only of those I want to take off.

- I intend to keep my clothes on this weekend if the nights are cold, M Van Cliff.

- And what about the next morning?

- You know the proverb. Wake-up every morning with determination to go to sleep at night with satisfaction.

- I can't get no satisfaction. Especially concerning you, beautiful Candice."

Chapter 21

Friday morning I wake up in a good mood. In reality, I feel incredibly good. Tonight, I'm going to see Olen. For a whole weekend. A quick glance out the window, that has now become a habit, let's me know how many paparazzi are present. I've learnt to look down, keep a polite smile and especially to keep my mouth shut. The video of me turning around crazed, letting out a strangled "What?" has already been viewed enough. Strange, there's a lot more paparazzi this morning. I'm in the middle of brushing my hair when I get a message from Paul:

"Stay home, Candice. Good luck."

I get a text from Jo:

"Candice, take deep breaths. I'm sorry, but you have to look on the internet, now. You've made the headlines. You… and Danny."

I boot up my computer with shaky hands. Photos of Danny. Dad. Mom. The car. The forensic report. Everything's there. Everything. The last years of my life, spent trying to forget it all, come rushing back, and I'm transported to that cursed Christmas eve. When I killed my parents and Danny.

I shoot Paul a text. "Thank you". I can't say more than that. Fat tears run down my cheeks, they're out of my control. Pesky old habits. I cry, I bite my nails. For an hour. Two hours. I'd like to go outside, but I can't. Now everyone knows. I'm trapped like a hamster in its cage. As if on auto-pilot, I head to the kitchen. A small knife, that's what I need. A non serrated knife. I sharpen it just the right amount. I press down on skin, where I can distinguish my old scars. I just have to fall back into my accursed old habits, that's it. I press down on skin, just the right amount. I breathe in. Cut while inhaling. You feel the pain all the more. On three. One. Two. Three. I breathe in.

Someone knocks on the door.

The knife hasn't moved. Knock knock knock, once again.

"Candice, open up. I know you're in there."

Olen's there, behind the door. I hold my breath and get up on tip toe in front of the door.

"You can breathe, I can see the shadow of your feet behind the door."

I sigh.

"Open up, I'm begging you."

I open the door.

He considers me a while. Me and the bags under my eyes that have become sallow in the space of a few hours. My runny nose. He takes a careful step forward. I'm on the lookout, like a wounded animal. He closes the door and takes me into his arms. Then, he takes another step forward and finally envelops me in all his warmth. I melt in his arms for a while, closing my eyes.

"Why didn't you say anything?"

I bury my head against him. Please, don't say anything.

"Because talking can be too hard."

He pushes me back by my shoulders and stares into my eyes. I swallow the lump in my throat and after a few seconds, the tears are pouring down of their own volition. I can't control myself any longer. No matter how much I purse my lips, try to look down, Olen takes my face in his hands and forces me to look at him.

"Say something."

Jo's face hovering over me and holding my elbow comes back to mind.

"Say something."

Jo, who takes me by the arm, at the funeral. I look at her, crazed, and no sound makes it past my lips. She gets up, tears in her eyes, and talks in front of the gathering of people. My parents' friends, Danny's friends. Our friends. I hear her talking about me, who appreciates their presence, and thanking them. I'm not there. It's someone else. Don't ask me to speak. Just tell me it's a nightmare and that I'm going to wake up.

Olen bends down and kisses me. I come back to the present immediately. I eventually manage to form a sentence:

"What do you want me to say?"

He finally lets go of me. Impassive.

"What do you want me to say? There's nothing to say. I'm alone, in the dark. In front of an abyss, in front of the unknown…. They left me alone. I…"

Breathe in. Breathe out. But fat tears fill my eyes, and run down my cheeks.

"I'm alone. They abandoned me. Because of me. And I hate them for that. And I hate myself for that…"

My voice is broken. I'm broken. Olen pulls me to him, breathes in the scent of my hair, and tightens his hold on me each passing second.

"You're not alone… You never have been."

His words set me free and set free the sobs that have been held back for so long. Olen picks me up and carries me to the couch in the living room, keeping me close to him.

"Tell me.

- It was three years ago. Danny and I, we had a fight a few days before christmas. It was when he was giving more and more Jazz concerts. Everything was going ok, well that's what I thought.

- Why did you fight?

- I wanted to get married, start a family. He wasn't ready. He was cheating on me. I don't know if fame went to his head or…

- Or what?

- I think he never loved me. I was the one who put all my energy into our relationship. And he thanked me by sleeping with someone else."

Olen presses his lips to my forehead, and holds me tighter still.

"I don't know if he loved you. But the timing wasn't right, he wasn't ready. Guys who cheat are lost, not in the right state of mind."

I hold him tightly in my arms, hoping to ward off bad luck: I hope you're not like him, Olen.

"Otherwise it's because the girl doesn't give him what he needs in the bedroom. But from what I've seen... you definitely have what it takes."

I pinch his stomach while smiling through my tears.

"Don't say it, Olen, please.

- Say what?

- That there's an explanation for everything.

- Alright I won't say it. And then? What happened?

- I went to my parents' after the fight. He still wanted to come, to fix it, I guess. When his plane landed on Christmas eve, I refused to go and pick him up. I hadn't told my parents anything. Just that we had a fight. My parents were the ones to go and pick him up. But a truck hit them... I ...

- But if you would have gone, you would be the one dead today," He says stroking my hair.

"I blame myself so much. I've wondered every day since, for a long time, if it was all a dream, and if I hadn't been so stubborn staying in that relationship that seemed perfect to me but was ultimately messed-up.

- What if, what if... Candice, you can't live your life by wondering "what if" every morning...

- It stopped. The day I met you." He strokes my cheek.

"And then?

- The police arrived at two in the morning. You can't imagine. You imagine that's what a car accident feels like. The impact. And then you realize, bit by bit what happened. Like a puzzle. Which barely put together, the pieces slip through your fingers. Because you've lost everything. Papers, always papers. Go to identify the bodies. Choose the coffins. Check there's room at the cemetery. Papers, more papers. Insurances, banks, taxes, the state. Open boxes, sort out, throw out, give away, sell the house. Put the money in the bank so you don't have to think about it again. Papers, taking a breath, forgetting. The space of a night. Waking up, thinking it was just a bad dream. Starting all over again.

- The scars on your wrist? Did you do that to yourself?

- Yes. And my shrink was very into new age stuff. He set me up with acupuncture sessions. And Dr Tran sees me often.

- Does it calm you?

- Needles can hurt just as much, but they don't leave any traces. But yes, it calms me. Helps me sleep better. I still go."

Olen stays silent.

"How do you feel?

- Silly. Stupid. Naked. Vulnerable. As if I was looking for a curtain to hide behind, without finding one.

- Welcome to the club of the flayed that the public love to pity.

- What do you mean?"

It's now or never, if I want to break through the shell of this little boy begging for affection. But Olen continues to stroke my cheek.

"You're very brave.

- Well… Only mountains don't break."

I show him my wrists. The deepest scar is on my right wrist.

"And then, emptiness. That you try to fill with your day-to-day life. I literally lost it in a meeting at the publishing company I used to work for. Just like that. All the anger against Danny needed to be let out. Obviously, they fired me."

Olen takes both my hands and kisses my wrists.

"Is it because of your anger that you do this?

- No that… it's what I deserve for killing my parents.

- Don't say that!"

And he repeats the process, rocking me in his arms.

"Don't say that. It's not true. It's nobody's fault. I'm sorry. I understand now.

- Really?"

I run a hand through his hair.

"Can you understand how much I want to wake up and be certain that the sun will rise the next day? And that there's always four walls solidly around me?

- And that you need to curl up into a ball when things go too fast?

- Yes.

- Like a hedgehog?

- Yes.

- And to sting people when they want to dig a bit too deep?

- Yes, Mr Van Cliff. There you go, you've worked out the Candice Evans mystery.

- I'm not sure. Listen. The best way to grieve is to live. To do crazy things. Your parents would want you to make the most of life. It's the biggest honor you could do them. Pack your bag, we're leaving."

Truthfully, it was Olen who packed my bag for me while I was in the shower. When the water runs down my body, I'm under the impression that I'm receiving absolution. Sorry Dad. Sorry Mom. To have imprisoned your memory in my sorrow and anger. It was

Olen's arms that delivered me. And you too, Danny, I'm setting you free. We could of had the world. And you preferred to ruin it, or you couldn't see it, it doesn't matter anymore. How I would like to only feel anger towards you, it would make it easier. I'm letting you go. I've had enough of this anger that's holding you back and has me prisoner too. I breathe out noisily, as much air as I can. It's time to move on, kiddo. Truly. Olen has loaded my bag in the car, and is in the middle of cooking when I come out, dressed and refreshed.

"Where are we going?

- You'll see.

- Is it far?

- Roughly three and a half hours drive. If the Lincoln tunnel isn't closed. We're going to eat this delicious spicy tandoori chicken and then we'll head North.

- What's three and a half hours North of New York?

- You'll see. Now fill up that beautiful belly that I'll pepper with kisses tonight."

I smile, eat the delicious meal he's prepared which I hope was made with love, and we "head North".

I mechanically check my phone, what's North of the state of New York.

"Stop and look at the scenery, Candice.

- You still not going to tell me where we're going?

- No.

- How far is it?

- If you start acting like a child, you'll get a spanking."

I smile. I let myself be lulled by the sound of the engine and when I open my eyes, night's falling.

Olen's stroking my hair.

"So, my little frog, sleep well?

- Why little frog?"

He runs his index finger over the corner of my mouth... where there's drool. I scowl, and wipe my mouth. How embarrassing! I try to distract him by nodding towards the window:

"Are we here?

- Yes."

We're parked in front of a house with a lit up porch. It's a big house in red brick, three storeys high, with a beige awning where a porch swing, that looks extremely comfortable, covered in its beige blanket and cushions, sits.

"Who lives here?

- My mother."

It's as if I'd just been slapped. Except it wakes me up completely. Olen smiles at me, gently taking my hand.

"Shall we?"

And without waiting for my answer, he gets out of the car. I can make out a woman with silver hair, arms crossed exit the house to wait for us on the threshold. I take Olen's hand while walking up the small driveway that winds through a perfectly manicured lawn, and as we get closer, I try to straighten my hair. Why didn't I straighten my hair earlier, for God's sake? What I must look like. I must have an ashen complexion. Once we reach the bottom of the stairs, Olen lets go of my hand and takes me in his arms.

"Olen, darling…"

I now know where Olen gets his delicate features, and a naturally distinguished look. Carefully manicured nails, silver white hair in an impeccable bun, she exudes dignity and the quiet education of intellectuals. A strong jaw, and piercing light eyes, she's dressed in a Ralph Lauren ensemble, comfortable yet elegant. I read somewhere that Olen had Danish roots. Before me was the typical beauty of Northern Europe.

"Mother, this is Candice. Candice, this is Chrysta Van Cliff.

- Pleased to meet you ma'am.

- I've heard a lot about you Miss Evans."

Right, well it seems like we're off to a good start. I follow Olen, who took a hold of my hand once more, into the modest house.

"You haven't had it repaired yet?"

We've barely set foot in the door, that Olen's pressing his foot down on the creaky floorboards.

"No, I haven't gotten around to it. This new paper on Makenda took up all my time.

- You're a political journalist?

- Precisely.

- Mom covered the conflicts in Western Africa, these past thirty-five years. But now, that's it, she's taking it slow. Retirement, remember?

- I'll never retire."

We sit down in the living room. The pre dinner drinks waiting for us. On the walls I see a few old photos withered by the constant exposition to light. I can make out an energetic, blonde woman, with a shotgun on her shoulder in front of a truck of African soldiers.

"Is that you?

- Yes. I still have the riffle, you know.

- They nearly took it off her at the border.

- I told them it was a toy.

- They let you keep it?

- Yes!"

Olen starts chuckling.

"Because it was a toy!

- As long as the guys over there didn't know that!"

We burst out laughing.

"Mom aimed at the Kondaru chief.

- Van Cliff's don't negotiate.

- What did they want to negotiate?

- My perfume, bought in Paris, imagine that!

- What a bunch of little bastards!"

Chrysta glares daggers at Olen with her steely blue gaze. My God... I can't imagine what she looks like holding a weapon.

"Sorry mother... but I feel things in an intense way and I need to let it out in my own words."

My God! He's giving her that look! A sideways glance, the lone dimple on the left side.

"Mmh... passion..."

She looks at me for a second and I can't make out what she's thinking. She gets up to go to the kitchen and I lean in to whisper in Olen's ear:

"You feel things in an intense way? That explains a lot.

- And what's that?

- Your incommensurate pain in the ass side.

We raise our glasses of martini to passion, not forgetting the salmon canapés. I'm intimidated by this great woman and I don't know what to say when Olen leaves me alone with her to go to the bathroom. After a few minutes in silence, I nevertheless feel obligated to talk to her.

"I'm surprised, sorry. Olen never talks about you. I mean…

- He has a childlike exuberance... and a secretive side.

- Yes, it's paradoxal and I didn't expect that he would have a feminine role-model like you.. A journalist with an incredible career.

- Thank you.

- I'm not sucking up to you…"

Chrysta raises an eyebrow and sententiously says:

"Well I'm not the one that gave him a taste for brainless bimbos, that's for sure."

I slouch down all of a sudden. What to say? If I agree I'll come off as a smug and prissy nerd If I deny it, I'll be a hypocrite. I content myself with a "mmmh". She stares at me with a small smile, that can't be good.

"You're very different from all the previous ones. Intelligent. Maybe a bit too much."

I stiffen, frozen, whereas Chrysta seems to contemplate the garden through the window. Night is falling like a murmur.

"Olen really likes you.

- I really like him too,' I say prudently.

Chrysta turns her green sparkling eyes on me.

"What are your intentions with my son?

- Generally, it's the shy young woman's father who asks the young man that.

- I don't believe in your shy facade.

- Believe what you want, but don't think I'm a promiscuous woman.

- I think you have your head screwed on properly, but what are you looking for, that's the question.

- Has Olen told you how we met?

- You came knocking on his door.

- Uh... no not exactly.

- I'll be frank with you Miss Evans. Polite but frank. In the event of a wedding, Olen will draw up a contract. I'll make him do it this time. Consider the leg up he already gave you with your career a huge favor.

- I didn't ask your son for anything. I was very happy with my life, even though to some it may have seemed insignificant.

- Really?"

Chrysta has a point. If my insignificant life was enough for me, I wouldn't be here. I would have turned down Olen's invitation to the party. I would have ended things before they even started. Yes, Olen lit a fire inside me. Bringing out my passionate side.

"So, shall we eat?"

Olen's standing in the doorway. Had he heard us? His lips form a straight line, and he seems deep in thought. We stand up, smoothing out our clothes and wearing fake smiles. I guess that the game with Chrysta Van Cliff has just begun. I recall that the queen is the most powerful piece of a chess game: Chrysta is Queen mother and I'm... I seem to be the bishop. This time a checkmate will be impossible.

Chapter 22

☐

Once we're sat at the table, Chrysta starts a conversation. Olen takes her by the hand and looks at her adoringly. The question then arises: where's Olen's dad? I let my gaze wander the old wooden walls, but only find very few photos. Only a picture of Olen with a young girl who has dirty blond hair retains my attention. His first girlfriend, probably. I notice that some frames have been taken down: photos of Clarissa maybe? I feel a hint jealousy. Chrysta is comparing me to the others. The Clarissas or maybe even those that didn't get a ring... Olen's phone vibrates, and I see him quickly check it. This man will never be completely mine. He belongs to the public, to his fans, to his entourage. Chrysta watches me, while sipping her drink, and the sparkle in her eye takes on a steely aspect. And what if she was like that with all his girlfriends? And what if she were a test?

"I got the spare bedroom ready for you Candice. I hope you find it to your liking.

- Oh thank you Mrs Van Cliff. I'm sure I will.

- It's right next to mine, in case you need anything.

- Thank you very much."

What she actually means: "You won't be sleeping with my son tonight, and as people say, keep your friends close and your enemies closer. And don't you dare leave your room to go and join him, I'll hear the floorboards creak. That's actually why I haven't gotten it fixed."

I force a smile.

"What's the plan for tomorrow?

- I'm going to take Candice to the park, the lakes, we're going to... spend time together.

- Get to know each other better," I say looking at him.

"Will you be home for dinner tomorrow night?

- No, I'm taking Candice for a change of scenery.

- Oh... But we need to get to know each other, Candice and I.

- We'll have the opportunity to do so, Chrysta, I'm sure of it."

The battle of wills lasts a fraction of a second longer, however the shock is present. Even Olen felt it. Yes Chrysta, I'm here, and I like him, and I'm going to fight for him, even if you're the one I have to fight.

"Right, well, we're going to bed."

I stand up and grab the plates in order to stack them and take them to the kitchen. I can hear Olen whisper something, but I don't want to give the impression that I'm eavesdropping by minimizing the noise while doing the washing up.

"Oh, leave that Candice, I'll show you the bedrooms."

I look at the photos of Olen on the stairs, in passing. The same cheeky smile at 10 years old, and a stray strand of hair falling into his eyes. If we had a kid, I'd want it to have his eyes. Easy there, Candice, you're losing it. And you deserve to be slapped.

I feel Olen's hands slide over the small of my back. I turn around and two magnificent eyes shine in the semi-darkness.

"This is your room, Candice.

- Thank you."

The bedroom is modest, a window giving out onto the perfect lawn that we crossed a few hours prior. The floorboards creak and the patchwork duvet is meticulously folded at the end of the bed. Everything's perfectly tidy, especially because the room is practically bare. A dark wooden wardrobe stands in the room, containing more bedding.

"Well, goodnight, Candice.

- Thank you, you too, dinner was delicious, Chrysta."

A polite smile and that will be all: or rather " I don't know when the second round will take place, but I'll load my rifle Candice, to smoke you when I see you again."

"I'll go and get your bag.

- Thank you, Olen."

I wait for Chrysta and her son to leave the room before falling onto the bed, eyes closed. I pay attention to the noises of the house, Olen's footsteps in the driveway, the trunk of the car slamming. Chrysta doing washing up in the kitchen, going up the stairs, getting visibly annoyed with one of the drawers in her room. I put a hand over my heart. Everything's alright. Everything's perfectly fine in my little world. It's silly but it calms me. I should put to use Dr Tran's advice more often. I left the door open and Chrysta could possibly see me laying down like an idiot, but I don't care. Everything's alright.

All of a sudden, I feel a breeze on my body. Olen's in the room and he's watching me, from his position leaning against the dresser.

"Do you know how sexy you are, Candice Evans... especially when you don't know you're being watched."

I hook my thumb in my jeans and put my other hand behind my neck.

"You know that you're not allowed to be here, Olen Van Cliff?"

Mischievous smile. Face half angelic, half demonic. A mix between James Dean and Marlon Brando advances on me in all his insolence.

"Are you going to tell on me?

- Maybe that way, I can get in her good graces."

He lays down next to me, his gaze on my midriff where my shirt is riding up slightly. He extends his index finger, and lets it travel between my jeans and my skin, along my belt.

"Olen...

- Candice…

- Your mother has the keys to your chastity belt.

- Don't worry about me, let me worry about you.

- I have a bag to unpack.

- There's other things that I can help you unpack…

- First, I'd like to…"

And I turn towards him, propped up on the bed, a hand in my hair. I take hold of his t-shirt.

"I'd like to know more about you."

He frowns. Mmh. Not good.

"So, you grew up here?

- Partly. I started off in New York. And then, at the age of thirteen, we came here. My old home burnt down when I was fifteen.

- And I'm the hundredth girl to come here, is that it?

- What makes you say that?

- Chrysta's attitude, kind of cold, and the floorboards didn't creak when you came in. So, you know the spots that could give you away like the back of your hand.

- Mmh. You would have made an excellent spy.

- You didn't answer my question…

- This used to be my room.

- Ah.

- And I found a smart way to sneak out early on.

- And there are a lot of photos of you.

- Yes.

- And your Dad? Did he… pass away?

-Yeah."

Silence.

"Ok," I say quietly.

I feel like the silence is going to thicken if I let this opportunity slip through my fingers.

"When did he die?

- Last year.

- Wow… that's not so long ago. I'm sorry.

- Mmh. We're weren't close anyway. But thank you."

He continues rather quickly.

"Right, I'll let you unpack."

And after pressing a quick peck to my lips, he gets up and leaves me alone, deep in thought. I'm not the type to complain, but if Olen was keeping his past under wraps, his childhood, maybe it was even more painful than mine. And what if it wasn't just him being reserved, but a wall hiding a valley of tears? While putting my clothes away in the wardrobe, I swear to myself that I will uncover the mysteries of Olen Van Cliff. What could I do to get him to trust me? What if, the source of the problem between us was this. That one word that doesn't fill the rift between us. Trust. I can't help but laugh when I open my bag and see that Olen picked out my best lingerie. After my shower, I doze off in my bed, when I feel a warm body slip in next to me. Surprised, I'm about to scream but Olen has already covered my mouth with his, and is in his birthday suit, already hard. I halfheartedly try to resist, but he has my underwear off within seconds.

"You can't say no Candice.

- And what if your mother hears us?

- She's already asleep."

And without waiting any longer he enters me, and silences my cry with his mouth, kissing me like a starving man. He very tenderly, caresses every inch of my body, with the tip of his fingers, then with the whole palm of his hand, becoming too much, clawing, my thighs, my inner thighs, my ass. I answer his call by wrapping my legs around his waist. He brings me to the brink of orgasm and I cling to him, biting his shoulder. To which he answers by pulling my hair back, and even if my eyes are closed, I know he's watching me, when with a movement of his hips he breaks through my last barriers, and the waves of pleasure submerge me. I feel as if I have a second skin, enveloping my body wracked with shivers, creating space between each of the molecules that compose me.

"My Candice, my safe haven," Olen whispers while pressing his lips to my temple.

I don't have the strength to form any words, and I give in to a deep slumber, inhabited by sparkling eyes, the laughter of children never born and my parents that are smiling at me with trust.

The next morning, Olen comes to wake me.

"Come on, my sweet."

I would have liked to sleep for a few more hours and roll over groaning.

"Come on, get up!" Olen slaps my ass.

"What's wrong with you?" I yell at him.

He bursts out laughing, not taking his eyes off of me. That's when I notice he's already dressed and has a glass of juice and some toast with scrambled eggs.

"Up, or I'll bite you on the ass."

I have an irresistible urge to say "go on, give it a try", however, judging by the way he's looking at me, I know that's all he wants.

"Doesn't your mother mind me eating in bed?

- She's still asleep. Unless you're shouting woke her up.

- She'd already be in the room," I say giggling and sit up in the bed.

"Well done, Miss Evans.

- Where are we going?

- To get some fresh air."

I wolf down my breakfast while Olen gets everything ready. Being alone with him. Without a driver, or a bodyguard, without family, or entourage, without friends who are nice but a bit overwhelming. I hug him in front of the car, and look into his eyes. Troubled, he strokes my temple with his delicate finger, and looks at me. However, a fraction of a second later, I notice he's looking at me and the house behind me. Olen suddenly pulls me into his arms, and breathes in the scent of my hair.

"Come on, let's go.

- I feel like we're running away.

- Nonsense, we're coming back tomorrow.

- But where are we going?

- I want to show you a special place. A magical place.

- Did you pack my pajamas?

- No need."

He starts the car with a small smile that I know so well now. I watch him out of the corner of my eye: his gaze turns hard, and goes to the road. Twenty minutes later, we stop. Adirondack Park dazzles with its flamboyant colors, and putting my hand in Olen's as we make our way down the central path, something comes to me as an afterthought: everything will be fine. Everything's going to be really really really fine. Is it the majesty of the trees? Is it the song of the unseen birds? We walk in silence in the wild nature that seems to be able to keep all secrets.

"I'm thirsty."

Obviously Olen has everything planned. He produces a blanket and a bottle of cold water from his backpack. I sit on a huge rock on the river bank, near him. I watch him out of the corner of my eye, wrapping his arms around his knees, observing the unattainable trees quietly, calmly.

"I've never seen you so calm.

- I love this place.

- Did you come here as a kid?

- I didn't have the time. I spent most of it with my mother.

- And were you and your dad close?

- Not really.

- I'm going to have to torture you to get to know you.

- Sorry."

He lowers his head and stares at the ground, eyes cold.

"My father used to hit my mother. He was an alcoholic who was too far gone. He died alone, just like he deserved. And if I could, I would go as far as erasing the name from his tombstone."

Chapter 23

He said that with such detachment... I can't believe that he was the one to utter those words. I give him a few seconds to cool off.

"I have a hard time picturing Chrysta with...

- A social case?"

I don't want to knock his father even further down than he already is. Who am I to judge his family? I tilt my head and ask as softly as I can:

"Someone who had severe problems and didn't know how to deal with them?

- They met each other in college: my dad played for the football team.

- And you mother was studying journalism?

- Yes. Everything was going well. And then my dad got injured. He never truly recovered. Impossible for him to keep on playing. And..."

Olen sighs and looks up as if he wanted to pierce the foliage with his eyes.

"And he ended up a housepainter and an alcoholic. Mom protected me a lot. We came here because an alcoholic as a father and the neighborhood in New York we used to live in, full of hookers and junkies was a lot to deal with, as a kid. It was good here for a while. Greenery, space. And when I turned sixteen, one day I came home, Mum was crying on the kitchen floor and he was crumpled on the couch, soaked in alcohol. He could barely move, that asshole."

The light that pierces through the incandescent leaves of autumn lights up Olen's face. His jaw has adopted an odd shape as if he was about to bite.

"When I saw Mum's face…"

His breathing becomes labored and his voice is so full of anger.

"I grabbed the bastard by the throat, and dragged him on the ground to the garden, and I hit him. Again. And again. And again. Mum was the one who stopped me."

I have a lump in my throat, tears running down my cheeks. However, Olen isn't looking at me, lost in his memories.

"I told him, if he came near us again, I'd kill him. With my bare hands if I had to."

I get even closer to him, I'm afraid he'll run like a wild animal if I go too fast. His eyes are so cold, I gently stroke his face to bring him back. He blinks, and turns his gaze on me.

"Sorry, I didn't know.

- I don't want your pity.

- It's not pity. It's tenderness. It's…"

I stop immediately, blushing. Olen takes me in his arms all of a sudden, and lays me down on the grass underneath him. He then undertakes to graze his lips over my neck, my shoulders, my cheeks.

"Do you think we're social cases, Olen?

- No. I know we both get a second chance. And you never were a social case.

- You think?

- Just a very serious case which I've decided to pour over, that's all."

And he buries his nose in my cleavage.

"My Olen's back," I say laughing wholeheartedly while he sniffs my neck like a dog.

"You don't have too many bad memories from New York, do you?

- No. When I went back at eighteen to go from one audition to the next, New York worked out pretty well for me.

- Did you make it straight off the bat?

- No, not at all, I had to sell my blood for a year to be able to eat.

- And where did you sleep?"

He has a small embarrassed smile. Olen's adorable dimple that no woman can resist. He admits candidly:

"I always found a place to sleep."

I see. Women. Indeed, how can you let such a man sleep outside?

"Why did you bring me here?

- It's beautiful. It's pure. It's outside of time."

He rolls next to me and keeps his eyes riveted on my cleavage.

"Are those beautiful words yours Olen?

- Yes."

I lay on top of him and kiss him while the sound of the river lulls us. I place his hands over his head and interlace my fingers with his.

"This is it.

- It, what?

- It between us, it's what makes us pure, beautiful and outside of time. It's what we have that transforms us. Here and now, and us, it's like Adam and Eve before the original sin.

- Ah, but we've already sinned, my sweet.

- No, sex isn't the original sin.

- Oh really?

- No. It's doubt. It's the ultimate poison that makes you mistrust life, and others.

- Is that of you?

- Yes, Mr Van Cliff. It's of me.

- You don't have doubts about us?

- Hush, Mr Van Cliff, shut up and kiss me."

And to ward off bad luck, I place my hand behind his neck and kiss him passionately. I breathe in his musky scent mixed with sandalwood. I'd recognize his scent anywhere.

He groans, when I start to feel his erection.

"This is a public place, right?

- Yes it is. You'll have to wait until tonight to remove my chastity belt."

I sit up, having for effect that my pelvis presses down on his hips all the more. He grabs my hips, and massages my rear, mouth closed.

"Are you teasing me?"

But I already feel his breathing deepen and even out. Pesky actor, too well versed in controlling his urges.

"My turn to be chased.

- We'll see if you can resist."

I roll onto my side, smooth my skirt down on my thighs, and stand up while arching my back, giving him a few seconds to admire the view. I feel Olen's gaze pierce through my back, and standing slowly, he slips his hand under my t-shirt, and grazes my nipples. I'm already electrified, but I focus on my voice that I will to seem natural:

"Right, shall we go?"

He gives a silent nod of approval, and we make our way back to the car.

"There's a great place not far from here, you'll see. A place I came across with my mother."

I admit tensing for a fraction of a second. I thought he was going to say Clarissa but her ghost was well and truly gone.

"I feel guilty towards Paul. I abandoned him yesterday morning. If... if the press doesn't calm down, I don't think I'll be able to go on. I'll have to find something a bit more out of the way. Far from New York.

- You're not going to change jobs because of the press, are you?

- Whatever the case, I leave Paul to his own devices every other morning because there's paparazzi outside my window. He needs someone who's unwavering, that's what being a good assistant means.

- It'll blow over.

- I don't know, they don't seem to be getting tired of me.

- And how could anyone get tired of you, my little Candice?

- Your little Candice?

- Yes mine, and mine alone."

He grabs my waist, presses a kiss to my hair, and breathes in my perfume. I'm dying to ask:

"Forever?"

But I hold back. You're going to scare him off, Candice! I pull out my phone to take a picture of the two of us. Of course, I look strange in it, one of my eyelids is a bit too droopy, and I'm not looking into the camera. Olen, on the other hand, looks perfect: his smile, his shiny ruffled hair, and eyes in which you want to get lost.

"My turn!"

He grabs his phone and pretends to put it under my skirt whereas I quickly flatten it against my thighs:

"You perv!

- Who's fault is that?"

He pinches my ass while I get into the car. You'll see, Olen, who's going to be the predator tonight. He starts the car once again and we're rushing down the main road. Olen has the music on full blast, and hits the small button. The car's top goes down, and I get up, holding onto the windshield: I feel like one of those small tibetan prayer flags that the wind rustles and reads. I'm free, everything's going to be alright…

We arrive in front of a wrought iron gate, where "The Point" appears in elegant lettering. I distinguish two figures on the right in the underbrush when the car flies towards a huge wooden building.

"Hold on… did I just see reindeers?"

Olen bursts out laughing in answer to my surprised expression and my voice which is too high.

"I didn't imagine it, did I: Those were reindeers, to our right, weren't they?"

The car comes to a halt in front of a big building completely made out of wood. It's welcoming, and exudes the feeling of a comfy way of life, even in the middle of winter. The lawn is impeccable, and wooden sun loungers with dark blue material makes you want to throw yourself on them with elegance and hot chocolate in hand.

"You'd think we were in Frozen!"

I get out of the car amazed, and Olen takes me by the hand while we walk into the main building. It feels like the perfect house from a TV show for a perfect family. And the thing is, it works: it feels like home.

"Mr Van Cliff, how are you? It's been a while."

The fifty-year-old man who welcomes us is very elegant and is paging through the old-fashioned register.

"Yes, Charles, but you know our family, we'd rather come in autumn.

- That's also my favorite season... all the colors..."

He fetches a key and slides it on the counter.

"Thank you, would it be possible to eat here... in thirty minutes? Madame is hungry.

- But of course."

A lopsided smile from Olen. An embarrassed one on my part. And we exit near the Boat House.

"Sounds like you come here a lot.

- I try and bring Mom here roughly every month," He says as he opens the gate for me.

Every month... what if his Mother was, in fact, my biggest rival? Stop it, Candice, make the most of the present.

A few minutes later, we're in front of a stone house that has a roof covered in dark tiles. The small wall out front, forming a purely symbolic barrier, covered in flowers soon to be withered, reminding me of the wild and charming Scottish countryside. Same impeccable lawn, same wooden structure than the first building.

"Wow. Is all this for the two of us?

- Sure is, beautiful."

Hand in hand, we enter a circular room, the decoration surprising me: so modern and graphic! The light and varnished wooden beams criss cross above the wooden table of the same color. The checkered curtains nearly blend into the wooden structure. A painting with dark tracery trones over the fireplace, and completes the room which is actually rather refined. The bedroom has more color to it, surrounded by pennants on the wall, and the four poster bed, covered in soft pillows, which is already calling out to me. No garish objects, simply good taste, and simplicity that makes it seem like a second home.

I feel Olen's hands run over my t-shirt and start to rub my lower back, while he presses a gentle kiss to my shoulder. And then another. I lean into him, and reach behind his neck offering him my lips. What a weakling, Candice, you didn't even resist more than two seconds. Oh go to hell! But Olen slips his hands under my skirt and takes a hold of my underwear in his fist. The fabric presses against my crotch, forcing a moan out of me. He grabs my ponytail in his fist and pulls my head back, arching it further.

"So, Candice, are you hungry?"

He then slides a finger inside me followed by a second one, pressing down causing waves of pleasure to course through me. When I'm nearing my end, he pulls his hand away and removes the small lace tanga I had on. However, instead of continuing his exploration, he smoothes down my skirt and pulls me to him to finally kiss me, and tenderly caress my neck and my back. He then pushes me away gently and leans forward to kiss my hand. He looks up at me from beneath his lashes and asks:

"Are you really hungry, Candice?

- I hate you.

- No you love it, my sweet."

He laughs while pulling me towards the balcony... which reveals itself to be a dock. It's the most beautiful view that I've ever laid eyes on since seeing Olen naked in my bed. The mountain is towering before us and seems to be saying to itself "Mirror mirror on the wall, who is the fairest of them all?" and its reflection answers "You my Queen are the fairest of all". The trees surrounding the lake bow before it, forming a carpet of wild colors. I can make out a boat house to the left, where two boats and their oars are floating.

A table is already set on the dock, and we sit opposite each other. It's so beautiful. Everything is so beautiful and … perfect. The clapping sound of the water on the pillars of the dock removes any remaining trace of tension from my body left over from yesterday morning.

"Thank you.

He tilts his head to the side.

"For what?

- For…"

I'm not very good with words. Maybe that's why I love to write. Unless it's hearing yourself say things that's hard...

"What is this place?

- It's where the aristocrats of the 19th century came for a small getaway.

- And today?

- There aren't any aristocrats.

- I think a lot of people in Hollywood think of themselves as aristocrats.

- People like who?

- Hank Wayne, for a start."

His shoulders relax.

"Relax, Olen, it was a joke."

And, once more, I gaze upon the calm and perfect blue as if nothing happened. Why does he think I judge him, for God's sake?

"So, once again, thank you. For New York and here. I'm happy to be here. With you."

It's an incredible effort, and I have to force the words out but I'm touched by his behaviour.

"You're not … the disrespectful and irresponsible jerk... that... I might have thought… a movie star like you would be."

My God, I feel like a donkey getting a cucumber shoved up his ass by someone, talking like this. I search for words in the grooves of the wooden table. But when I look him in the eye, I bite my lip. What an idiot. I hurt him. I hurry to add:

"But you're… not like that."

Too late. I hurt him. His eyes are already turning towards the lake. I cling to his hand, to keep him with me and I can no longer control the words coming out of my mouth:

"Sorry. I… I'm having a hard time finding the right words, and to bare my thoughts completely. I shouldn't have said all that, but that was before I knew you. I only thought it for a fraction of a second at Masquerade. But since…"

Suddenly, his phone rings.

"Sorry. It's my agent."

Shit, Candice, the one time you had to shut your mouth, you screwed everything up. You just called him a disrespectful jerk, when he was kind enough to bring you here. His hidden paradise, and you take that trust and trample it. You're the one that deserves to be trampled.

All that's going through my head, whereas I try to take a natural pose, relaxed in the armchair, hands crossed in my lap. I put my sunglasses on. Olen's silhouette stands out on the dock, a hand in his pocket, the other on his phone. I can't hear what he's saying. I take a mental picture of every detail of him and the scenery. I want to remember this last perfect memory. Of the moment that I understood I was madly in love with Olen, that I could no longer go on without him. That I was on my knees, despite my pride, my sidesteps and my aloofness. And he knew it. The question is: what is he going to do with this victory?

Chapter 24

How to build a relationship when the other party puts up a glass wall? Should you try and break it? Pretend as if nothing's wrong, even if you miss that sweet warmth? Or maybe try to break the ice? The thing is trying to break through that kind of ice takes time, and I'm afraid of dying outside in the cold.

How to trust, when I get that unsettling feeling that he doesn't love me? I'm a security blanket for him. But maybe that's what he is to me too? I feel abandoned and rejected at the table on the dock. What should I do? Should I join him? And what if he rejected me completely? Let him come to you, Candice. However, I feel that the fear and incomprehension rising in me is creating a palpable tension, nearly electric... instead of warming the atmosphere between us.

All of a sudden, a young woman approaches and smiling at me, says a few words to Olen, who nods and answers something that I cannot hear. He'd hung up, and still carried on looking out at the lake. What's the problem, Candice? Being in love, in my opinion, was forgetting yourself as individuals, and being one. As long as I feel my heart beating, I'll share his suffering, his indifference, his joy, everything! For a charming smile, a caress, a look from Danny, I was ready to do anything.. Except today, I've come to realize that the more I resist this magnetism, the more addicted to Olen I become.

Have I changed? Have I really become wiser? In my mind, that word seems absolutely incongruous be associated with love. Maybe I haven't changed. What if Olen couldn't give me my fix? My fix of passion, my blood pumping… I've lived these last years like a bookworm. I don't want to destroy anything or hurt anyone. Don't mind me, I'll just go on with my little life, nothing special, but impossible for you to understand. I've always disappeared in a puff of smoke when things became intense. Disappearing. I whisper to myself, gazing into space:

"And I've taken a liking to you, Olen, light of my life."

Olen finally turns around, and comes back with a rather tight-lipped smile. Without a word, he takes his seat opposite me once more, and takes my hand, in silence. We stay a few minutes, and it takes all the inner strength of a mouse turned hamster, running around it's wheel that spins infinitely, not to scream at him:

"Right, now you know what I feel for you, what about you? What are we going to do now?"

"I've ordered some trout. It's very fresh and light, you'll see."

Why is he still not looking at me?

"Very well."

His gaze fixed on my hand, slowly, he brings it to his lips and kisses it with fervour.

"I need to know. What do you think this is? Truthfully?"

He finally looks at me, but I don't find what I want in his eyes. It's as if he'd veiled them, and is watching me from behind his wall of ice. My Olen, we're so much alike.

"I think you're a good person. I like who you are. I like it when we're together. You do me good. And I hope I do the same for you.

- Yes. You do me a lot of good."

He averts his gaze to the lake once more. My God, I've never seen him so deep in thought.

"Did you enjoy the party at the club? My birthday?"

Why on earth is he bringing that up again?

"Well apart from that pervert, Hank Wayne, and that model that pressed every square inch of her skin to yours... yeah it was cool.

- That's my life, Candice. Does that life appeal to you?

- It's your life, currently, but it doesn't define you.

- Those are the people I meet everyday, the people I hang out with, that I have to hang out with.

- Why?"

He sits up, choosing his words.

"That's the way it is, going out is part of the job description as an actor, partying, too... so that people see you, to make them want to see you on the big screen. And that, I can't give up on that.

- Surrounding yourself with young nymphs and aspiring models that eye your bank account, that's part of the job?

- They don't mean anything, you know that... and yes that's part of it.

- If your career should end tomorrow what would you do?"

Olen looks at me, half choking.

"What makes you say that?

- I don't know, just curious, we're talking frankly so might as well think out loud and study all the options. The Oscars are snobbing you and have been for a while... I'm not saying that you'll never get one, I hope you do... sorry. I shouldn't be voicing my thoughts about your career.

- Tell me. I want to know what you think.

- I think that some part of you is aware that all this... isn't real. What's real is getting up in the morning, walking the dog, picking up after him, making dinner, making sure not to make too much of a mess so you don't have to waste too much time on cleaning. It's taking walks on the beach, and meeting new people who do something completely different to what you know.

- It's staying at home watching an episode of "Game of Thrones" while eating pizza?

- Yes. That too."

Before I could make a move, he slides his hand behind my neck gently pushing some stray strands of hair from my face, kissing me tenderly. Both of us leaning halfway across the table, we seal our lips and all doubt flies away.

"Is it that too?

- Yes," I breathe out.

Olen presses a kiss to my forehead, my cheeks, my eyelids. I take hold of his neck with my hands, and forehead touching his, I whisper to him with closed eyes:

"Listen, you don't live in real life, but I'm real, I can be that for you. Whatever happens. Seriously, Olen, if everything ends tomorrow, what would you do?

- Please. I don't know."

I once again see the scared little boy that grew up with an alcoholic and violent father in his eyes.

"I've always dreamed of rearing horses in Montana."

He looks at me, taken aback. I never got the impression that it was something absurd.

"What?

- I'm just imagining you, cowgirl in the hay."

His lopsided smile makes me melt, and he throws himself on my lips. My God, please let the trout get here, I won't be able to hold back much longer. Olen kisses me, again, and again, and still pensive, he runs the tip of his thumb over my lips:

"If I was no longer Olen Van Cliff … you wouldn't love me anymore."

"What??"

I suddenly pull back, ready to run. His eyes widen. Good God. It's as if someone had slapped me.

"I thought I made myself very clear. Since the beginning. Do you think I'm a gold digger or something? You really don't get it."

I get up. I need to go for a walk, but he holds me back by my wrist. I have no other choice but to sit back down.

"I didn't want to hurt you. I don't think you're a golddigger.

- Apparently, your mother does, and I don't know. Maybe you still have … that doubt. Deep down.

- No. It's just, I tell myself that people don't really know me. And don't really appreciate me for who I am.

- And do you know who you are, Olen? If your career was over, you'd still be Olen Van Cliff. It's simply that you won't wear Armani suits anymore. It's just another side of you. If you take away the hyped parties, the girls that throw themselves at you, and the easy money for a photo in the newest popular club, well … it's ok. Back to normal life, and believe me, there's nothing bad about it."

"Normal life, that's fine by me. Especially if I'm with you. But those parties, that life-style, it's part of the job.

- Yes, Olen, but it stops people seeing the real you.

- But that's what being an actor is!! People don't care who you really are. You sell a dream. If you stop being the person who lives a crazy life for them, if you stop being that name... then people won't give you the time of day. You disappear."

Poor Olen. The most powerful man in Hollywood doesn't know who he is.

"No you don't disappear. Never. I don't know, it's like the characters you portray. When you leave the set, you're not the same person, are you? Well, when you leave the club, you become yourself again. Olen. My Olen."

And I bite my lip while the young woman comes back, all smiles, and puts our two trouts in front of us, expertly orchestrated on a plate. All these women around him, are trying to get his attention, all these people who want an autograph, a signature from him... they don't let him be who he is. And he doesn't want to be the real him. He needs the attention. It's his drug, his very own, the child beggar of New York that became a Hollywood star. He doesn't think he has enough talent for people to remember him. I suddenly feel very ill at ease. I think back to that small boy who had to sell his blood to survive. How could anyone hold it against him? I've never known what it's like to be hungry. My parents always had money. They pampered me, loved me, probably more than I deserved. Olen Van Cliff may be a billionaire, but he thinks like a beggar. And it's his heart that's begging: affection, recognition, love, to whoever can give him his fix. I raise the white flag by saying:

"Bon appétit!"

The trout melts on my tongue, and the vegetables are crunchy, simply perfect.

"I have an idea Olen.

- Hum?

- Why don't you do something for charity?

- Like ?

- A foundation or something like that?

- For what?

- I don't know … cancer or Alzheimer's?

- I never had those so why would people listen to me?

- And what about the environment?

- Already taken by someone else!" He chuckles while eating some potatoes.

"Alright, so what moves you? That has something to do with personal experience? That belongs solely to Olen Van Cliff? I don't know … why not benefactor a university?

- Me? Benefactor a university? I never paid attention in class. Actually quite the opposite, I messed around all the time. I never managed to fit in when I was in high school, so going to give speeches at a university … they're going to laugh in my face."

Olen chuckles again: this is the hidden part of the iceberg.

"No my sweet, apart from this pretty face, and a bit of talent, and luck at getting parts at the right time.. I haven't got much to go on.

- Stop talking about yourself like that. It … It's not true. You have a lot of talent as an actor. You're actually really really good. You have... a bulletproof survival instinct, a lot of inner strength and… you think of the future. You're already thinking about investing in real estate when most would blow it all on a jaguar or drugs."

Olen's finished his plate, and elbows on the table, interlaces his delicate fingers. He puts his head in his hands, sighing, averting his gaze towards the mountain.

"Listen, I had an idea, you can come up with the details. Finding a cause through which you can put your fame to good use. That will… mean that you don't have to go out clubbing with brainless bimbos and pervert producers to… exist in the public eye. So that people hear about you. Something that will make you feel useful, because maybe that's what's missing in your life: a meaning to your career. Your only goal can't be money. It's not enough. You need to dream."

Olen looks at me with a half amused, half admiring expression over the top of his hands that are still linked together.

"Well, there's definitely something in that pretty little head.

- You have no idea.

- Now, get your ass into that bed, you little minx!"

And he gets up, sliding his hands beneath my thighs, hoists me up from my chair to carry me to the bedroom. I let out a small shriek of protest, a not very convincing one at that. He gently lays me down on the perfectly soft bed, slowly taking off my shoes. From my ankles he makes his way up stroking his finger across my veins, and presses his lips to mine, the ones between my thighs. I close my eyes and savour the feeling. I can't take anymore of his touch, push him away and cling to him. How can two imperfect beings unite so perfectly? Both our scents intermingle to become one. The taste of his skin, the music, the perfect harmony of our fingers and the crinkling of the sheets. I don't exist anymore. I dissolve under the weight of his body, strong and tender, and his husky voice that tickles my ear. I give in to the waves that come in quick succession: skin, muscles, smells, face half-light half dark, I let Olen enclose me in his delicious grip from which I don't want to escape.

Later on, I'm tracing the muscles of his back with my finger.

"What's success like?

- Well … It's like pain. You're not in control anymore. You're still alone. I met Clarissa on a crappy TV show in which I made my debut. We dated for two months and then I knew success. For four years I didn't stop. I did four movies back-to-back, without going home. I slept two nights in my own bed and the rest of the time I was in a hotel. I celebrated my birthday four times on my own. I missed Mom and my friends. When I got back, I didn't want to come back here. I went to New York. I ... partied a lot and I saw Clarissa again. Suddenly...

- You fell in love all over again?

- No. I think being alone for so long... success is something you need to share, with someone. And all of a sudden, there she was. She hadn't been swept up by damned success yet. Full of joy. And after three months, when it was time to get back to set I thought to myself, why not. I'm going to settle down with this woman, and we'll see."

I let silence fall, not between us but in my own mind.

"I'll think about what you told me. You're right, I need to invest in something. Other than my career and your thighs.

- That's nicely put.

- I want ... to be useful. I like that idea. And I'll do anything to not end up like my father.

- You're nothing like him ... that I'm sure of.

- This society ... is warped. Plagued with absentee, irresponsible and selfish men."

He presses himself to me, wrapping himself around me.

"Your turn. Tell me about yourself. I want to know everything, where you grew up, all of it.

- Well. I grew up in a small town, Culpeper in Virginia, and I spent half my time in the States and the other half in France.

- Why?

- My grandmother. Every summer, I went to France.

- Wait, do you speak French?

- Yes, a bit, my sweet and gentle, Olen."

He props himself up on his elbow, biting his lower lip, intrigued.

"Is it near Paris?

- No it's in Cantal. Near Aurillac. Far from everything. Well, there's a few castles. The countryside, cows, my grandmother, green beans from the garden to hull, chickens, a pig. We spent the day in Paris when I was six years old, I don't remember it."

I resist the urge of asking if he'd want us to go together. Stop, Candice, make the most of the present.

"My parents still went, just one summer in two, instead. I haven't had time to go back since the end of high school. With my studies, and Danny, and everything… But I often give my grandma a call. That time … with my parents was very hard.

- Does she live alone?

- Yes but … she keeps herself busy. She sells eggs and her vegetables at the market twice a week. She's a part of an association of hikers, nordic walking, you know, the one with the sticks. She's seventy-five and is still full of life, but I can't help but worry a bit. I'm afraid she'll take a fall one day. You know, old people, can really hurt themselves.

- Yes, I get it. You know, you can pay someone to check up on her.

- Yes. Yes that's a good idea.

- Come on, we'll go out on the boat to take it all in."

And we spend an incredible afternoon, talking about our favorite Disney movies, how cereal in the morning is addictive and how the French weren't very good at making romantic comedies, until recently.

"Why did you want to become an actor?

- I realized that you could make a lot of money clowning around.

- So it was for the money?

- Studies, that was impossible for me. For an actor there's worse than being poor.

- Which is to say?

- Being anonymous. Being nobody. I didn't get any work my first year in New York. It was horrible. I was in the middle of a physical transition and I definitely felt it."

My heart breaks thinking back to the fair-haired kid with delicate features, giving it his all in an audition and getting rejected, only to starve in the streets.

"Crappy TV ads, a secondary role in a TV show just for several episodes and a secondary role that didn't make the cut... all that for nothing. It's my best friend, Dennis, who told me not to give up.

- What? Dennis?

- Yes."

I stress my lip. Could I have misjudged him? In my opinion, he's a parasite without any talents, and who auto-proclaimed himself assistant, he however managed to see Olen's talent.

The reflection of the foliage which had become incandescent with autumn was defying the blue of the sky. And in a few powerful strokes, Olen directs the boat towards the house, then let's us drift. As we get closer to the hotel, we become more and more silent. I'm the first to enter the bedroom, and involuntarily stay back to the door.

"This weekend was amazing.

- Hush, it's not over yet."

He slowly takes the clip out of my hair and slips the light jacket I had on, off my shoulders. And with the tip of his fingers, he starts to massage my lower back, drifting up the length of my spine, stroking my shoulders underneath my t-shirt that I'm dying to rip off so I can throw myself at him. I wait, however. I give in to the delicious shiver that runs through me. It's a game of who gives in first. He's now running his fingers over my stomach, and his lips playing along my clavicle. It's driving me crazy I press myself to him further, while he takes my t-shirt off one handed. And I keep my arms above my head, wrists crossed. He doesn't resist and strokes my breasts with the tips of his fingers before laying a kiss on them. Head thrown back, I let his hands run through my hair, on my shoulders.

"Touch me," he implores, leaving no space between us, as if he wanted to melt into me.

"I think, your work isn't done," I say slowly moving my hips.

He chokes on a shout of rage which is, at the same time, laced with excitement and comes to kneel before me, pulling my shorts and my underwear down in one go. I place my hands on my hips, and watch him while I spread my legs. He's still kneeling, and looking at me pleadingly as he caresses my thighs. I ask him, candidly:

"Do you love me?

- I adore you."

I close my eyes, and throw my head back in acceptance of his reddition while he dives on me. I have a grip on his hair while he strokes me with his tongue bringing me to the brink of ecstasy. To the brink only… smartass, he wants to play till the end. He suddenly rises catching me at the top of my thighs and impales me, still standing. I let out a strangled cry clawing at his flesh while he carries me to the bed where he hovers over me, without letting go. I capture him between my thighs, and he answers by rocking his hips slowly, watching me with a small smirk. I'm already sweating: "I love it when you tease me."

He smiles tenderly at me and enters me more deeply with every thrust, taking me even closer to the brink of orgasm. When I scratch his back, however, he suddenly takes a hold of my wrists, pinning them to the bed, going even deeper, merciless. I whimper, begging in turn. He lets go of my hands and I seize the opportunity to lay a slap to his ass. He holds back a hiccough:

"I take your breath away, don't I?" I say mischievously.

"Little minx."

He pulls out and roughly turns me around, grabbing my hair.

"Do you think you can win, Candice?" He says through gritted teeth.

"Maybe…

- Fine."

He enters me slowly, just right, bringing his hand down on my ass.

" All for fun, right?

- Yes…"

He enters me again, insistant, back and forth, keeping a rhythm, never going faster, always leaving me wanting more. He whispers gently in my ear:

"Do you love me?

- I adore you."

He bites my neck as he pounds into me, which throws me into the waves of pleasure, freeing us both, leaving us panting, heart beating fast. He wraps his arms around me, holding me tight in his arms and presses a kiss to my forehead.

"Candice, do you really want to be with me?

- Well I'm here aren't I, you idiot, what do you think? Why do you ask?"

And I fall asleep in his arms, dreams of gliding over an azur blue lake intermingling with Olen's gaze.

What time is it? I roll over to see Olen fast asleep, blissed and satisfied of my body. I watch him with tenderness. All men look like kids when they're asleep. I felt lucky to get to watch him like that... him, who's an insomniac. Abandoned to sleep and the aftereffects of our caresses, I take a deep breath, filled with pride. I gently lay my head against his arm, and touching him, I was certain that I touched a piece of eternity, somewhere between protection, tenderness, new-found innocence. I was lucky. My life was back on track. I got a second chance. And suddenly, I have the urge to do something, something I hadn't done since high school. I get up slowly, and bust a few moves: until I hear someone clearing their throat. I freeze instantly. Olen's watching me, bemused, hair all over the place:

"What are you doing?

- Uh… a victory dance…

- A victory dance?

- It's something I used to do with my parents when we were happy. When we wanted to celebrate something."

He smiles at me, jumps out of bed, and starts dancing with me. We look ridiculous, but we couldn't care less. He then takes me in his arms, and spins me, until he throws me on the bed:

"Right, now, for the dance of sex!"

Chapter 25

"Where the hell are you??"

- What?"

Liza's overly excited voice even manages to wake Olen beside me and I'm having a hard time collecting my thoughts.

"Candice, it's Jo. She's in labor."

I jump out of bed to get dressed.

"I'm on my way."

Olen breaks through his sleep-induced fogginess.

"What's going on?

- It's Jo, a friend of mine, she's in labor.

- It was planned, wasn't it?

- In two months time."

He jumps out of bed and gets dressed within seconds. A few minutes later, we're hurtling down the road towards New York.

"Did everything go well with her first one?

- Yes, but this time she had a few small complications. Nothing serious, but she was a bit more worried. I hope the baby's ok. That they're both ok."

Olen takes my hand and strokes my fingers with his thumb. I'm touched, which reminds me of Jo, who I briefly told him about.

"I'm sorry, that we had to shorten the trip because of this. But I don't think I would be able to enjoy the evening there.

-Yes, so, you owe me a yes.

- A yes?

- Do you want to spend Friday night in two weeks, with me?

- Well yes. What's going on in two weeks on a Friday night?

- New York film festival. Could be fun, right?

- Fun? I'm going to be crucified by journalists on the one hand, and your female fans on the other.

- Of course not."

Olen's beside himself laughing.

"Nathan will help you.

- Who's Nathan?

- My stylist. He'll teach you how to smile when you say "screw you".

- I already like this Nathan."

When we get to the hospital, Liza's at the front desk:

"It's ok, the baby's here."

We get into the elevator and Olen pauses in front of it:

"What are you doing? Come on, Olen!"

He gets in and after a small awkward silence, I say:

"Liza Cole, Olen Van Cliff, I believe you've already met. Bali... the impromptu get together, all that, you know...

- Oh yes. Great to see you again, Liza.

- Same."

But Liza keeps her eyes riveted on me. She's evaluating whether he made me cry this week-end or not. I smile and she relaxes. In the room, Jo's rather pale, eyes shut.

Ilan's stroking her hair, and straightens up when he sees us. I hug him.

"I'm sorry, I didn't bring flowers, we got here as soon as we could.

- Don't worry about it. She'll be happy that you're here. We were so scared."

Ilan turns to the incubator where a tiny body's resting.

"It's a girl.

- Congratulations, Ilan. She's beautiful.

- Thank you.

- Ilan, this is Olen. Olen, Ilan is Jo's husband.

- Hi, and congratulations. I'm glad everything's ok.

- Thank you.

- Can I get you a coffee, Ilan?"

Ilan turns to Jo. Never have I seen someone as tender and loving as Ilan. His daughter's going to have him wrapped around her finger. I reassure him:

"Don't worry, we'll keep an eye on her."

Ilan smiles at me, thankful, after one last glance at Jo, he leaves the room with Olen. Liza sits in an armchair and I stay close to the baby, talking to her.

"Your mommy and daddy love you very much, so you have to be ok, you have to get big and strong. We all love you very much."

A nurse walks in, soon after, to check the baby's and Jo's pulse, the latter opening her eyes. I go to hug her while the nurse leaves, with a reassuring smile.

"Are you ok Jo?

- Shit, I've just had my stomach cut open on 20cms and she's asking me how I feel.

- Sorry Jo, you're right. What happened?

- I don't know. Contractions at lunch. Ilan made fun of me thinking I was stopping myself from … you know what.

- Yes, I see.

- And God, it hurt so much, I wanted to punch him.

- Mmh.

- And it made me think back to the first time I went into labor. Same, I wanted the same thing, to punch him.

- Yes, I remember.

- But I told myself, this isn't right at seven months. So, Ilan went pale and we came straight here. C-section right away. Didn't think twice about it.

- Your daughter wanted to see you, that's all," Liza says relaxing into the armchair.

"Yeah, queen of pain in the asses … like her mother.

- There you go two men, two women in the family, it's even now.

- Right Candice, where did he take you?

- To Adirondack Park.

- Nice!

- Yes.

- Is he here?

- Yes

- Did you tell him about me?

- Yes.

- He's scared, isn't he?

- Yes, I think so. But maybe more of the baby than you."

Jo pulls a face:

"Shit, stop making me laugh, I've just had a C-section for God's sake."

Suddenly, I notice Liza"s bright eyes.

"What's wrong?

- I … I think that it's starting to go to shit with Jake.

- What?

- I think he's trying to dump me.

- What do you mean ?

- Well I told him we could see each other this week-end, I wanted to see him."

I can't believe what I'm hearing, Liza asking a man out.

"Well, it's been a few weeks really, we always see each other alone. I wanted to eat out, a double date with Ilan and Jo… and he told me he had a football match. But, the last time, I mean I got out the heavy artillery, my Chantal Thomas lingerie, come on!

- Oh I see," Jo agrees.

"I don't know, normally they can't get enough.

- Right, Jo should we tell her?

- I don't know.

- Come on.

- Shit, what, tell me what?

- You're in love, Liza.

- No.

- Yes.

- No.

- Liza, don't make me want to punch someone again.

- You're addicted.

- What about him, isn't he addicted?

- Maybe he doesn't know yet."

That's when Ilan and Olen come back.

"What's going on?"

Ilan slips in next to Jo and strokes her hair. I tell him what happened and Ilan says pensively:

"Well, maybe he needs a bit of time."

Olen chimes in too:

"Yeah so he can think about what place you can hold in his life.

- Yes that's for sure. How long have you been together? Two months?

- You come crashing into his life, turning everything upside down. And, to you, that's normal, but maybe for him … he needs time."

Liza, woman of action, had crossed her arms, staring at the ground. I look at Olen: are those words only meant for Liza… or maybe for me too?

"Right, and what do I do now?

- You stop wanting to control everything.

- Alright.

- And let him come to you."

I take a step towards the alcove where the baby's sleeping:

"What are you going to call her?

- Kate.

- Like…

-Like Ilan's mother… and like Catherine the Great. A strong woman.

- She's going to drive you crazy," I laugh.

I hug them again before Olen and I leave, arms linked.

"Right, that was a quick introduction. But there you go, you know my most important friends.

- They're very nice.

- Thank you. Thank you for bringing me here.

- Do you want to grab something to eat?

- Yes. No…

- We can get take-out and eat it at yours, in peace?

- Perfect."

We get some sushi and while sitting on the couch I look at Olen and Olen looks at me.

"I enjoyed this week-end.

- Me too, my little Candice.

- We know each other better now.

- Oh we've got a lot more to learn about each other."

My legs draped over his, he straightens up and kisses me. But instead of laying me back on the cushions, he gets up and clears the table.

"Nathan will call you tomorrow."

A few kisses, and Olen slips out of the apartment. I can barely stand, I'm that tired. And tomorrow, I have to face the world.

Obviously I'm mortified standing before Paul, who's being too sympathetic for my taste.

"Listen, I talked about it with Olen, thank you, but if the situation doesn't improve, I'll have to resign.

- Candice, it's such a shame. You're efficient, well you're a great second when ...

- When I'm here.

- Maybe you could work from home?

- Maybe, but I don't see myself living as a shut-in. You see, that would mean they've won.

- And until they calm down?

- Yes. In fact, what would be nice, is if a reality TV star or a singer's sex tape was leaked. The press would find me much less interesting.

- A piece of advice, block news sites and if you want, come and work on an adjusted schedule.

- That's a great idea.

- Shall we start working on Cannes festival?

- Great !"

I go out for my lunch break, sunglasses and hoodie firmly in place, to grab a salad and a small sandwich. The newsagent's has set up its display, and I can't ignore the magazine covers with pictures of the car crash. The yellow headlines, pictures of mom and dad, the car wreck everything about it is aggressive. But apart from exasperation, I feel nothing at all. No guilt. Olen, well and truly, does me good.

"Candice?

- Yes ?

- This is Nathan, Olen told me that you needed me!

- Oh Nathan, great! You're the one who's going to help me prepare for the festival?

- Absolutely I'll prepare you to face what they have in store for you.

- Wow.

- I'm joking."

We meet up at Liza and mine's Monday night. "No time to lose," Nathan told me. I pushed the couch out of the way as he had asked, and I have no idea what to expect. He's a large brunet with features slightly reminiscent of Asia, and a well-tailored shirt, who observes me from head to toe so pointedly that I wonder if he's gay. He shakes his many bracelets crossing and uncrossing his arms while watching me.

"Well, let's make this a bit more ... Grrrrr.

- Grrr?

- Yes we're going to bring out the fiery red Ferrari that lies within you.

- Right. Because what am I at the moment?

- Herbie, the Beetle."

Before I process the jab, he gives me a binder with various looks for brunettes, with different hairstyles and makeup. Clothes of different brands, known or not.

"Look, I've prepared this folder, you can keep it, and use it as inspiration for your next outfits."

I wince when I lay eyes on some pieces with a low neckline.

"Thank you Nathan, but I don't want to become a bimbo.

- I don't want that either! But leaning towards something more feminine and more polished, would you mind that? A femme fatale, does that speak to you?

- I don't really feel up to it. On Halloween, why not! Everything goes on Halloween!

- But in Hollywood, everything goes too.

- Except me: I think people won't let anything slide for me.

- Poor darling! You want me to shed a tear for you, is that it? Have you even made a small effort?

- Why ?

- To get people to like you!"

Take that. Another jab. And here I thought he was going to be on my side.

"Have you ever seen the photos of you? You never smile except in the ones taken in Bali. My first piece of advice, smile all the time, it would make you seem less dramatic and a bit nicer. The nice girl that all the other girls envy. Not the minx who has a face three feet long and who thinks she's above it all.

- Wow. Are you going for a knock out before the end of the evening or something?

- Better it come from me, now. I express what no one dares to.

- Well ... thank you ... Do I really come off prissy?

- It's a wonder what Olen sees in you, he's so cool ... and affectionate with everyone."

I'm beginning to understand all this fuss with the press. Nathan's now sporting a satisfied smile. He stands up and claps his hands.

"Okay, let's try something else. Here."

And he plops three books on the top of my head.

"What's this ?

- The complete works of *Gone with the Wind*.

- Is it so I stand straight?

- It's to seek excellence."

I smile, and take a few steps.

"Look up and smile! You look like a lobotomized giraffe. And clench your buttocks! Good. Now, for the hard part. Here: it's the right size, right?

- Yes."

I put on the heels and Nathan puts the three books back on my head. Suddenly, he pulls out a flashlight, worthy of a cop, and yells at me:

"Come on! Faster ! To the right ! No to the left! Look this way."

I nearly drop the books but manage to catch them just in time.

"God damnit, what was that for?

- The photographers on the red carpet," He replies stoically.

"Right, we have two weeks to coach you, I'm guessing you eat pizza?

- No. Sushi.

- Well from now on, if you want to fit into the dress I'm going to get for you, forget snacking between meals.

- Your going to get me a dress?

- Yes darling, seeing as it will be a loan and it's been tailored for a starving model from Eastern Europe, you better opt for spring rolls, and smoothies from now on. No more carbs. Adios!

- Adios to gnocchi and cheese too?

- Yes.

- Olen's the one who isn't going to be happy.

- Olen much prefers your gnocchi.

- Nathan! I have to introduce you to Liza.

- And I need to introduce you to Konjac. You know, the pasta that doesn't make you put on weight. Right, from here on out you'll drink the juice of a lemon or a spoonful of apple cider vinegar diluted in water every morning.

- What? That's disgusting!

- You've got to work to get your ass in a tight Yves saint Laurent or Versace dress, darling. Then, you"ll take two charcoal vegetarian capsules before and after meals. On top of that, you'll eat carrots in a crudité salad for lunch with fish and greens. And I'll make appointments for two tanning sessions.

- Hey, you've planned a Navy Seal training!

- No: the red carpet, the largest roast for ingenuous people like you. And if I don't prepare you, the journalists will eat you alive.

- So what ? After all, if they've decided to tear me apart, they will.

- Do you love Olen?

- Yes.

- More than anything ?

- Yes.

- Then consider this as you supporting his career. Right now, Olen can, with the snap of his fingers, get a movie to be made if he wants to. Nowadays, his name alone can launch a whole butterfly effect that will generate money, jobs, projects worth several million dollars ... in short, you're by his side, to support him, and you have to take your place. I worked for a politician's wife, same thing. Now, in a week you have an appointment at Laya's Institute to cleanse your skin. And three days before that, you'll be there for a full body scrub and full body wax, eyebrows included.

- Full body?

- Do you want somebody to see the hedgehog peeking underneath your Versace?

- I don't have a hedgehog anyway. A mouse at the most.

- Well, my mouse, the day before you wash your hair, and mani pedi.

- My God, I didn't do this much for prom.

- Was Olen at your prom?"

I smile, blushing.

"Right, I'll see you on the day, for hair, makeup, and helping you with the dress. And, please, stop the sushi, convert to Konjac, and follow my advice, you'll thank me later.

- Okay, so I put on the dress, the shoes, and ... I smile blissfully while hanging onto Olen's arm?"

Nathan gets up, laughing his head off.

"No, that's where the hard part starts.

- What?

- Do you have any idea why stars wear dark sunglasses?

- To not be recognised, obviously.

- Yes and because if you smile, it has to reach your eyes. To show you truly feel happiness, joy, and above all, self-confidence.

- Oh yeah, that really is the hard part.

- The perfect smile, the lips are parted, and you show only the upper row of teeth. Like this."

And he turns his back to me, and resting his chin on his shoulder slightly higher than the other, he barely opens his mouth.

"Wow ...

- Your turn."

I mimic his pose.

"Right, well, you look like a giraffe who just smoked a joint. Maybe if you try closing your mouth."

I now laugh wholeheartedly at his quipps.

"There, that's true emotion, and it's always better than poses that you can't really handle. Right, now, for the last tip: keep your head up, and create some asymmetry.

- Like what you did with your shoulder?

- Exactly.

- Now, pretend to point to something using the tip of your nose, and chin up.

- So, like a giraffe then?

- Perfect !

- And then do a quarter turn with your body. It will show off your curves.

- And what about my hands?

- One will be holding a pretty little clutch, matching your shoes, and the other will be on Olen's ass!"

He puts his hand up, and I give him a high five.

"Being a journalist is a piece of cake Candice. Knowing how to dance around their questions and remarks,that's being the icing on the cake.

- Yeah. It's still a mouthful to swallow.

- You'll manage, giraffe."

And Nathan pulls me into a reassuring hug ... and slaps my ass. Definitely gay!

Chapter 26

The orgiastic craze could begin. Fans flocked and flowed against the barriers screaming Olen's name. Some girls were crying, holding up pictures of various actors. From behind the tinted windows of the limo, I could make out a banner "Olen, marry me.". I grab a hold of Olen's hand while he watches the crowd through the tinted glass. Impossible to read his expression. I need to hear him say it, now:

"Tell me again that I mean something to you Olen."

He turns his head slowly, rousing from his thoughts.

"Of course I do, I introduced you to my mother!

- Yes, like you've probably done with others and your mother must have seen a lot to size me up from head to toe like that.

- A few ....

- I get the feeling that you're still that young seventeen year old guy. And that you've been with ... so many women ..."

I feel stupid asking him this again right now. He contemplates me somberly and as if shaking himself from his thoughts, pulls me to him, holding me in his arms:

"We've had great times together and I'm happy with you. YOU. Okay ?"

He returns his gaze to the crowd through the tinted window.

"We'll talk about it later. Do you remember one of the things you told me when we first met?

- At Masquerade?

- Yes.

- Not really.

- You told me to go and see how many flowers I could get my hands on and I asked you what type of flower you were."

It comes back to me in flashes. I burst out laughing, falling back against his shoulder:

"Yes I think I remember.

- My little cactus. My hedgehog. Stay close to me, you're my shield."

He holds me against him pressing a kiss to my forehead. I wrap my arms around him and inhale his fragrance. Here's hoping they never stop making his cologne.

"I'll have to buy myself a bottle of your cologne, keep it in storage for the days you go off filming."

He smiles, memorizing each and every detail of my face.

"Ready ?

- No.

- You're right. Nobody's ever ready to deal with this. But I'm here."

Someone opens the door to the limo with tinted windows, and Olen gets out first, magnificent and proud, causing a screaming chant of his name. He spins around and around, taking the time to wave to every part of the crowd. Wow. They're going to throw rotten tomatoes at me, I can't possibly make it through this evening in one piece.

When I get out, I'm so blinded by the flash of cameras going off that I no longer hear the shouts. I try to put on a smile, not showing teeth, and I link my arm through Olen's. But his attention is already directed towards the crowd and the photographers. Something struck me then, with unprecedented abruptness. He's in his element on the red carpet. He already has his feline grace: penetrating gaze, cheeky dimple and predatory smile, he embraces the crowd, his fans, with his eyes.

Journalists are in an uproar to see us make an appearance together, and I hear Nancy O'Brian take the first shot, in front of the camera, microphone in hand.

"What a great feeling to cling to a man's arm. Even an ugly and badly dressed one, still gives you a lot more composure than a handbag or a pair of shoes from a famous brand. It's their greatest power. What's left to say when they're well dressed and confident ... every woman would love to find that match. Elegant, unique, stable, he gets noticed and causes the envious murmurs of the women. Sometimes he's coveted, sometimes he pops up unexpectedly ... the most mischievous accessory, the most reassuring ... and most dangerous, I name Olen Van Cliff."

We pass them by, and Olen ignores them. Dennis has already chosen who's entitled to an interview. Two commentators on a platform are broadcasting the event live:

"A Marchesa dress. Great choice. But making a relationship official on the red carpet, isn't that a touch overrated ..., Helen? What are your thoughts on this Candice?

- Brad, dating a celebrity's like graduating using life-experience. It' a great illusion, but deep down, you know it doesn't have the same standing.

- Why's that, Helen?

- Because a " normal " person will never have the glamor of an actresses, a model or a singer that can electrify crowds. In other words, she's no star. The petite bookseller will remain a mere impostor, on who the fairy godmother through luck bestowed her magic... or was it by mistake?

- Helen, well you've always had a way with words ... put your claws away! Any chance you're jealous?

- Maybe ... I've had the pleasure of interviewing Olen early on in his career. He was adorable. As for his partner, or should I say latest conquest, who knows... it's not that I don't like her ... I just despise her life choices."

I focus on Nathan's advice, smile, chin up, drop the one shoulder, and after the death row surrounded by photographers and TV journalists, Olen abandons me, called over by Dennis:

"I have to go talk to him.

- Okay, and what am I supposed to do?

- Go behind the wall of photographers and wait for me inside. Here's your pass."

With that, Olen waves over one of his bodyguards, who steps forward immediately, smiling, shows me the way. Olen presses a quick peck to my lips, and I follow the friendly hired muscle, behind which I just might be able to hide while I await Olen's return. But once we make it to the reception, he melts into the tapestry, and I have to face the crowd alone. Candice calm down, it's not the Met, for God's sake. A festival in New York, amongst professionals, a few journalists, nothing serious. Olen says his piece, presents the award to his favorite director, everyone smiles, a few appetizers and we can slip out. I saunter through the guests, who are staring at me, not sure if they recognise me. I smile, and make my way towards the buffet. Alright, grab a drink to seem at ease. For a split second I'm tempted to give in and have a petit four, but I can already picture the look on Nathan's face if I do. I have to admit his plan literally had me shedding off weight and the Marchesa dress wrapped around my body with near to no effort. I turn around, sipping some champagne, and come face to face with Maria, Becky Sparks' rival, reality TV star.

" Oh ! You're Olen 's fiancée?"

It seems like I'm face to face with a carbon copy of Becky Sparks, a latino version : same heart-shaped mouth and eyes fluttering in disbelief. Other women look up, astonished. I feel like a fly caught in the spider's web. I can't decide between being panicked and being irritated as she flutters her eyelashes at an incredible speed. Quick, Candice, find a diversion. Anything.

"Can I take a picture with you and Olen later? I'm a huge fan of your relationship! Do you know what they call you? The " Olenices ".

- Uh ... you must be mistaken," I say, as sweetly as possible.

Olenices. Seriously ! I choose to retaliate using a distraction:

"Hold on a second! Are you Maria Gonzales? You were with Becky Sparks on that reality show, weren't you?

- Uh … yes ! Absolutely, yes that's me! Did you recognise me?

- Well, you'd have to be living under a rock to miss that PlayBoy cover!

- Oh thank you. Usually Playboy uses blondes ... it's an honor to be the first Latina to pose for the magazine.

- It's a great combination. Best of luck, Maria."

And I get out of there. Maria had the ambitious project of demonstrating her presence on the internet for a week, as much as she could. Between fake breast cancer, a false pregnancy and a fake break up ... she was successful. She would have done anything, and I had learned my lesson with Becky. Maria's all the more dangerous because she's that much smarter: she's here to find a part even a secondary one. Attract attention, create a buzz, and break through walls that once were well partitioned but that were porous nowadays, as long as you can triple the investment of the financier. Olen please convince me tonight that you're not just a dice thrown by a financier on the board of this vast masquerade.

I make my way amongst the guests and, finally, manage to find Olen after a few minutes.

He's deep in conversation, glass in hand, with last year's Oscar winner. A tall redhead, with a beige satin dress that clings to her curves and sublimes them. Olen's in deep contemplation of her face. Calm down, Candice. It's only natural, he's networking. She gets a bit closer to him, and puts her hand on his chest, her fingers trailing along it. Olen mesmerised, looks down. Well, he likes beautiful women, it's only natural to admire beauty. I think she's beautiful too. A bit cheap for the likes of her, but that's a word men are unable to associate with women. Right, how long is this going to last exactly? I have no idea what she whispers while she gets even closer, but Olen looks up at her, contemplating her face in surprise. Really !! He just took her in his arms, kissing her on the cheek. My mouth's dry.

"You should watch yourself miss. And change your bets while you still have time."

It's a lady in her fifties, elegant in her sheath dress. I think I recognise her as one of the people who organised the festival, without being sure. She continues sardonically:

"The rich, the powerful and the beautiful intermarry. To make sure they're not surrounded by leeches. And to perpetuate the race of genetic miracles.

- I'm not trying to take advantage of him.

- Look at him. Can you not see the truth, Candice? You're not part of the same world. You never have been and you never will be. Do you know why you make the papers? Because people like criticize, but they can't identify with you. They want to identify with Clarissas, and Olens. With Marlon Brandos and Marilyn Monroes. Even if it ends badly. They're wild animals that fascinate us and that we convince ourselves we've tamed, but they never belong to us. They consume as much as they consume themselves. And one day, when they no longer need you, they toss you aside.

- You seem very bitter. Personal experience, am I right?

- A little."

She takes my arm, almost maternal:

"There will always be a gap, you can already feel it, and it will only get worse. He's barely starting his career. Movie stars, and above all actors, are always surrounded and courted by women ... they don't want our reality. In their eyes, we have something that's annoying."

Averting her gaze back to Olen, still in deep and hushed conversation with the redhead, she continues thoughtfully:

"And they need to shine in the firmament. Far from us. Excuse me, the projection's about to start."

And she glides through the guests while I gulp. I have to get out of here. I head for the exit, quickening my pace as I go: suddenly, a hand stops me. Olen's looking at me all smiles.

" Hey ! Where are you going ?

- I'm looking for the toilets.

- Over there."

I don't want to make a scene in public. Fear, worry, doubt: the face I see in the mirror is so unlike me. It's hidden behind a mask of makeup, that's now crumbling. For a long time, I knew what I didn't want: to be the latest conquest, a trophy wife, a celebrity. But what do I want? I want a home. I want a normal life. But I also want to dance in a dress that flatters my skin in the same way Olen knows how to charm my body. Is this what life's all about? Coming and going between dreams and reality?

I shake my head, stop getting yourself worked up. And what if it were true? And what if he just got caught up in it for a few months, before going and cheating on you at the next party where he had too much to drink. And everyone will know about it before you, thanks to the tabloids. And the rumors will drive you crazy until you break, and you'll push him until he can take no more: then, he'll give in and cheat on you. I can't spray water on my face, it would ruin my makeup. I understand now how Olen can feel trapped! I take deep breaths in and out. Olen. He's behind the door. He needs you, Candice. I go back out immediately.

" Everything okay ?

- Yes. I drank a bit too much champagne. My head was spinning."

He takes me by the waist, and when we look at each other, the world around us and their jealous whispers don't matter any longer. I'd like to tell him again, "This, between us, Olen. That's what makes us pure and timeless. " However, I'm not given the chance, Dennis has already returned to the charge.

"Olen, someone wants to meet you."

I feel my hands tighten around Olen's waist. But I don't want him to feel guilty.

"I'm sorry. I promise, I'll make it quick."

It's a tanned, youngish, skinny man. His face seems familiar, and I need a moment to put my finger on it. That's ... Moktar, Ben Ousour's son, the son of the infamous dictator of Kyrgyzstan!

"It's an honor to meet you, Mr Van Cliff. I'm a huge fan of your work."

I carefully approach Dennis and discreetly ask:

"What's a dictator's son doing here?"

He stiffens, ignoring me, and throws over his shoulder, all smiles:

"Okay! Ha ha! Shall we take that souvenir photo Mr Ben Ousour?"

"Olen, no!" I shout a little too loudly.

Everyone spins around to look at us. Olen has his eyes riveted on me in shock.

"I'm sorry, Olen can't take this picture.

- Candice!

- Trust me, you really can't take this picture. Sorry."

Ben Ousour's face is expressionless, and he glares at Dennis who shrinks. However, Olen takes me aside, clutching me by the shoulders, and staring at me, he says:

"Let Dennis do his job, okay? You're acting weird tonight.

- Me, I'm the one who's weird? Do you realize you were about to take a picture with a criminal's son?

- What? Listen, let me do my job, alright? What the hell's going on with you?"

Everyone's heading to the projection room looking at us askance. I'm aware of the fact that all my fears are breaking through and catching in my throat, becoming hysterical, but it's too late: it slips out.

"I think Dennis was about to make you do something stupid, the question is why.

- Leave Dennis out of this, I feel like what's going on here has nothing to do with him.

- You're right ,we'll get to the bottom of this. Right, what's going on between us, Olen?"

He looks at me stunned. He hesitates for a second, looks around, and quipps,

"Well, it's casual.

- You call a pair of jeans casual, not a relationship.

- Well well, little bookseller, in my opinion, you're thinking about this too much. "

He's trying to lure me in with his sidelong glance. But I'm not in the mood for his charming number, and I backup. He gets angry:

"You know what's wrong with you?

- I talk too much and I'm too smart for you?

- It's making you pretentious and snobbish. You don't even know how to give in and enjoy the present.

- I gave in and enjoyed the present with you. A few times and I think you rather liked it. It's been three months now. What happens to us in all this?

- Well ... we keep going.

- We keep going ? Hiding every other day to avoid being photographed together? Withstanding everyone's criticism saying I'm not good enough for you? Shutting up and standing by your side? Is that what it's like to be with you, Olen?

- I thought you understood what dating me involved. It means remembering your place. So remember it.

- Oh! Would you give it a rest, you're an actor, not the center of the universe! I don't have to bend to your schedule and your rules all the time.

- You know what you are? You're a pain in the ass.

- I'm Sorry, what ?!

- Yeah a pain in the ass.

- Okay, you win, fuck you, Olen Van Cliff! You'll end up alone like an idiot. Or better yet, with a model twenty years younger who's going to ask for a divorce after 2 years of marriage, and after having a kid, and she'll get half your fortune. You'll have to take quite a few photos with dictators to pay the alimony.

- Dictators? What the hell are you talking about?"

However, I turn and run. I pass in front of the photographers, the crowd. Someone grabs a hold of my arm. I spin around intent on telling him to grow up. Fire that parasite, Dennis, who's going to cause a shitsorm of trouble. But Olen's not the one who grabbed me. It's Dennis, who's just about ready to pull my arm out of its socket in the middle of the street.

"Fuck, I'm going to smash your face in. I just lost two hundred thousand dollars, you idiot. A photo, just one, three seconds, and we would've gotten two hundred thousand dollars!" He seethes.

"We? Of those two hundred thousand you would have gotten a percentage? And this picture would have appeared in three months time on the internet with the headline " Olen friends with a family of dictators. " Great publicity!

"You're a pain in my ass, you're a pain in both our asses, Olen's and mine, have been for three fucking months, you and your principles.

- Don't worry, I'll get out of your way."

I try to free myself from his hold, and the photographers turn up, cameras at the ready. I struggle more and more, but Dennis has a vice-like grip on my arm and tries to drag me away, anger coming off of him in waves. I nearly lose my balance with these heels.

" Enough! "

And in one last effort, I manage to abruptly break free and smash my fist in Dennis' face. He processes what just happened, and backs off in shock, holding his nose.

"Touch me one more time, and I'll send you to kingdom come."

He doubles over in pain and I think I glimpse a trickle of blood bead between his fingers. He takes a moment to process,

"What?"

I hear some people snickering at him "It means death, asshole" but I've come to realize that the sneers don't necessarily mean they're on your side. Just that they liked the show. I clamber into the first taxi I can find to get away from this feeling of being a circus freak.

Jo and Liza are sitting down at the table, nervously waiting for me. I throw myself into a chair. Jo has already served up the chicken curry, and Liza's looking at me dumbfounded.

"That dress is sick! I didn't get to see it!

- I think it's over between Olen and me. We blew up at each other tonight.

- Go on.

- Do you know the person who organizes the festival?

- No.

- I wish you were there, Liza. She destroyed me. But she was only telling the truth: I don't belong with Olen. Class, charisma, poise, fortune, I don't have those things ... I'm just me. We're different in every way. And I stopped him from doing something stupid, but Mister didn't like it.

- What do you mean by something stupid?

- Omar Ben Ousour's a dictator in the Middle East, imposing a rule of terror. His son was there, he wanted to take a photo.

- Wow, that would give the tabloids grist to the mill.

- You said it. But I was ... put in my place.

- By his agent?

- And Olen himself ... There you have it."

We had nothing left to say to each other. Liza seems nervous.

"I'm sorry I know this isn't the time, but ... Jake asked me to marry him!" She blurts out while stressing her napkin.

I'm stunned. Already? What's it been ... three months? And he was about to dump her!

"Congratulations!

- Yes, congratulations, Liza, I'm really happy for you. You deserve it.

- Thanks, Candice. Look, I'm sorry it didn't work out between you and Olen ...

- Stop, don't say that, nothing's lost.

- That's not what I mean. But ... you have a lot of insecurities about this relationship.

- Says the person who was dead scared two weeks ago in my hospital room.

- I was scared because I'd never fallen in love before. I was a little worried about the difference in our walks of life, and ... people's outlook on the difference in skin color. But they were just concerns, I realized that it didn't matter. And everything else, I'm ok with."

I stare at my chicken curry, thoughtfully…

"The question is: Is this relationship worth fighting for ? Is Olen worth it?

- Who knows."

I start eating without much appetite, and try to change the subject:

"Just one thing though, three months, isn't that ... a bit too short to decide to get married?

- I want to take my time. First, we're … going to live together. You see, we're engaged. But I'll start the wedding preparations in six months. That gives me time to plan, and be confident in my decision. Besides for the apartment ...

- Look, you don't have to worry about that. Don't put your life on hold for anyone. You're the one who told me that."

Liza looks at me teary-eyed, and takes my hand.

"Thank you.

- No, thank you. Both of you. I'm lucky to have friends like you."

And Jo, eyes hardened, but puffy, shining with tears says:

"That's not true. Stop it or I'll knock you out."

That night, I go home both sad and anxious: I look at my phone. No news from Olen.

I spend my weekend writing, writing and writing some more. Everything that goes through my mind. Becky Sparks, Hank Wayne, the ruthless red carpet. And it's only on Sunday night, when I hear Liza discreetly come in and start packing boxes, that I manage to fall asleep. I give into the darkness. Drained. So drained that I don't have any dreams, for the first time in years.

Chapter 27

"Hi Nathan!"

Nathan looks at me apologetically when I open the door. A lot has changed in three weeks.

"Can I come in?

- Yes."

He comes in but stays near the door. I grab the satin Marchesa dress, looking sad on its hanger like the empty shell of an insect, and give it back to him.

"I didn't take it to the cleaners, like you asked. But I think it's as good as new.

- Thanks, that's great, don't worry I'll take care of everything.

- You want something to drink ?

- No thanks, I'm going to give it back straight away.

- Thanks again for everything ... But it didn't work out. All my efforts were in vain."

Nathan nods, a little sad, biting his lip:

"You were stunning. You were perfect. I saw the pictures. And the meme too.

- The meme ?

- A short animation that people made for the fun of it, of you and Dennis. It's going round the Internet. Actually that was one hell of a punch, honey. Respect."

Damn.

"Ah. Well ... thank you. How long has it been up for?

- It was up that very night.

- Of course it was. Is it funny at least?

- Oh yes. It's really well done.

- At least I took my bow in a memorable fashion."

Nathan blinks and quirks an eyebrow. After a few seconds, he says softly:

"What do you mean take a bow? Aren't you going to try and piece things back together with Olen?

- I don't think he wants to, Nathan.

- What about you ? Do you want to ?

- I don't know. I have to admit I don't feel up to it.

- Wait a second, what's the problem? He loves you and you love him. Simple.

- What about in three years? And in ten? When he's even more famous, and what if I haven't changed, haven't evolved. And he's cheated on me with all of New York and Los Angeles?

- I can't tell you what to do, I'm no shrink. But I like love stories. Especially the ones with happy endings.

- Thanks Nathan.

- You're welcome."

He marks a pause, hesitating in the doorway and turns around at the last

Minute:

"Listen, Olen's organizing a party Thursday night. Go. Explain what you feel after you've slept on it, tell him your fears and tell him you love him. It's at 225 Warren Street. Go.

- Thanks Nathan."

He gives me a hug as my grandmother would and kisses me on the forehead.

"Go, giraffe, chin up!"

He slaps my ass before leaving. Why does everybody do that? I closed the door and went back to writing. I don't want to get worked up about it anymore, or rather, I rediscover how good it is to write. I write for a long time, without worrying about spelling mistakes or about the possible perfection of my writing, because I'm a living imperfection. I am a scab, painful and irritating on the face of the earth. I sit back down at my desk, with my rosé cider, and go on to the last chapter.

"Right, what name can I give Becky? If I call her Becky, it could give too much publicity and she could sue me ..."

The modern starlet in my novel makes a name for herself in Hollywood, pretending to be ingenuous amongst shady producers, merciless rivals and slightly arrogant juvenile leads. I empty my glass bitterly and put my rancor on paper. Obviously, I'll scrap some passages, but those few notes jotted down some months ago have matured and are now taking on a new dimension that I never expected. I read over the last few sentences, quite pleased with myself and feeling calm, I close my computer. That's when Liza gets back.

"How are you ?

- Fine.

- You want me to give you a hand with the boxes?

- No thanks. Jake's coming to pick up some furniture, I'm mainly going to pilfer the linen.

- Can I borrow a nice dress tonight?"

Liza stares at me a moment and smiles showing her immaculate teeth:

"Do you have a date? Are you ... going to see him again?

- No. I'm going out with someone else. Someone I met before that.

- Oh. Right, of course, help yourself. Feel free.

- Thanks, Liza."

I chose a blue dress with an empire cut, a strap on one shoulder and I go to meet Alec when night falls. The latter is waiting for me outside the restaurant, the front of which is blocked from view thanks to red curtains. He nervously runs a hand through his hair. Delicate features and a leather jacket, he's just as cute as last time.

"You look gorgeous.

- Thank you."

I congratulate myself on my choice of dress. And I let him look at me for a few minutes once we were seated.

"Thanks for sending me that text.

- I wanted to see you again. I thought you'd be a little more ... available. Some Merlot please."

I smile as the server turns back around asap.

"So, what's new? Are you still working at the same production company?

- Yes. But I'm going to quit.

- Why ?

- It's become complicated because of recent events. And it reminds me too much of a lifestyle I can't cope with. Feeling a need to move on.

- So, have you been thinking about what options you have?

- For now, I'm writing.

- Really ? And I can have a preview?

- Oh, it's not a movie, it's a novel. A novel about this business actually.

- So you can't cope with it, but, at the same time, it inspires you ...

- Yes ... yes that's true. It's a business filled with wild animals. We're all fascinated and drawn to them. Until they devour us.

- And what's it about?

- A deceptively innocent woman who ... you think will be walked all over by someone smarter or stronger than her everytime she does a scene, but she always manages to get by. I tried to paint a picture of it all: the press, the internet, cinema ... everything's blurred now. It's scary and interesting.

- Is it pessimistic?

- No. It's just an observation of human nature.

- Does it end well?

- I like happy endings.

- Me too."

And we look at each other, smiling. The music is soft and breezy, the waiter returns to take our order.

"Enough about me! What about you? Any news?

- I still run the diving club in Mexico. Still full of stressed out execs.

- Cool. So, what are you doing in New York?

- I've come to meet some investors, to open a second one. And, why not, attach a rural gîte to that, ecotourism that kind of stuff, you know.

- That's great!

- What about you? Planning on staying in New York?

- Who knows. This city, has a hold on me I think."

Alec contemplates me thoughtfully. Our order is served: braised pork ribs with honey, and fresh vegetables.

"If you were to move, where would you go?"

- Second excellent question of the evening. First, I have to move my roommate, got engaged, so I need to find a new roommate or move out.

- You want a fresh start?

- I think life just sent me a lot of signs. So, a new apartment would be welcome.

- You're welcome to come to Mexico. I'll hide you if you want," He says winking at me.

I burst out laughing, and we discuss Mexico, the food, the incredible colors, Michael Kenna's next exhibit and my love for black and white photos. Alec then leans over and takes my hand,

"I love this song."

Time stops when Alec puts his hand on mine. Except the warmth that's trying to seep in, remains on the surface. In a split second I realized: it'll take a lot of work to get Olen off my mind. He's embedded in every inch of my skin, like a heavy metal ingested in small doses over a long period of time, which has crystallized to form another barrier under my skin. When Alec raises his hand to stroke my cheek, I lower my head.

"Sorry."

He withdraws his hand, and closes off with a polite smile.

"Sorry, I am really sorry Alec, I truly thought I was actually available.

- But you're not.

- Not in my mind or in my heart ...

- I don't have an answer for that. I understand, don't worry."

I go home, on foot, pitifully. It's killing my feet but I need to walk, I'm tired of pacing in my apartment. I'm tired of going round in circles period. When I get home, I open a bottle of Colombelle and pick up the novel this time backwards to correct spelling mistakes and check out the last additions. I quietly close my computer. I don't know who I can get to read it, I don't even know who I'm going to send it too ... Time will tell. If I survive until Thursday.

***

When I arrive at 225 Warren Street I see that something's wrong straight away. The people in front of me are dressed in tuxedos and evening gowns. And I dared "come in sneakers", I can tell what they're thinking. What kind of party is this? In a private apartment? The two security guards see me coming. I stand rooted, stupidly, in front of them.

"Good evening, I'm here for Mr Van Cliff's party.

- Do you have your invitation?

- Uh ... no.

- Miss, we can't let you in. It's on invitation only.

- Don't you recognize me ? I was at the festival with him.

- Yeah, sure. They all say that."

I'm internally seething. What an idiot. I should have asked Nathan for more details.

"Listen, if I can't get in, can you just tell him that Candice is here? I have three words for him.

- Three?

- Yes.

- Send a message.

- I wanted to talk to him face to face.

- Let the other guests past please. They paid to be here."

I swallow my pride, pull up the hood of my sweatshirt and retreat. Paid to be there? He charged an entrance fee for his party? I kick a pebble on the pavement: Dennis has got Olen completely under his influence and he let him do it. What can I do?

That question haunts me the whole walk back. And the awful truth hits me: I can't do anything. You can love people, you can't make the right choices for them. I start crying. It's stupid. I haven't cried so much since I met Olen. Is it because I feel crappy or because I finally allowed myself to open the gates when needed? It's anger and rage that come over me when I close the door of my apartment. Jo started a family, Liza's getting ready to fly the nest ...

everyone seems to be finding their place in the world. Except me. "Don't forget your place," he told me.

I allow myself another glass of Colombelle and play my favorite game, sitting opposite the window, feet on my desk.

"Slug droppings," I curse out loud this time.

"Olen Van Cliff, you're a bunch of slug droppings. Tiny droppings, very wet and sticky."

What else can I come up with?

"Olen Van Cliff, you're a monumental pile, of slug droppings on which even Jo's baby wouldn't defecate. You little shit ... where was I?"

"You okay Candice?"

Liza's standing in the doorway, arms crossed, watching me.

"You went to see him?

- I went there, I didn't get in. Needed an invitation.

- What are you doing ?

- I'm writing a novel.

- About droppings?

- A little.

- Will you let me read it?"

"If you don't read it, who will?" I shoot back, sneering

In two seconds Liza's crossed the distance between us, turns my chair and lands a monumental slap across my face.

"Stop feeling sorry for yourself. That's enough. I thought you bounced back easily, by seeing other people, but apparently you chose to drown. And you have no right, you hear me?"

I'm still in shock from the slap. In recent months it was on my ass that people have been hell-bent. Makes a change.

"Get back in the saddle, now. Anything, you have to keep your head above water."

I look at her, teary-eyed, lump in my throat. What good is it Liza? Can't you see nothing's working for me? I was ostracised a long time ago and I'm still reeling, wondering where I am and where I'm going.

"To do what ? I have no right to be happy. It's obvious."

She carefully kneels in front of me, and puts her hands on my knees. Looking deep into my eyes, she says:

"Because you think happiness is a right? You think I had a right to study? Me, who had a slave as an ancestor five generations back? Me, a black, head of department in a huge marketing and communications company?

- I'm not as strong as you Liza.

- You are still alive: so you're strong. Period. Each time you want to cry, cry, but do something straight after. To keep going.

- You're right. Alright, I'll stop whining.

- I don't know, look for agents that might be interested, or put it online on a self-publishing site, something like that.

- Sorry ...

- Sorry for slapping you.

- No, it did me good, thanks.

- You want me to do it again?

- Uh no. That's okay. Thank you. Alright, now, let me work.

- That's what I like to hear."

Liza leaves the room to go back to her packing. She's absolutely right. I empty my third glass of Colombelle in one go. Damn. I still haven't eaten, and it's starting to go to my head. That's the thing with this sweet white wine because it's sweet, it's soft, you drink it like you would a juice, and it takes you by surprise. Like Olen.

That's when I realized something: I'm boring. Worse, I bore myself. That's why I'm on my third glass of Colombelle. I'm boring myself with these fears. I turn towards my bed. My fears are there, lurking underneath, coming up with a plan to tie me to the mattress so that, by God, I don't go out, leaving me to cry on my fate. What do people think of me ever since my relationship with Olen? Since the festival? What will people think of my novel? Will they want to crucify it with their pens? Damn.

"Lizaaaaaa!

- What?

- Thank you for slapping me!

- You sure you don't want another?

- No, it's okay I'm doing the rest on my own, thank you."

Honestly,when was the last time I fell in love? Sure, it destroyed me but Liza was right, I'm still alive. So not made of glass. And I still haven't finished a novel. When was the last amazing trip I had? I have to admit, apart from Bali and the suburbs of New Jersey, there weren't many. I look at my fears and tell them:

"I understand, don't worry, you can stay. But hush. I started to create something, and I'm not stopping. Yes, I'll make a good life for myself."

I'm not going to watch my life pass me by instead of living it. It would be like living your life on one leg, when you have two. And I have to admit it's Olen who made me want to run and dance. And I clamor loudly to get it in my head:

"So what if it's not him!"

Then, I upload my novel: So what if nobody likes it! I'm already a failure so ... It's as if a door opened releasing what was locked inside. The truth crushes me. Fuck it. I think that's how I'm going to put it. The "fuck it" will remind me that I don't owe anybody anything, nobody owes me anything, and that I'm not that weak.

I turn around facing the bed: fears coming out from under the mattress, and I dust them gently having them sit around me. Now hush, I'll throw the bomb that might just be a damp fire-cracker, but ... fuck it. For now, it makes me giggle. And following Liza's advice, "it can be anything but do something", I post my novel online on the most popular of self-publishing sites. There. One thing out of the way. Take that Olen, and the world, take that. Or as Lion King's Timon would say, "If the world turns its back on you, you turn your back on the world."

Right, next, I send a concise email to Paul where I apologize, but I quit. I'm not there for him, he deserves better and I'm sincere. I don't say it, but it's also a way for me to distance myself from Olen.

I had a comfortable life. But it was so unlike me. Could I lead a slightly less comfortable life but one that's better suited for me? Without this fame or fortune madness, just a life where I wake up happy. There'll be good days and bad days. Do less but better. With more of me to go around.

Could this be the beginning of Hakuna Matata?

Chapter 28

The next morning, I have a terrible headache, and my thoughts on Olen aren't any clearer. Accusing me of being a desperate girl who needs to be told that someone loves her every five minutes? Apologizing for the psychodrama at the Festival? Candice do something, anything. Alright then. I take my laptop and look up Olen's number. Cards on the table, somehow or other, we'll see.

"Hi, Candice.

- Hi, Olen."

Awkward silence.

"Listen, I wanted to talk to you ... First of all, I wanted to apologize for my behaviour last time. I ... actually it would be better if I saw you. Explaining over the phone is ... hard."

Long silence.

"I need time to think, Candice. About us. About a lot of things. "

Those words said in a nonchalant manner, drop like a stone, heavy on my heart and finishes breaking it into pieces.

"You need time to think?

- Yes. Don't you ever need that, to think?"

The icy tone makes me shiver and I'm lost for words. How can you get everything so wrong? I slide to the ground, against my bed, where my fears sat around me, patting me on the head, muttering, you see, we told you.

"Candice, are you there?

- Yes. "

That's my problem. What am I still doing here? Why hasn't God put me out of my my misery? God doesn't exist. He wouldn't have designed a creature like Olen to, then, give him my heart. It's so unfair and cruel to give men your heart. The sun setting on my world was fast approaching. And there was no luminescent plankton to help me find my way.

"Goodbye, Olen."

And I hung up. I start to giggle nervously. Is it possible ? My life isn't like a movie, but an old Z series that don't hold a candle to a telenovela. My life is worthy of a script, the first three pages of which were flicked through only to be thrown in the trash. Last night, I thought I managed to get things in order, that everything was going to kick off, that pushing my fears aside would be enough. But I was wrong about Olen. He really went dark side.

I'm choking. I rush to the window to open it, and stay there a few minutes gulping in all the air I can. Change of scenery.

When I open my eyes, the sky blinds me. Change of scenery. Yes. I call Dr. Tran to make an appointment, urgently, and I pop a few clothes in a backpack with my passport. I'm ashamed to leave without saying a real goodbye, but I leave a note for Liza.

An hour later, Dr. Tran looks at me and listening to me for over ten minutes now peering over his glasses, taking notes as usual:

"I find that men and women aren't ambitious in their expectations and are content with little. It's hard and tiring to be idealistic in this world.

- tiring ?

- Yes, I feel tired. Like a senior citizen who collapses from within. I thought I was special to him. I'm not special or different. I'm just naive and stupid.

- Don't say that. You have a super power.

- What do you know about super powers?

- George Lucas got his inspiration from samurais and martial art masters for *Star Wars*, if I were you I'd be nice.

- Sorry.

- The press and all ... they're kryptonite.

- I'm Superman?

- You're from another planet, that's for sure. But you have a super power. Hope."

I nod without much conviction, as long as he jabs a few needles where I need them, and prescribes me what I need to sleep on the plane. I want to sleep, to sleep and wake up in France with the birds, with a pain au chocolat full of butter for breakfast. If Olen Van Cliff's my kryptonite, then I have to get as far away from him as I can.

Luckily, there are some tickets for the Paris-New York flight.

I fall asleep a few minutes into the flight: I'm so shattered, and I've cried so much that I slip into a strange dream: I'm back at the New York festival. Someone tell these girls to stop shouting ... But I notice that a giant picture of Olen is looking me up and down from all the screens of Times Square. He's beautiful, and looks at us in all his splendor. A Rudolph Valentino of modern times that crushes us all with his perfect angelic features. Suddenly, his eyes are riveted on me, and I feel crushed. I become so small that he has to bend down to see me and the more he bends down, the smaller I become. I'm alone now, overwhelmed by Olen and his beauty. I wake with a start, my neighbor staring at me strangely. I cover my eyes with my mask, embarrassed. Only a few hours left ... I read a book without much conviction, and swallow my lunch without paying it much attention. The friendliness of the hostesses irritates me more than anything else because they remind me of the blissful and perfect beauty that would define Olen's ideal partner so well. But no, honey: he'll treat you like the last courtesan left, just to prove that he's a man, just to be able to look cool in front of his friends with a girl who seems exotic, and after a few months, he'll dump you at the slightest reprimand on your part. Who would dare contradict Olen Van Cliff? No one. I was right to blow him off. I did well punching the other idiot. I try to convince myself that I have done everything in my power whereas my conscience looks at me idly eyebrow raised. I punch her as well and fall back to sleep after a few pills. Note to self: don't fly in the breakup phase. The risk of losing it is only accentuated by the whole flying tin can thing.

   ***

I'm in Aurillac, and I'm waiting for Grandma. Like the last times when I was a student: in sneakers, jeans, hoodie, and sitting on my suitcase wich is relatively small seeing as I know I have a lot of things in my room at her house. I know she kept it the same. A small woman gets out of a green and yellow van, wrapped in a purple wool sweater and bottle green studded boots.

"You're lucky it's not raining!"

I stand up and hug her tight. She starts to cry, but looks down so as not to show it. I can't help but pull her to me once more. She smells like roses, her favorite perfume, apart from a few more wrinkles, she's doing great.

"*Tu es ravissante.*"

My French is a little rusty.

"What?

- You're pretty. *Belle*. Pretty as a picture.

- Thanks grandma."

And we're talking half English, half French. We *"baragouinons"*, as the French say, but we understand each other. That's the main thing.

"You scared me, you know.

- Why?

- Your message, it wasn't like you.

- I wanted to see my Grandma, it's been a while, what's wrong with that?

- Was it a man that made you want to see me all of a sudden?"

I give her an embarrassed smile. Grandmothers know everything, they're life's warriors. You know the grandmother of Red Riding Hood? I always imagined her with an ax, ambushed in the forest, ready to do battle with any big bad wolf that would deem wise to annoy her. She has no time to make jam, and if the Little Red Riding Hood comes to visit, it's because she was injured in single combat during her latest duel against the wolf.

"He hurt you.

- I'll tell you later. Have you got chocolate?

- Yes honey. I have a whole a stock.

- You're the best, Grandma."

And she broke into her laugh showing beautiful white teeth. I see her from another perspective. The perspective of a woman now. Did she have many lovers before my grandfather? And after Grandpa's death, had she known other men? I'd never noticed before, but despite her farm clothes, Grandma remained very pretty: a clip with a floral pattern in her hair, a pretty scarf, her perfume, and a little lipstick, earrings, small and discrete but which added an extra sparkle to her already glimmering eyes. Or how to remain dignified despite the fact you're ankle-deep in mud. I hope to have inherited some of her genes.

We arrive at the farm: nothing has changed for the most part. I'd changed. I became a New Yorker, well and truly, and my love life now has two monumental failures. Could I live here? Start fresh?

"Come on! Grab your suitcase, we're going to take it upto your room."

Once in my room, I smile. Everything's as I left it: my vanity that I found downright ridiculous when I was a teenager and that, now, delights me. I open the drawer and contemplate my hair brushes, my hair straightener, and the few makeup palettes. I just make out Grandma's presence, as she leans against the door jamb.

"I haven't touched anything.

- I know. It's good to be here. I should have come a long time ago.

- Don't beat yourself up. Look, we're here. We'll make up for the last few years."

She holds me in her embrace, laying her chin on my shoulder, and we both look out onto the garden through the window when it starts to rain.

"Let's get something to eat."

On that note, Granny makes her way down with a bounce in her step, proud of her cooking. Yet, I can't manage to let myself be transported by the smell that reminds me of sunny afternoon amidst the long grass of the garden. I painfully swallow the starter, a garlic soup. Grandma brings out her secret weapon: a delicious mouton stew in puff pastries. I pretend to push my plate away, but Grandma fills it up anyways:

"Go on, I don't want to see anything left on that plate. Appetite comes with eating!"

And it's true. I gobble up half the stew, and three portions of puff pastry. Grandma, looks at me, smiling, and pours me some wine while she asks:

"You like the sauce?

- Yes, it's delicious. You have to give me the recipe.

- Will you have time to cook?

- Alright, alright, you got me. No."

And we burst out laughing while I dip the bread in the sauce and push my plate away, full up.

"There you go, I've put on three kilos in fifteen minutes.

- No you haven't! A few grams at the most. And tomorrow, you'll help me on the farm. I go to the market on Sunday morning. Will you take care of the chickens?

- Of course! I'll come with you to the market.

- You don't have to, if you want to stay here...

- I want to. I want to see something else.

- How many days off do you have?"

I look her in the eye and smile.

"Well, I'm not going to leave you guessing all night. I don't have days off, I resigned. I broke up with a man.

- Wasn't he nice?

- I thought he was. We had some good times. He said nice things...

- You judge a man by his actions."

I try to push Olen's face from my mind. Olen on the lake. Our embrace in that wonderful timeless park. His words did me so much good.

"Is he handsome?

- The beauty of the devil and an angel's smile. The body of a god.

- Oh dear. Do you have a picture?

- No. You'll succumb to his charm.

- That bad?

- Yes.

- Well then don't show me. Tell me.

- I opened my heart to him, with all the fears that were hidden there. And he didn't like it. He doesn't want to see me. I think he saw me in a different light, and he, too, showed another side of him.

- He became cold and distant?

- Yes.

- Pfff. Your grandfather did that to me. After a few months. In my mind, we were going to get engaged, and he thought he could consider other options. I mean, there were a lot of hussies in the village, believe me.

- Wait until you see New York, Grandma. And what did you do?

- I went to Italy for four long weeks to learn Italian.

- Wow... you never told me that!

- I'm telling you now. I wrote a few letters to girlfriends in which I talked about my Italian teacher, a charming and well-educated man. Guy came looking for me in Italy. He was too afraid that I'd get engaged over there.

- How manipulative!! Why didn't I inherit your genes??"

Grandma leans over to stroke my cheek gently, so gently that I get teary-eyed.

"You're like your mother. A cold expression that impresses, but a soft heart... and no filter.

- Grandma... what about you? How are things since the accident?

- Good. Don't worry about me. I'm waiting for God to take me. He takes care of my Sylvia, and of your father while he's waiting for me. And then, there's you, you're here."

I keep her hand in mine, pressed against my cheek.

"Do you mind if I stay here a little while?

- As long as you want.

- You have wifi here? I'll have to check my email at some point.

- Yes, you'll find the code on the box, there. It has its moments and it's a little slow, but it's okay.

- You have a computer?

- No.

- A tablet ?"

She points to the small side-table.

"Yeah, well, tomorrow afternoon, we'll go back to Aurillac, I have a lot of things to show you.

- You want to convert me to gadgets?

- Yes.

- I have my books and my TV.

- When was the last time you went to a bookstore?"

She grumbles fetching some compote.

"Well, you're not going to teach me how to live now, are you?

- If I go back to New York, I'd like to talk to you once a week thanks to the internet. Wouldn't you want to see me every week, to chat? You can do that with a computer or a tablet."

She stops eating her compote, and looks up from her bowl.

"What do you mean 'if' you go back to New York? Are things that bad?

- I... I'll do a little performance overview while I'm here. Why not ... turn a new leaf for a lot of things..."

Grandma considers me in silence, shaking her curly white hair.

"He really hurt you, huh…?

- Yes."

Grandma's the only person I can't lie to.

"You want to watch TV?

- No thanks. I'll unpack my suitcase, take a shower and go to bed. Goodnight, dear Grandma."

I'm ready to pass out due to nervous-fatigue but I slept so much on the plane that I toss and turn, hardly getting any sleep.

Note to self: don't go on the internet when you're depressed. I don't want to shop online, and anyway, I don't even know if they'd deliver here... And I refuse to check my emails ...

I know I came to change scenery, burning bridges but I can't help but rehash it. I know I shouldn't, but I can't resist: I type his name in the browser. I'd barely finished that I was already regretting it. My God, how long has it been since the festival? He must have gone out every night, judging by the number of photos. Olen scoured all places likely to contain pretty girls, models and young actresses. Brunettes, redheads, blondes, he's made the most of it, prolonging the drunken evenings with after parties, always well surrounded and photographed. He really turned a new leaf, when I'm looking at pictures of him having fun and enjoying life, like a jerk... I'm in shock. And the more I look at the photos of Olen smiling, arrogantly, the more it allows me to tear up this bond that I believed we had. It isn't sadness, it's rage bubbling under the surface. Except I've never been good at finding revenge strategies. I scroll through the articles, laying the final blow to my heart and my pride. All these statements, the sweet words, were a small break from his reality. Before he showed his true face to the world. Before showing me his dark side: Olen the megalomaniac hungering after bimbos and admiration from others when he's backed up against the wall.

I feel my blood boil when I see one of the headlines: "Candice takes advantage of Olen Van Cliff's fame to launch her novel!" I'm stunned. How can they bend the truth like that? I hope people won't believe this kind of crap. Unfortunately, I know these kind of sentences are like poison. Does Olen look at these websites? No, I'm sure he doesn't. What can I do? I log on the forum section and go back to the comments:

"You're a bunch of haters! You don't even know her! I bet you didn't even read the novel, how can you judge it like that???"

What a bunch of morons. I close the page, and try my breathing techniques. Everything is fine. Everything is fine in the world that is mine.

Damn, what am I going to do now? I could leave New York. At least for a few years. Two years would be enough for people to forget about me. Candice, try to get some sleep! This might be the perfect opportunity to go to Paris... I could start a blog. Like an American in Paris telling of her life. I like to read... Apparently you can stay for free at Shakespeare and Company. And it would allow me to be closer to Grandma, come and see her a little more often. What about Liza? And Jo? And your career? Yeah not a great career ... you could say that I'm back to square one, and as for friends they can get on well enough without me. Yes but can you get on without them? I feel stupid and alone. The only solution that my brain comes up with is to sleep: so I fall asleep after a few hours with my head on the perfectly soft pillow.

The next morning, I don't know if I have the night's sleep to thank, or the mist rising in the courtyard and the birds singing softly on the ledge of the well (which gives me the impression of being in a Disney movie), but I feel soothed. I look at my watch: six in the morning. I hesitate a moment and then finally I leave the room still in pajamas. Grandma's door is closed, so I tiptoe downstairs so as not to wake her. I freeze upon my arrival in the kitchen. A man with graying hair is silently going through the drawer and pulls out a knife putting it on the worksurface. He hasn't seen or heard me. I feel my heart start to beat erratically in my chest. Did someone follow us from the station? I was probably easy to spot, me, the typical tourist. I grab a copper pan that was hanging on the wall and wield it as I get closer. If I aim for the head, at his age he could die. Don't do anything stupid, Candice. I approach cautiously. Alright, go for the legs. If I take them out from under him so that he falls, I can tie him up. Fuck, does Grandma even have string? I get closer still on tiptoe, I'm less than a few feet away now. Otherwise, I can pull a Kevin Costner from *The Bodyguard*, I block him with a chair. Suddenly, the man turns around and screams upon seeing me. I brandish the pot a little higher, and he puts a hand on his heart.

"Shit, what the hell are you doing here?"

The man raises both hands in the air, and seems to run out of breath. He waves towards the table. I realize that I spoke in English and he may not have understood. I give him a nod indicating he can sit, still brandishing my pan. He drops onto the chair, breathless, one hand on his heart. It was at that moment that Grandma came storming into the kitchen, panicked, and takes the man into her arms.

"Who the hell is that???

- It's Jacques... he's... he's... he's my boyfriend.

- You have a lover?

- Yes... well, no! My… *amoureux* you see.

- You're in love ?

- Well, yes. In fact, we've been living together for a few months now."

I'm flabbergasted. My grandmother? In love? MY GRANDMOTHER ? With a lover? My brain, after receiving that scare, is in shock and refuses to picture it.

"Well, what, you only warned me the day before yesterday that you were coming, and you weren't in any state to listen, so I thought... well it was a bit soon.

- But... you..."

Anticipating my question, Grandma answers instead of Jacques who was about to:

"He came to meet me when you were asleep.

- What a… little sneak!"

I'm almost impressed. Poor Jacques looks at me and raises his thumb questioningly at me, to which I answer with a laugh, that becomes infectious seeing as Grandma starts laughing too.

"Tu peux lui dire de baisser la casserole maintenant?*

- Sorry, Jacques."

*Can you tell her to lower the pan please?

And I approach him taking him into my arms in a typical American hug. He blushes, surprised.

"Sorry Jacques, I thought you were a thief. Of course you can come back," I tell him.

- No no no. We're going to spend a few days just us girls first. To make up for lost time.

- I chased after your grandmother for six months before she accepted to go on a date with me. I can wait another week.

- Oh, that doesn't surprise me, we can be tough in this family. You ... You should stay for breakfast, Jacques, okay?"

I then pull out a chair so that Grandma can sit next to him while I make coffee.

"I ... I bought croissants and pains au chocolat.

- Oh thank you, Jacques."

Ok, now I feel really guilty. I try to make small talk with Jacques by asking lots of questions and after a few minutes he has completely relaxed and even manages to speak in a coherent English.

"So, ladies, what's your plan for today?

- We're going shopping.

- Ah... pretty dresses?"

He winks at me and gazes lovingly at my grandmother who blushes a little. My God, I didn't hear anything last night, and to say they had sex. Wow. I'll never wrap my head around it.

"No, we're going to buy a small computer or a tablet for Grandma so that she can get in touch with me easily.

- I already have a phone.

- Yes, but with a computer you can watch movies online, chat with someone as if they were here.

- If you can convince her, hats off to you. I had to court her by writing her letters."

I burst out laughing.

"Yes, Miss Candice, exactly, letters, poems, all the palava... like in the olden days!

- That's so cute.

- Alright, that's enough, let's go shopping."

On that note, Grandma starts to clear the table while I stand up and go to get dressed. From the corner of my eye, I see Jacques steal a kiss from Grandma before doing the dishes. A few minutes later, after feeding the chickens and rabbits, we leave for Aurillac.

"I'm sorry I warned you so late.

- No no, not to worry. We're adults, we can survive a week without seeing each other.

- Jacques seems nice.

- Yes. He likes to drive me up the wall sometimes. Well, we're going to treat ourselves this morning, what do you say? We'll get a manicure," She says, taking my hand affectionately.

Two hours later, we're settled in armchairs for a pedicure and a well-deserved massage: I managed to convince Grandma. I bought her a tablet. It was only natural for us to sit in a comfortable chair so that I could explain how to video chat. Now, I close my eyes for a few minutes to enjoy the massage.

And then I turn my head to look at Grandma, and how dolled-up she'd made herself after seeing Jacques. But she frowns typing away on her tablet. She was no longer grumbling about computers. That was something. Something else was going on though.

"What are you doing Grandma?

- I'm reading...

-What are you reading? Jean Paul Sartre to be pulling a face like that?

- I bought an ebook at random, based on the recommendations of the "users".

- What is it?

- *Fifty Shades of Grey* ... Well, well ... isn't life complicated for some people…"

It's been three days since I got here. Wearing my muddy boots and the dress I've had since I was fifteen, I no longer feel like a fish out of water, I'm in my element. Blacky, looks at me with an evil glint in her eye. She's the only one I haven't managed to tame. The other hens let themselves be held and stroked rather easily. Grandma shakes her head, looking at me:

"They're chickens, my darling, not kittens.

- I know, but I can't help it, it reminds me of when I was little.

- Yes, you had a habit of naming them."

We load the truck with crates of eggs, some vegetables and rabbits before leaving for the market in Aurillac. It's mostly due to her rabbit stew that Grandma has such success at the market. Just imagine, it's ten in the morning, you're strolling through the market, and you smell the delicious scent of sauce. A nice lady smelling like roses, with a clip in her immaculate white hair, smiles at you kindly and asks how things are going. Provided that you're feeling a bit lazy, you succumb and buy a portion of rabbit stew ...

and Grandma makes you pay ten times more than anywhere else. One hell of a business woman, right?

Grandma didn't really need my help with the stand, so for the first few hours, when there weren't many people, I saunter through the flower market just next to us, true festival of bright colors and incredible scents. I don't know anything about flowers but I want to buy them all to arrange part of the garden. I take some photos to send to Liza and Jo. I was very laconic since my arrival at Grandma's so I appease my guilt with an enthusiastic and colorful message. I go back to help Grandma with the stand and when we sold all the stew, she says to me in passing:

"What do you say about going to visit the castle of Pesteils?

- Yes!"

The castle stands proud not far from Aurillac and I laugh when we stop in front of the building whose creeping ivy is seeking to cover the walls of light stone.

"A castle straight out of a fairy tale!"

We spend the afternoon touring the inside, looking at the tapestries, the dungeon which dates back to the Hundred Years' War, and I can already picture my next novel: yes, that's what I'll do. Stay here for a few months and write about whatever I feel like. No matter if nobody reads it. A princess who killed princes. Right, nope, no one would read that. A princess that none of the king's court liked? Why not. A terrible and capricious princess who even causes a hundred year long war. Wow, calm down Candice. Grandma sets the tour guide down while we make our way out and we take a photo in souvenir in front of the fortress.

"Thanks Grandma, this was a great idea.

- Yes, I'm glad. We had a good day.

- And I'll take this opportunity to visit the area.

- You can stay as long as you want, you know that," She says, slamming the car door.

Grandma parks the truck in front of the farm when my heart stops.

I get out of the truck, shaking and furious. Candice stay calm, you've got this.

Olen was sitting on the woodpile, wearing sneakers and shapeless jeans, a backpack at his feet. Bags under his eyes, he gets up upon seeing us. I'm not going to let him call the shots, out of the question:

"Two questions: how did you find me and what are you doing here?

- Liza tipped me off and... I came for your three words.

Chapter 29

He made me lose my composure. Three words... Grandma lays a hand on my shoulder with a worried look.

"It's him, isn't it? I'll get the gun.

- No, please don't Grandma, go inside and make us some herbal tea.

- Are you sure?

- Yes, please."

Grandma passes by me and stops next to Olen staring at him. Uncomfortable, he smiles, bringing out his dimples, but it's not working. Not with Grandma, who then resumes her slow and determined walk through the mud to the house.

"Can I come in?

- No. Leave.

- Three words. I came here for three words, and I want to hear them.

- It's over."

He was speechless. Perfect, now you know how much it hurts. Rejected, abandoned and you now know what it feels like. Now, go away Olen. However he doesn't leave, doesn't back up, instead he stares into my eyes,

"I don't believe you.

- Alright. Actually what I wanted to tell you would be more than three words. You don't want to find happiness Olen, you want to feel the power you have on people. And you know what? You have none on me. Did you really think I was under your spell? I'm never under anyone's spell! For a moment of happiness with you, I have days upon days of doubt and fear. That's not love. And playing with others and their feelings that isn't seduction.

- I never played with you. I wasn't sure of myself, but after that weekend at my mother's... everything changed. I wanted to change for you. And that's when you went crazy.

- I didn't go crazy, it's just that... I saw the rift between us.

-What rift?

- Look around Olen and listen. Everyone says we don't belong together, a difference in money, in fame, in backgrounds, and success.

- What?

- That might be the problem, you know: you live in your little world, your world that has nothing to do with reality. You don't see what's real."

It's as if I'd slapped him. But he takes my face in both his hands:

"Who cares what people say. We're above that, you hear me. Us, this thing between us, that's real."

I gently take his hands off my face.

"And that night, when all my doubts came to haunt me, you told me to remember my place. Well, maybe this is where I belong.

- What amongst chickens?

- I saw you with that redhead. I saw how she looked at you, I saw how you looked at her. I don't want to wait around just to be cheated on. I couldn't bear it. Your betrayal... coupled with public humiliation.

- What Eddy? I would never! Instead, you should be happy.

- What? You want me to be happy at seeing you making eyes at other women?

- No! I... You told me to find a charitable cause. I've done it. I've founded one. I created a foundation for education.

- Wha... What?

- Yes... I wanted to tell you the night of the festival, but I didn't get the chance..."

I bite my lip. I didn't give him time to.

"It's a foundation having to do with the education of young people from families with problems... like me.

- Wow... Olen... that's great.

- Eddy didn't have time to call me back before that, but she organized a charity dinner on invitation...

- At 225 Warren Street...

- Yes... We raised over five hundred thousand dollars that night."

I take a step back in silence. I feel so stupid, relieved but still mortified.

"I don't believe you. I don't have faith in your sincerity. I can't believe in the sincerity of someone who lives in a world of illusions. You're surrounded by leeches and women. Actually you made the most of it over the last few weeks.

- Let me convince you. A lot of things have become clear to me, I fired Dennis. I understood much later who that man really was, the one who wanted to take the damn picture, so thank you. You helped me avoid a lot of trouble. I... I didn't grow up surrounded by righteousness, kindness and benevolence. My heart isn't used to it. And I need your good and benevolent heart to learn. Teach me."

It's only been a few seconds and I'm ready to give in. To throw myself into his arms. But what about the peace I've managed to find here.

"You'll cheat on me. Someday.

- No. I went out to forget and..., " he adds ruefully, looking at his feet, "to make you jealous."

"Well, it worked, except for believing that I was going to come running, that's misjudging me.

- I wanted to hurt you.

- Job well done. I called to pick up the pieces, or at least to end it on good terms.

- I know.

- And you pushed me away. You needed to think.

- I know it was wrong to hurt you like that. But you hurt me too.

- What?

- You abandoned me!

- What are you talking about?

- You left, you ran away that night. What did people think, left there alone, like an idiot? I get there with the most sublime woman on the face of the planet, we fight at the entrance, in front of everyone, and she ups and leaves me. I've always felt alone, and I thought I'd never feel that again. And, in the end, I never felt so alone as that night. You... you abandoned me."

My heart aches with shame and sorrow.

"So yes, when you called me, I tried to delay it. I didn't want for us to be over. I... I was planning to come over during the weekend so we could talk.

- You said it... with such detachment. It was almost a sneer.

- I know. I 'm sorry. I wanted you to hurt as much as I did in that moment."

He pulls me to him once more.

"I tried to give you the best. I introduced you to all my friends, we had a great weekend, we get along well. We're good together."

His body pressed to mine ends up breaking my will... almost. With incredible effort, I gently push him away and tell him as delicately as possible,

"Yes nothing but us. But being with someone isn't being just the both of you. It's being together, in the big wide world."

I shake my head,

"You leave first thing tomorrow."

He watches me and after an indecipherable silence, asks:

"Can I take a shower? It was a long journey.

- Yes. Follow me."

We enter the house and Olen follows me up the stairs in silence while I hear Grandma busying herself in the kitchen downstairs.

I wait fifteen minutes in the hallway and go into my room.

Obviously, he's still shirtless. He's really trying everything to get you to give in. Candice. I mark a pause, he still has a huge effect on me, but I don't show it. I try to seem indifferent, but he's not fooled. I bite my lip. I fix up the bed, patting it with a ridiculous amount of concentration.

"You can sleep here tonight.

- What about you?

- I'll sleep downstairs, on the couch."

He closes the distance between us and puts a hand on my shoulder.

"I'm sorry for telling you to remember your place: it was tactless of me. You belong by my side.

- No.

- Yes.

- I'm too tired, I don't have enough energy to get into a debate with you. Your bed."

He gets dangerously close.

"Are you tired?

- Yes. Very.

- What did you do today?

- I went to sell eggs and vegetables at the market.

- Did you sell out?

- Yes.

- How much did you get?"

I know what he's playing at, he's trying to prolong this conversation.

"I don't know, fifty euros.

- Wow. You'll be able to buy a new apartment with that.

- I don't need your sarcasm.

- What do you need?"

And before I could so much as move, he brings me tenderly into his embrace. I want to give in, but I feel one last barrier: the fear of suffering, silent, stiff and throbbing which is keeping my heart in its trembling claws.

"I know I can be an immature and irresponsible idiot, but you're good for me. You make me become a better person. I'll protect you from the evil journalists, from my ex wife, from everyone.

- And who's going to protect me from you?

- I've changed."

I search his face: yes, he'd changed. He'd lost weight, his features were drawn. I see a flash of Olen walking through his apartment, alone, beer cans littering the floor, and picking up a slice of cold pizza. Maybe he suffered a bit too... I slowly break away from his embrace, realizing that I feel something other than satisfaction. I feel hope. Out of the question!

"Goodnight, Olen.

- Hold on."

He takes ahold of my face and puts his forehead to mine.

"Please, if you have to leave me, I have one last favor to ask. Spend the night with me.

- What?

- I'm not asking you to sleep with me, even if I really want that, and it would lighten the mood. Just have a drink with me."

I think about it for a while. What's the catch?

"Okay, fine. I'll go and ask Grandma.

- What time does she get up in the morning?

- Usually around six. But don't worry ... you can leave a bit later.

- Yes. But in the meantime, we're going to spend an evening together."

I try to decipher his expression once more, but there's no trace of his smile that brings out his dimples. Just a polite smile and that... is it possible? Almost submissive. I go down the stairs and find Grandma in the kitchen:

"Your friend staying the night?

- Yes. He's leaving tomorrow.

- It's him, isn't it ?

- Yes.

- He's very handsome. The face of an angel and the eyes of the devil.

- Yes. He's handsome.

- And smart. He knows how to use carnal pleasures to keep women around, like flies. I know those type of men well.

- Oh, Grandma!

- Right so, I'll leave you two to eat. You need to talk.

- Yes and no. He leaves tomorrow.

- I saw how you looked at him, and how he looks at you. Those type of men don't fall in love easily. They have all the women in the world at their feet.

- That's for sure...

- You have to send them packing from time to time. Like parrots. You have to throw them to the ground sometimes, otherwise they get too much confidence and start pecking!"

I like her wisdom. She knows about life, and doesn't hide the truth. She smiles calmly as if she has all the answers, and has the power to protect me from anything that could cause me pain.

"I love you Grandma, you're a true Hakuna Matata.

- What?

- No, nothing.

- Well, there's mushroom soup, and we've got some bread and cheese left.

- It's going to be fine. Thank you, Grandma."

She kisses me on the cheek making a loud smacking noise, holding me tight.

"What about you?

- Well, I'll go out with Jacques.

- Oh ... I see ! Well ... have fun.

- And you, be careful, don't be fooled. He's charming, but that's not enough.

- I did tell you he was handsome.

- He's to die for darling. To die for."

She kisses me on the forehead and after I hug her, she leaves. It's only when I hear the van start that I go back to the stairs,

"Olen! You can come down, now!"

I see his blond head emerge from the darkness, peering around he asks:

"The coast clear?

- Grandma went out ...but your still on dangerous grounds."

I busy myself in the kitchen by setting the table and reheating the mushroom soup.

"Can I help?

- Get the napkins from the cupboard to the left of the fridge."

Olen obediently does as he's told while I feel him watching me out of the corner of his eye.

"Has your grandmother always lived here?

- She lived in the village itself before, but my grandfather inherited the land from his family. So, when they got married, they came to live here.

- Did she have any other children besides your mother?

- No.

- And have you thought about what I said? To get someone to come out every week to check up on her?

- Actually ..."

I take the pot full of soup to the table, trying not to spill any.

"That won't be necessary ... She has a boyfriend.

- Wow that's great, meeting someone at her age!

- I think he's a bit younger than her."

Olen starts laughing wholeheartedly and I feel my heart ache. That smile, that lightness, his head falling back slightly. The face of an angel and the devil's eyes.

"Thank you for letting me stay the night," He says, taking my hand.

His hand gripping mine, I feel its warmth creep into my flesh. God, I missed that.

"Can you pass the salt please?

- Of course."

And flustered, I pass him the salt with shaky hands.

"How's your mother?

- Fine ... and besides, she complimented me on your novel."

I stop, the salt shaker hovering over my plate.

"My novel? Your mother read my novel?"

The thought of Chrysta leaving heinous messages on forums about me, and picturing her face, always so dignified, crumpled with rage makes me giggle. But I restrain myself and ask politely,

"Oh, and did she like it?

- Yes. She even told her friend about it, a literary critic. She called me to tell me she didn't like you but ... you were special and talented. And that you need to keep special people in your life."

I'm speechless. Though, admittedly, I was deeply affected by her words. She acknowledges my work, that's something.

"That's nice of her. How's Paul? I resigned.

- I know. He told me.

- I feel sorry for him, I hope he finds someone good that can bring it.

- Yes, he found someone, not as good at multitasking as you, but he's good.

- That's great, I'm happy for him."

I eat in silence, and he seems to be searching for a topic of conversation amongst the bread crumbs.

"And how's Jo?

- She's fine, the little family's doing fine. Ilan's making a new album, he's a huge homebody, because he's going to leave on tour in three months, and that's about it.

- Family changes everything."

I get up cautiously to start clearing, but he stops me.

"I read the beginning of your novel.

- And what did you think?

- It's a good vitriolic portrait ... of everything. Of the business, of easy money, of the world and what it's become."

He pauses.

"Paul would like to make it into a TV show.

- A TV show?!

- Yes, there are some characters that you can really develop. I love the former movie star, the woman struggling to return to the front of the stage.

- Yes, me too. She may be cruel, but you can understand her, she's angry.

- Yes, I think you're going to get offers.

- I'll call Paul first, it's the least I could do. However, given the time difference, he might need to call me in the middle of the night to get ahold of me here.

- You'll ... see to it when you get back."

I look at him silently while getting two yogurts. He bites his lip.

"You are coming back?

- I haven't decided yet.

- You can't just drop everything like that !!

- And why not? Both you and Liza, in fact, all of you, you're always telling me to take risks. There you go. I'm taking a risk."

He shakes his head, running a hand through his hair nervously. I almost withdrew satisfaction from it. Yes, Olen, you can't do anything about it, I'm not under your control. Hurts, doesn't it?

"And what are you going to do for a living here?

- I'll go to Paris. I've wanted to go for a long time.

- Visiting and living in a city are two completely different things.

- I'll start by visiting and then I'll live there.

- And what will you do ?

- I'll be a waitress, or I'll write ... become a journalist. An English teacher ! I'll see when the time comes !

- You want to teach English to the French? Good luck !

- Come on, I'd like to see you try to learn French!

- Ah, *mais mademoiselle*, it would be a pleasure to learn *avec vous*.

- *C'est vrai? Tu voudrais des cours de langue petit monsieur?*"*

Olen's stunned.

"How do you say 'I just got an erection' in French?

- *Va te brosser.**

- *Va te...*"

I snigger.

"That's not it, is it?

- No. It's an elegant way of saying no."

And finishing my yogurt, I get up but Olen's quicker and he clears the table.

"Well... good night...

- Wait. You promised to spend the evening with me.

- We've talked enough, don't you think?

- So let's drink!"

I think about it. What's the catch? Ok, Candice, be nice. This evening is the last you'll spend together. You'll never see him

*Really ? You'd like lessons in French, young man?

again. Never again. I sit on the couch, where I settle cautiously in a corner, and he follows suit.

"Okay then."

We dig up a bottle of rum and Olen removes the cork which emits a triumphant pop.

"To us!

- To our respective success."

And we do the shot.

"To your career as a writer which is off to a good start.

- Writer, screenwriter... let's go crazy!"

And we empty yet another glass of rum. Olen pulls a face.

"Tell me, your grandmother isn't a lightweight, is she? She drinks this as a shot, right?

- Given the dust on the shot glasses, I'd say she uses a cup.

- A whole cup?

- Yep! One hell of a grandma "

I do another shot, slightly euphoric.

"Something tells me you take after your grandmother.

- Maybe!"

The visual of Olen's forlorned face staring at his plate of food comes back to me. I already beat him that day.

"You're very sure of yourself on that one, dear little Candice.

- Oh you wanna bet?"

He refills our glasses.

"Do you want to play never have I ever?

- Hmm, I knew there was a catch.

- There's no catch, just the truth. If you lose, you give me a second chance. If you win ... what do you want if you win?

- You have to learn French!

- Alright."

He gets out his phone and types away for a while.

"What are you doing?

- I'm... getting inspiration for questions."

I watch him for a minute, snuggled up and hug a cushion to me. I feel relaxed, soothed. Where did it go wrong between us? Candice, shut up.

"I'll start: never have I ever cried after sex."

We look at each other in silence, then we burst out laughing.

"Oh, we're badass.

- So... Olen Van Cliff... I never lied to a girl to get into her pants.

- Ouch... but no... I hope you're not too disappointed."

I avoid answering, and push my hair back.

"Let's see... I've never... flirted with the girlfriend of a friend or an acquaintance."

He shakes his head and rolling his eyes, empties his glass.

He casually asks me looking at his nails,

"I never liked being spanked."

I blushed, and empty my glass.

"I never regretted sleeping with someone."

He grimaces, emptying his glass.

"So ... Miss Candice ... let's see, I never watched porn.

- That's low. Really low," I say, doing my shot.

"There are no rules, dear Candice.

- Alright, in that case I was never given a footjob."

He empties his glass after pulling a face.

"It happened once, it was so weird, I swear. Well... my turn... I've never stuffed my bra.

- Pfff... I was fifteen, ok? High school was hard."

And I empty my glass, closing my eyes. My throat begins to burn. Hopefully, I don't throw up.

"Alright, my turn... Olen, have you... No sorry, I never... tried to see my neighbor in her underwear?"

For a minute, I'm sure he's going to snicker and say that he never had to, as his bed was never empty... however, he empties his glass without saying a word.

"I never put a dick between my breasts."

I suddenly feel very hot. I see Olen's face above me, his body against mine, and my nails on his back. I sit up taking a deep breath, and empty my glass. I see his lips stretch into a thin, evil smile through my glass. Olen Van Cliff's asking for war. I feel myself inexorably sink into the couch, while the heat continues to rise. I take off my jacket, under Olen's watchful eye. I say to him:

"I never fantasized about another woman in the presence of my other half."

He marks a pause... and doesn't so much as blink. Then he leans over slowly and empties his glass. I knew it. Victory. I stick my chin out slightly, and smile sardonically in turn.

"Never with you. With my ex-wife."

We look at each other in silence.

"I never used a sex toy. "

I drink. I was expecting that one. He slides his hands down my calves and while he leans over he gently pulls me towards him. No. Resist. I whisper in his ear while he looks at me, his face mere inches from mine:

"I never cheated on anyone."

He doesn't stop his progression, and grabs my wrists to position me under him. I'm no longer master of my body, the lips of my dry mouth part as he puts all his weight on my hips.

"You want to make me out to be the big bad wolf, sugar, but if a wolf leads a pack, and loves freedom he has only one companion. Only one."

He then lays his full length on me, and whispers:

"Clarissa and I were separated when we met, you and I. And you, I've never cheated on you. But... we all make mistakes. Especially at sixteen, right?

- Not all of us had an all you can eat buffet of promiscuous models and actresses offered to us at the age of sixteen.

- Are you jealous? You wouldn't like it. There's not much to get your teeth into."

I shove him away angrily and jump to my feet:

"Always an out, huh? "

My head starts spinning: I collapse and fall into a black hole trying to cling to the two stars that shine in Olen's face.

Chapter 30

I don't recognize the smell of my sheets. But they're so soft. I keep my eyes closed, tossing and turning under the duvet. Bits of last night come back to me. Olen ... rum ... rage ... I've never been that drunk in my life. I hear someone moving beside my bed: an aspirin starts to bubble in a glass of water. I open one eye and my head starts spinning. What...? I'm in a huge bed, with silk sheets, white walls, a huge bouquet of peonies on a marble fireplace. Huge blue curtains frame the windows where I see cars and buses honking. I have to blink three times to see it, through the fumes of alcohol that are wearing off, the Eiffel Tower. The fucking Eiffel Tower! I'm in Paris ?

"Did you sleep well ?"

I'm lying on my stomach, offering a spectacular view of my ass. I grab the phone sitting on the marble shelf next to the bed and throw it at his face with all my might. He used a pillow as a shield on which the phone crashes.

"Damn it! You kidnapped me?"

And I lunge at him trying to land a blow with my pillow, but he lifts me from the ground to better pin me to the bed, like a wrestler. I remain on the bed for a few seconds, stunned.

"You lost!"

That sentence helps bring back the last of my memory. He repeats it, insistent:

"You lost. So..."

And he let's go of me, cautiously.

"I'm entitled to a second chance. Can I at least try? I just chose another location. A more ... romantic one."

I glare daggers at him, getting up slowly. I'm completely aware that I'm topless and in panties, but now every cell of my skin is radiating anger. He raises both hands in a sign of surrender.

"And if I don't succeed ... You don't have to worry about me leaving, the airport is even closer so that I can disappear from your life. And I can get you a ticket for a flight back to Aurillac," I don't stop my slow approach, seeing red.:

"You knew I was going to lose.

- Yes.

- How?"

He looks at me with a sad smile.

"Genes. It's in my genes to hold my liquor better than you.

- How did we get here?

- I booked an uber during the game.

- When you looked at your phone?

- Yes.

- My grandmother ? Did you tell her?

- We left as soon as you passed out. I left a note saying that you weren't feeling very well. Here."

And he hands me a tablet already connected to the internet.

"If you want to call her, tell her you're okay ... I don't know if the phone's still working."

I rip the tablet out of his hands, furious, and return to the bed. Typing in my Skype username and password , I empty the glass of aspirin in one go. Phew, Grandma installed Skype as I recommended. As soon as she sees me online, she calls me.

"Candice! Are you okay?

- Yes, I have a huge hangover, but I'm fine. I passed out last night. I think, partly due to my emotional state. Everything's fine.

- You emptied my bottle of rum I see!

- Uh ... yes, sorry.

- Were you celebrating something?

- Uh ... no. Not at all. We'll spend the day here, in Paris. We'll relax, and then ... I'll be back tomorrow, probably.

- Well ... if anything changes, you let us know.

- Yes of course, say hi to Jacques for me.

- Yes darling, enjoy Paris. And make that boy work for it, teach him not to let a girl like you go!"

I switch the tablet off, relieved. A good thing done. Well, Olen's right, I lost. True to my word, I'll give him a second chance, in Paris. IN PARIS !! It could be worse. I admit I'm getting as excited as a kid on Christmas, the Eiffel Tower's taunting me.

"Olen?

- Yes ?

- Did you bring clothes for me, from my room?

- I got a jacket on the way out, your pumps and ... the dress you were already wearing.

- You didn't think to bring a change of underwear by any chance?"

He points to three large bags that I hadn't seen sitting on a round seat next to a vanity. He has a little proud smile that warms my heart:

"Thank you ..." I say, smiling.

That smile seems to give him wings because he perkily throws over his shoulder while returning to his room,

"I'll let you take a shower and get dressed. We're going to grab breakfast."

He closes the double doors of the suite. I check my phone, because he even thought of bringing my purse. Now, I'm totally impressed. After a quick shower, I spread the clothes he selected for me out on the bed: Chantal Thomas underwear, jeans and an Isabelle Marant blouse, adorable red sneakers made by 1083 and a red trench coat from Comptoir des Cotonniers. But how did he get these clothes when it's barely ten in the morning? A personal shopper had to be tasked with opening the shops before he got there, and all that, while I was sleeping. Or maybe the hotel, is a palace with a private shop ... I run my finger across the knotted Hermes scarf around my neck. Had I missed luxury? A little, I have to admit. Any of dad's fortune, the money from the house, I put it all in the bank to forget about it, and I got hung up on work, with dad as a role model, hard working, the only sure thing in this world. But ... what about fun? And what if it was time to have fun again? Olen interrupts my thoughts:

"Nice ... does it fit okay? Did I get it right?

- I think you've seen it all, from every angle."

I detect a slight blush creep over his cheeks. Obviously, he knows me like the back of his hand.

"Even the shoes fit perfectly."

Shut it, Candice, seriously. Olen smiles, content.

"Thank you. You have very good taste. I wouldn't have chosen better.

- Are you hungry?"

A few minutes later, we're in the living room of the palace and I already wolfed down a croissant, a pain au chocolat, an omelette, and several coffees. Olen looks at me in admiration and the people at the next table, an elegant elderly couple, are shocked by my man-sized appetite. I finish my orange juice in one go.

"Are you still hungry ?"

I burst out laughing.

"Yes, but I'll save room for lunch."

I feel so embarrassed at this luxurious and cozy environment, where everyone almost apologizes for breathing. Olen must feel it because he leans over:

"Why do you care what these people think?

- I don't know, it's so pretentious.

- It's norms. Each society has their set of norms. Look. It's your job as a writer to observe, isn't it? That doesn't mean you have to be a part of it and become like that. I take what I like, the rest I don't really care about."

And it's true that Olen also stands out with a simple pair of jeans and a white shirt, sneakers, and tousled hair.

"Besides, we're all different, all unique. Some prefer to fit in, to fit the damned social norms. Not us."

He takes my hand and leans over the table,

"Got it?"

I nod. Olen Van Cliff decides to seriously get on my case.

"Why did you kidnap me Olen?

- I saw you on that farm, you can't settle for that."

I brush away the few crumbs around my plate with the tip of my finger. He annoys me, always being right. Obviously, after a few weeks, I would have been bored. I keep my gaze cast down, and I know my mouth turns into a pout:

"It was a very comfortable situation.

- You little brat, you never admit you're wrong, do you?"

He leans over the table and lowers his voice:

"You like comfort and certainty too much, my little Candice. That's what that farm is to you. Love, life, that's not it. That's your problem, as soon as things start to get hard, you retreat into your shell and there's no one there. Do you really want to be an empty shell one day, little hedgehog? "

I open my mouth to protest, but have nothing to say to that. It was true. Horribly true.

We walk next to each other, brushing slightly against one another, and I let Olen guide me. Paris is an open air museum where people discuss everything. Should you say chocolate croissant or pain au chocolat? It taunts us, Americans, on the other side of the Atlantic, with its Eiffel tower, never stumbling, just light and so chic ... and she's calling to us. It's different from Rome, the matron firmly rooted in its history. It's different from Venice whining on its lost past, it's different from Edinburgh, Empress of the North, rough but never haughty. It's not the joie de vivre. The bed of the Seine is lined with dead bodies, you'd know if you took interest in history. Paris breathes provocation, always alluring, but never vulgar. "Fluctuat nec mergitur" is its motto, it's tossed by the waves but never sinks. Paris, the proud, has injuries, but responds with mockery to all self-righteous people who would seek to cover the nude statues in the garden of the Louvre. This is Olen's favourite city: provocative, a little light but a philosopher when he hasn't partied too hard, they have so much in common! He obviously planned everything and we enter the Louvre through a security line to contemplate the Mona Lisa and her eternal smile for a few minutes only. Then Olen takes my hand, leading the way out,

"Come, I'll show you somewhere special."

We arrive at a church not far from the Louvre.

"This is the church of Saint Germain l'Auxerrois. Church of artists."

I'm surprised that Olen knows churches outside of Notre Dame. I let him carry on, passionate.

"It dates back to the seventh century, can you imagine?

- Wow... Like... before the Romans?

- Well,the French aren't the most peaceful people in the world, while the church was destroyed and rebuilt over the wars. The porch dates from the fifteenth century. Look."

I'm impressed and moved by his passion for architecture. He shows me the gargoyles of the buttresses, with its bestiary of birds, griffins, dogs, cats, rats, bears, and wolves... We go in and I ask:

"How come you know Paris so well?

- I shot a movie in Paris.

- In French?

- No, an American movie by an American director, a love story in Paris.

- Typically American.

- Yes."

We halt before the statue of Mary, naked with three pebbles, long blond hair framing her face. She's so moving in this chapel which serves as an encasement that I press myself against him.

"Magnificent, isn't she?

- She seems so vulnerable.

- But never fragile... ," he says, taking me in his arms.

I dodge the kiss by pressing my cheek against his shoulder.

"It's here, that artists displayed in the Louvre, had the privilege of being buried, the royal church, hence the nickname of the church of Saint Denis of genius and talent.

- Greatness, before the Creator.

- Yeah... greatness."

Without looking at him, I whisper:

"You're one of the gods Olen and I'm mortal. Anything in this world can kill me: starting with people's wickedness... And an enchanted break in Paris won't change anything.

- You're not doing so bad.

- I just have a strong temperament..."

He turns to face me, and takes me in his arms. Unable to escape his two big blue eyes.

"You're my goddess. My goddess of innocence always in the right place.

- Seriously, Olen, I have no one to protect me, you can't control the press, the people's wickedness. I left school early because of it.

- You don't control them. That's everyone's mistake. You need to subdue them, you've already done very well in that department. You subdued me by being yourself.. Your problem is your lack of confidence. Do you trust me?

- I want to trust you. But living in this crazy world ... it isn't for me.

- You don't want to do something crazy in your life, Candice?

- I did a crazy thing the day I entered your room in Bali.

- What if every day was crazy? I live in a crazy world, and I'm crazy, but I'm crazy about you. And I'm crazy to hope that you'll be a part of my life. But living without you is worse.

- Hmm.

- What?

- I'm not sure that Steinbeck would appreciate it, but I tip my hat to your stylistic effort."

He pinches my ass while holding me pressed against him.

"Stop being a smartass. Stop giggling or I'll take you here and now.

- I'm not sure the French would appreciate that.

- Quite the opposite, they're unstoppable when it comes to sex."

I wanted him. Right here, right now. Confronted with my dilating pupils, Olen presses me harder against him, ready to get back to the hotel. But no. I needed to think, and let the bond reform, slowly.

"Shall we continue?"

While leaving the church, Olen stops, hesitant, and changes direction by slightly shaking his head. And we arrive at the Café de Flore. I didn't need to beg Olen, we had a reservation. I'm aware I look perfectly stupid smiling blissfully, it's not my fault that all the great French writers and artists of the modern age have been here. I suppress a gasp, opening the menu.

"Let's get out of here.

- Why ?" Olen wonders, surprised.

- Twenty two euros for a club sandwich?

- So what ? Who cares. Order what you want."

I shake my head in grumbling and eventually choose the duck confit. Olen orders two Ladoucette, (which proves to be two glasses of house white wine).

"That's it ? Are you done smoldering at the menu? It's not going to blush, you know.

- Uh, yes.

- We make the most of the present, right?"

And I close the menu putting it aside. He's practically lecturing me while taking my hand to kiss it. I can still see us at the dock, above the lake, in a park with wild colors. Damn it, Candice, focus on the present.

"Stop thinking about the past, and try to feel it instead!

- What?

- The genius of the great writers going through your butt to your brain."

I burst out laughing and it brings me back to the present immediately:

"I can't believe it. You know this is the birthplace of surrealism? André Breton, Philippe Soupault and Aragon met here. Apollinaire had a newsroom for the magazine *Les soirées de Paris.* And the war didn't change anything.

Then, it was the turn of the movie directors Marcel Carné, Jean Vilar..."

Olen looks at me, happily listening to me. I hold back. Candice stop being a know-it-all.

"Sorry, you probably already know all this, because you thought of bringing me here.

- I brought you here because this is a laboratory where everyone presents their idea of freedom. Their words, their colors, their vision... I have a very important question to ask you, Candice."

Taking ahold of my hand, he looks deeply into my eyes with his gaze that removes all trace of doubt:

"What's your vision of freedom, Candice? If you feel trapped in my crazy world... how can you be free at my side?"

I sense it's an important question, perhaps the most important one. I close my eyes for a moment and try to picture it. Him in LA, me in New York. Or are we both in Los Angeles? Why not. I can write there.

"I want to keep writing, and I want to spend time in New York, away from the madness of the paparazzi which will be even worse in Los Angeles.

- That's for sure. That's why I love New York. It's my place of freedom. What else?

- I want to spend time with you, but not on the red carpet, or in night clubs with your buddies. Like in Adirondack. That, that makes me happy."

Olen nods. Here we are. Meeting each other halfway. Is he ready to give up easy money, gained through an appearance at a club? Is he ready to be less accessible to leeches and to prioritize those who truly love him?

Chapter 31

It's slowly taking shape.

"Good. I think I can change some things, my agenda, my organization."

We look at each other in silence for a while and eat as soon as our food arrives. I must admit the duck's delicious, and the atmosphere shifts, becoming more relaxed, like a ball of yarn that unravels gently pulling strings one by one. In front of my plate now finished, I look around. Obviously, people recognized Olen, and are watching us.

"Are you happy to be here?

- Yes. Even if people watching us ruins the mood.

- All that, it's just bullshit.

- What?

- It's a lie. Look around you, there are more movie stars, like me, who come to be seen by writers and artists. When genius and creativity disappear, all that remains is the superfluous. Crumbs.

- That's a little harsh, don't you think?

- No. Look, even that twelve year old girl's looking down on the server because she's wearing two thousand euros worth of clothes on her back.

- You're the one who told me not to worry about the price of a club sandwich ...

- Yes, because you were placing too much emphasis on it! That's what I want you to understand. Freedom and truth. In my opinion, that's what's important. And the day I deviate from that, please, slap me. Put me on the right path as you did that night at the festival. Thank you for that. That's what I liked about you, what drew me in, right off the bat. You had no filter.

- Yes, but you're not going to like it.

- I'm not saying I'll like it, I'd have to be masochistic, but I need it. I can feel it.

- Okay, so if we're eating at the Café de Flore too, we're hypocrites then?

- No, we have the right, as long as we're not fooled. This is a lie: the truth is that writers are too poor to get a coffee here, and there are only parasites that come to profit from the glory incrusted in the seats. To shroud themselves in perfume. It's like reality TV starlets who come to Hollywood. It's not about the time period, it's human nature. But there's nothing wrong with that, it's just human nature. You look, you laugh about it, and you manage to create something else.

- Thank you for this lesson. That's why you brought me here, isn't it?

- Uh, yes. I'm an actor, my job is to put myself in other people's shoes and give them what they need. What's your job as a writer?"

I think about it... extensively. The first thing that comes to mind comes from him.

"People watching, and writing ... the truth."

He watches me with a satisfied expression.

"That's right, my Candice. Now, once you know the truth, you can play with it. No need to let it stick to our skin. No need for everything to be dramatic. Your freedom is to write about it but also knowing how to react with...

- Temperance?

- Reflection.

- You? Reflection? But you're always ... spontaneous!

- That's carefree abandon.

- Well we're not going to split-hairs over words!

- Sorry, how dare I play on words with a writer?

- Alright, ok," I grumble.

- You have the choice between being caught up in appearances or distancing yourself from them and laughing about them."

In that moment, I think that Olen might not have finished high school, but life taught him well. I smile and say to him,

"Shall we?"

And we leave the café after settling the bill. It's only once we arrive in the Luxembourg garden that I realize I hadn't paid attention to the heads turning as we walked by, so absorbed by what Olen had said.

"Come on, we're going to do something I love doing."

He takes two chairs in front of the pond, and we contemplate it.

"Listen, you'll be able to understand what they say."

I strain my ears and students talk about the political crisis in Europe, it all started in two thousand and eight with Greece, and that Europe was created by bankers. They munch hurriedly on their sandwiches reading over their notes from the Sorbonne and gesticulate debating the future of Europe. I don't dare translate for Olen lest they understand me. They look at us for a few seconds, but Olen takes my hand and smiles gazing into the water. That way, we seem like two blissful lovesick tourists so absorbed that we could never understand their heated debate.

"This is the laboratory of creation and freedom: in parks, cheap and dingy cafes, associations, popular theaters, student groups ... not in the presence of the well-off bourgeois society."

I listen, I learn. And I feel the touch of the spirit of Crazy Paris, before the war, after the war ...

"That spirit never died, it's polymorphic and changes location, changes social class, changes political side, changes nationality ...

to paraphrase the Lion King, "it lives in you"," Olen says with a wink.

We get up to walk across the park, all in all, not that big, but so quiet until Vavin street where Olen makes a sharp right for a ride by the Lucernaire, small theater where he took lessons during filming.

"Depardieu, Michael Lonsdale ... the greats have played here.

- And you ? Would you like to do theater?

- Already done, my little Candice."

I take note of that, he has regained his soft intonations. My little Candice. How I missed that.

"You've done theater?

- Yes, in this very place."

We remain silent for a minute in the small courtyard with its fountain that serves as an entrance to the theater's restaurant.

"Damn, that's where we should have gone.

- Next time, my little Candice."

And I feel warmth spread through me.

"So you did theater here?

- Yes here, while I was shooting the movie I took classes here. I loved it. I didn't understand a lot of the director's instructions, but I was able to suggest some things."

I was discovering a new side to Olen thanks to Paris, and another Paris thanks to Olen. This town suits him so well. We get a pastry at Colorova, where a young waiter welcomed us with the biggest and brightest smile in the world.

"Hello Mr Olen.

- Hello Thomas…, right?

- Do you remember me ?

- How could I forget the place where I enjoyed myself most in Paris?"

The smile of the waiter with tousled hair becomes even wider and he brings us two menus. I can see why Olen hasn't forgotten this place, hidden in a street behind rue de Rennes.

"This is one of the best patisseries in the city," Olen whispers, already overtaken by delight.

I chose the vanilla and tonka mille-feuille with red fruits and Olen orders a Youzou. The kind waiter spent ten minutes explaining patiently what a Youzou was, as the name doesn't sound French but Japanese: I keep in mind that there's lemon, whipped cream and cheesecake. Basically. However, you don't talk about pastries in France, you eat them, you enjoy it with iced tea or hot chocolate.

"Well have you finished making eyes at him?

- I'm not making eyes at him, he's nice, so I'm being nice.

- Yes, well, he's doing his job, that's all.

- Well, all waiters in Paris should be like that."

He grumbles something incomprehensible and I giggle.

"What?

- Are you jealous?

- Yes. You can laugh, you should see yourself when you're jealous.

- You look like grumpy from Snow White.

- I'm not going to tell you what you look like when you're jealous, otherwise my pastry is going to end up in my face and it's too delicious for that.

- You're right even throwing it at your face would be a waste."

When we leave, I have to close my eyes and let Olen guide me completely. Supreme act of faith because for one, given the size of Paris' sidewalks, an overpopulated city, I'm afraid to walk into someone, and secondly, I learn to completely ignore how people are looking at me. We walk a little, Olen holds me behind his back, making his way down the street, protecting me from passersby. I make out a polite "Good evening, Sir", and we take the elevator.

"Can I open my eyes now?

- No, Miss Evans, not yet."

I feel my way along before Olen takes me by the shoulders and I can feel the wind blow through my hair. I feel his hands slide down my arms, and guide my hands to a metal railing.

"There. You can open your eyes."

The view is breathtaking. Night has fallen, and the Eiffel Tower, that I can see in the distance, illuminates Paris in its thousands of lights.

"Oh my God... it's so...

- Candice...

- Olen...

- Is your heart... still open to me?

- I no longer have a heart Olen... I might not want to fall in love again.

- That's impossible.

- Oh yes it is. I carefully avoided love for five years. I can do it for the another fifty.

- Even your grandmother wanted to fall in love again.

- My grandmother's very strong..."

He didn't let me finish and turns me to face him.

"What if I promised you that I'd never do you wrong.

- You can't, it's in your nature to love having people on their knees. I'll never bend to the demands or requests of your assistants, agents, publicists. I will for a while, and then I'll say to hell with all of them and you with it. You think that's balance?

- What if I changed life?

- Your job is your life. You can't stop being an actor. Not after everything you've built.

- No my life, my life plan is us and my job comes second.

- Yeah, sure..."

I push my hair behind my ear, pulling at it harshly, despite the wind, as if to clearly articulate my thoughts:

"I was attracted to you because I thought you were charismatic, strong and carefree, so carefree and spontaneous. Actually, it's a lot of derision, and all that energy you have, you inject into your career."

I lower my voice, and I take his hands, saying quietly, as gently as possible,

"Olen the truth of it is that you love to have power over people. You love the cheers, the applause. It's natural, you're an actor. If you didn't have that motivation, you wouldn't have that fight in you, and you wouldn't have been successful. Because talent isn't enough in this world. But all that energy that I feel... it's all for your audience. And there'll be nothing left for me. Nothing that can be used to fuel our love. I would take care of you, but nothing will make it possible for me. Neither your world nor your lifestyle.

- Who said you need to be the one to take care of me?"

He's starting to get on my nerves, forcing me to shut up.

- You really want to be a superhero who saves people? Come with me, the Olen Van Cliff foundation really needs people like you. Let me take care of you. And I assure you, I'll make time for you. "

Olen takes a deep breath and takes a knee, pulling out of his pocket a Cartier jewelry box. I stop breathing.

"I promise you a crazy life but we'll be together. Never spending more than three days apart. I promise you that. You could write what you want, you don't even have to work at all, and I want your help with my foundation. I want you by my side."

I remained silent for several minutes, and other tourists stop, touched at seeing Olen down on one knee, holding a ring. Then their mouths drop into a surprised O upon recognizing Olen. He whispers:

"I think we're starting to attract attention.

- I can hear it.

- What?

- My heart."

I have tears in my eyes, and amongst the applause and Bravos, when Olen puts the ring on my finger, all my fears climb over the railing and throw themselves over the ledge. I think they're still flying over Paris.

***

Liza opens the door abruptly and grabs me by the shoulders without giving me time to breathe.

"You little..."

But the right word doesn't come to her, she then just holds me in her arms, and when I show her my ring, she weeps for joy.

"Oh my God... I knew it!"

And she turns to Jake, who has a beer in one hand, and the other in the pocket of his jeans. He stands trapped between the couch and the coffee table, and gives me a polite smile. He's actually really cute, and very muscular. My God, will he manage to calm the exuberant Liza Cole?

"I knew that I was right to give him your address in France. He needed to think... I mean, come on!

- Pipe down, Liza, he's coming.

- Yes, I'm here."

Olen comes into the living room and puts our bags down near the door.

I say hi to Jake, a bit awkwardly, and rush over to embrace Jo, Ilan, and the kids. "We're only missing Grandma, to complete the family portrait.

- Does she know?" Jo inquires.

"Oh yes. I'll let Olen tell the story.

- Well, she had left the shotgun in the backseat when she picked us up from Aurillac. Just to make sure I knew that I better not be messing around, but she was thrilled... I think. She said something I didn't understand.

- She said "twice already that an American has snatched my little girl". But she's going to like you."

We all take a seat around the pizzas we ordered. I was beat.

"Well come on, show us the ring," Jo orders.

"Actually, it's a wedding ring. And I have the same one. Just so that everyone knows we're together. Nearly married already.

- There aren't any diamonds, that's original," Jo says simply being guarded.

"It's the Trinity designed by Jean Cocteau, a French poet. White, pink and yellow gold: purity, love and divinity.

- Yellow?

- Yes. Yellow gold is the color of the gods," He says simply, kissing my forehead.

Liza grabs two beers out of the fridge, and thrusting them into our hands, we toast:

"To the two of you! Congratulations!

- To our reunion. To friendship."

And we drink in silence. I wasn't particularly hungry, and I quietly sit down on Olen's lap while Liza watches me and squirms.

"What's the matter?

- Go on, tell her!" Jake says, pinching her stomach.

"Candice.

- Liza?

- Have you checked the reviews for your book?

- Uh, a little, in the beginning, but I gave up."

She looks at me, taken aback.

"You gave up?

- It's as if people liked bad-mouthing me, so I read them in the beginning and then when I saw a headline saying that I wanted to benefit from Olen's fame, I stopped straight away. And now..."

I look at Olen who starts stroking my hair.

"I don't care. I think I'm cured."

Liza suddenly throws a cushion at my head:

"Read this, miss nothing can touch me anymore because I'm engaged."

I take the newspaper dating back a few days and begin to read, stunned:

"Candice Evans manages to chew out, without vulgarity, the portrait of our world mesmerized by the sirens of fame, through a kid whose insolence... "

My words are lost. I read the rest as quickly as I can in silence, I can't believe what I'm reading.

"Miss Evans Is the Billy Wilder of American literature of this century?"

Oh my God. Olen's hands snake around my waist out of happiness, while I kiss him with everything I've got.

And for the first time in a while, since the weekend in that magical park, I get up ... and I do the victory dance. Liza, and the rest of the group look at me speechless. But I don't care. You hear me ? I do not care. And I hold out my arms to Olen, who joins me, laughing.

Epilogue.

The media dubbed our marriage the event of the year, those who dragged me through the mud made amends since I was named a true writer by real journalists. Clarissa cried her eyes out several times, but mostly focused on the remission of her cancer to get a reality show in her name, plotting her return to Hollywood. Liza cried at her bachelorette party, she cried at her wedding, and she cried for joy in discovering where they were going on their honeymoon: Senegal. Jo and Ilan continue to regale me with comforting chicken curry when the paparazzi get to me a bit too much, and she taught me a few insults in Hindi. The video assistant asks me:

"Are you ready Candice?

- Yes."

I smooth out my dress one last time, a slinky knee-length strapless black dress. I now always choose something simple for my appearances. I take a deep breath. I've learnt my process now. And I'm no longer stunned, as I was before, when I made my entrance. I make my way forwards while some cameras click away and begin my speech at the school's lectern where we're going to intervene with young people. This is where I wanted to announce the plan for the Olen's foundation. Not on a TV set, but here in the field, close to the people:

"I'm often asked: What writing is? How one becomes a writer? Is it to do with technique? Where does the rumored inspiration come from?

Healing, imagining, expressing, dreaming, traveling, communication, passing something on, telling a story... Writing is a lot of things, not just jotting a few words on paper.

There's magic in writing... because when the soul takes action, magic happens. It's our soul, our mind, that we use to create. And imagination is magic in action.

I believe that everything must come from you. From who you are when you were a child. You're a seed, so rich, even when you have no parents, even if you grew up poor, or a part of the middle class. You're rich in everything that makes you up. You are a "once upon a time." Because oddly enough, the famous "once upon a time" gives us the impression that it's beyond the notion of beginning. This is a dawn, obviously, but amongst other things, it has a reassuring feeling at its epicenter, there always has been and there always will be. Once upon a time: as soon as you write, you have a creative power that defies the blank page. That defies life itself and also defies what it had planned for you.

The blank page. Everyone's afraid of that damn blank page: the writer, the scholar, the entrepreneur. But every day is a blank page. Our life is a blank page. And if you start with 'once upon a time', if you pour into it some of your dreams, then you'll get there. I suggest this exercise for the rest of your life. Start your day by saying "Once upon a time ".

I believe there's magic, and perhaps a religious aspect in what we write. Each book should be a profession of faith. In what you believe.

What are your dreams? Martin Luther King had a dream. Disney had a dream. And so did I. I make it come true a little more each day. It's that dream that has a force of attraction as powerful as the sun's.

We live in times of despair, darkness, distrust, malice ... and all that was created by humans. We don't have a sweet angel on our shoulder and a little devil that tempts us. We can be that angel, and we can be that devil. I believe the Olen Van Cliff foundation can be a leverage for youth. It's not charity dinners and empty interviews. You know I'm no good at this, right?"

The room erupts in laughter.

"It's an integration program that this foundation provides. I'm proud to say today, that I have a dream and I'm going to share it with you. We have a dream, and we want to share it with you. Education: the challenge of America. How could people who had nothing be able to succeed in building our beautiful country? With their inner riches! Yes, the world is, but it evolves thanks to us. I'm proud to present Vicky, who will be in charge of reviewing your applications for the merit scholarships, and Nagee, who'll be at the head of the personnel development and brainstorming workshops. And look! These are men and women dedicated to this cause, to this dream. Do you believe in this dream? I believe in us!"

The crowd gets to their feet in thunderous applause. Olen promised me we'd never spend more than three days apart: he managed to catch his plane and sneak into the front row. I no longer see the crowd of students, parents, teachers, our team or the journalists. I only see Olen in the front row, looking at me with indescribable pride and I get off the stage to throw my arms around his neck. The world is watching us kissing, but I don't care, I told you, I'm cured. And the world needs more love, right?